Country Place

Country Place

Ann Petry

MARINER CLASSICS
New York Boston

This is a work of fiction. Names, characters, places, and incidents are products of the author's imagination or are used fictitiously and are not to be construed as real. Any resemblance to actual events, locales, organizations, or persons, living or dead, is entirely coincidental.

Originally published by Houghton Mifflin in 1947.

FIRST MARINER BOOKS PAPERBACK EDITION PUBLISHED 2023.

Library of Congress Cataloging-in-Publication Data has been applied for.

ISBN 978-0-06-326009-2

22 23 24 25 26 LBC 5 4 3 2 1

Country Place

1

I HAVE ALWAYS BELIEVED THAT, WHEN a man writes a record of a series of events, he should begin by giving certain information about himself: his age, where he was born, whether he be short or tall or fat or thin. This information offers a clue as to how much of what a man writes is to be accepted as truth, and how much should be discarded as being the result of personal bias. For fat men do not write the same kind of books that thin men write; the point of view of tall men is unlike that of short men.

Therefore, I hasten to tell you that I am a bachelor; and a medium kind of man—medium tall, medium fat, medium old (I am sixty-five), and medium bald. I am neither a pessimist nor an optimist. I think I have what might be called a medium temperament.

It is only fitting and proper that I should openly admit to having a prejudice against women—perhaps I should say a prejudice against the female of any species, human or animal; and yet, like most of the people who admit to being prejudiced, I am not consistent, for I own a female cat, named Banana. Though I am devoted to her, I am well aware that she is much closer to the primitive than a male cat.

For example, the sight of the town taxi-driver, who is called The Weasel, arouses a kind of fury in her. Her tail swells to twice its normal size and she swats at him with her claws unsheathed. It is true that he dislikes cats, but that does not justify her snarling at him whenever he comes into the store to make a purchase. But like most females she makes no effort to control her emotions.

I see that I have used the words "town" and "store" without explaining either the one or the other. I am a druggist and the store is, of course, a drugstore.

In a city a drugstore is all wiggling neon lights and cosmetic bars and aluminum cooking ware—a place full of the hot, greasy smell of hamburgers being cooked in rancid fat.

My drugstore is not like that. It belonged to my father and to my grandfather before him. They installed the old-fashioned ice-cream parlor which remains much as it was in their day. It is separated from the rest of the store by an arched opening. In this separate section there is a fountain. But no stools upholstered in imitation leather, no coffee-makers, no electric grills. There are instead six small, round tables whose slender legs are made of wrought iron, and there are chairs which match the tables.

I make my own fountain sirups: lemon and cherry and orange and all the other flavors. When the chocolate sirup is cooking in a big open pan on the kerosene stove in the backroom, it fills the store with a rich, mouth-watering smell. One rarely finds that smell in drugstores these days—or any of the other smells so typical of this store. For I sell green ginger root and horehound candy and those round hard peppermints called Canadian mints.

But I dispense penicillin and the sulfa drugs, too. I tell you this lest you think of my store as a place untouched by time. On the other hand, I sell kidney plasters for backaches, and an amazing quantity of powdered sulfur, for there are many people in the town who blow sulfur down their children's throats as a remedy for sore throat—and a strangling kind of remedy it is, too.

The town of which I speak is Lennox, Connecticut—a quiet place, a country place, which sits at the mouth of the Connecticut River, at the exact spot where the river empties itself into Long Island Sound. Thus, Lennox is almost surrounded by water, and it is filled with the salt smell of the sea and with the yammering sound of the gulls. At certain seasons of the year, the sky over the town is enlivened by the comings and goings of water birds. For the coves and inlets and creeks that edge the town offer a perfect resting-place for migrant birds.

We have a town green, a large open space in the center of the town, where cows and sheep once grazed. My drugstore faces the green. The Congregational Church is directly across the way from it, on the other side of the green.

The town of Lennox is easy to recognize because of the Gramby House. If you ever take Route 1 to Boston, you will see a great brick house, facing the Post Road, about eighteen miles outside of New London. Motorists refer to it as the "pink house" because the brick appears to be a delicate pink when the sun shines on it. Whenever this house is spoken of, or written about, in the town, it is called the Gramby House, never the Grambys' house. I do not know why. Perhaps because it is the largest house in Lennox; or because it is the only brick house; or possibly because its occupants, Mrs. Gramby and her son, Mearns, were the town's wealthiest citizens. Perhaps for a combination of all three reasons. In any event, the presence of its imposing façade distinguishes this town from all the other villages that are strung along the Boston Post Road.

But like the other small New England towns we have a great increase in population during the summer months. Many refugees from cities spend their vacations here. These summer people leave about the first of September, and with their departure Lennox becomes, to all appearances, a quiet, sleepy village.

I say to all appearances because wheresoever men dwell there is always a vein of violence running under the surface quiet.

Last year, for example, during a period of great "outrage of weather" (as my friend Mrs. Gramby would have put it) Lennox could hardly have been called a quiet, sleepy village. Many untoward events occurred during, and after, that storm. I think that most of these things would have happened, anyway, but because of the storm they took place sooner than they normally would have.

I am the only druggist in the town of Lennox, and for that reason I believe I am in a better position to write the record of what took place here than almost anyone else. All of the people concerned were customers of mine. I have known them so well, and for so many years, that I can tell you what they loved and what they hated, what they hoped for and what they feared.

I was born in this town, as were many of the people of whom I write. Over the years I have acquired an intimate, detailed knowledge of all of them: Johnnie Roane and his wife, Glory; Mr. and Mrs. Roane, who were Johnnie's mother and father; Mrs. Gramby and her son, Mearns; Ed Barrell; The Weasel; Neola; The Portegee; David Rosenberg; and, of course, Lil, who was Mearns Gramby's wife.

In the following pages I have reported what happened to them and how it happened. I have written it in exact chronologic order, even inserting, in the proper place, my own reaction to various happenings. I believe this to be a true account, but truth has many sides, and, as I said before, I am not wholly without bias where females are concerned.

This record of events contains, of course, something of life and something of death, for both are to be found in a country place.

2

I DID NOT SEE JOHNNIE ROANE when he got off the train at Lennox. Nor was I an eyewitness to what happened afterward.

The Weasel told me of Johnnie's arrival in such detail that I might just as well have been standing on the station platform when Johnnie got off the train, and have looked inside his head as well.

His mother, who is an old friend of mine, told me much of what follows in these pages. In addition I have observed the actions of Johnnie's wife, Glory, for so long a period that I can tell you with a fair degree of accuracy what she thinks about when she wakes up in the morning.

This is how it was:

By the end of September the railroad station at Lennox is deserted and quiet. The summer folk have long since packed away their slacks and shorts and bathing suits and returned to the cities from whence they came; and the town, relieved of their presence, has begun to settle down for a long and peaceful winter.

The Weasel, who drives the town taxi, did not get out of his car when he heard the long whistle that announces the approach of the morning train from New York. He lowered the newspaper he was reading to watch the engine slide into the curve of the track. Then he glanced across at the Catholic cemetery without really seeing it because it had been there so long he would only have become aware of it if for some reason it had disappeared.

When the train stopped, he was absorbed in the newspaper. He was quite nearsighted, so he held the paper close to his eyes, poring over the detail of a hatchet murder case that had occurred in New York.

Thus he lost the opportunity to see young Johnnie Roane swing himself off the train almost before its motion ceased; to see young Johnnie Roane, tall and broad of shoulder, walk along the station platform with his barracks bag slung across his back. Johnnie could not believe that he was in Lennox, whole, all in one piece; and he kept thinking that perhaps he would come to or wake up and find that he was somewhere else; and it showed in his face.

And so young Johnnie Roane, just home from the war, paused on the station platform for a moment, looking around him with an eagerness that took in all the detail of the wooden flooring under his feet, the shape of the boxcars pulled in at the siding in back of the station. And he kept thinking, Glory, Glory, Glory. It has come true; I am here in this town once again; and tonight I shall hold her in my arms.

Then he walked over to the taxi. All he could see of The Weasel was his hands—small hands for a man, silhouetted against the bold headlines of the newspaper. He hesitated, half-expecting the man would sense his presence and lower the paper; and when he didn't, Johnnie tapped on the car window.

The Weasel lowered the newspaper and Johnnie saw his

sharp ferret's face, the close-set eyes, an out-of-shape cap turned backward on his head. The cap had been light gray in color, but it was covered with grease marks and darkened from sweat. There was a cigarette behind his ear. He looked Johnnie over carefully before he lowered the car window.

"Where you want to go?" he said, leaning toward him.

"Mrs. Roane's house on the River Road."

"Okay." He laid the paper down with a sigh. "Put your bag in the back."

Johnnie shoved the barracks bag on the floor of the car, then got in the front seat beside the driver. He didn't remember him. When he left Lennox four years ago, Old Man Crandall drove the town taxi.

A fast freight rumbled past the station, making conversation impossible. Johnnie watched it, reading the names on the cars: Lackawanna, B & O, Chesapeake and Ohio, New York Central—

As the last car disappeared from view, The Weasel started the motor. "You must be Johnnie, Mrs. Roane's boy. She's been expecting you," he said.

"Yeah," Johnnie said. He hoped the little guy wouldn't want to talk. He'd been waiting for this moment for four years and he wanted to hold it close to his chest so he wouldn't lose any of it, not even the smallest detail. It was a long ride out to his mother's house and if the guy was going to talk, none of it would be the way he wanted it. He had planned to look at every last detail, the trees, the houses, the streets; twisting and turning his head so that he could see down the little side roads, so he could swallow the whole place up.

But if the driver was going to run off at the mouth, he'd lose half the stuff he wanted to see; his attention would be diverted and he would not notice the rough wood that formed the station platform; and that the shed was almost laughable because the supports were spindly when you considered the length of roof they had to hold up; and that the station was covered with layers of grime and soot.

He closed one eye and squinted at the station house. Yes, when viewed like that it still bore a great resemblance to the gingerbread house in *Hänsel and Gretel.* And he let his breath out slowly, softly; because all of it was exactly as he had remembered it. None of it had changed.

With that freight gone he could see the Catholic Church across the tracks. It was just the same, too. No, not quite. It used to be whiter than that. The soot from the trains had turned it as gray as the station.

As he looked at the church, he almost smiled, remembering how the kids who lived in this neighborhood used to scuttle past the cemetery even in broad daylight. They called it the Irish graveyard and they swore the tombstones rocked and moved when they walked by. Of course there was a fast train called the East Wind which roared past the station just about the time school was out and it may have set up a vibration that made the stones move.

In any case, neither kids nor grownups walked by here at night if they could help it; because restless Irish ghosts were alleged to rise and walk on dark nights. And on nights when the moon was full, they were supposed to grow so uneasy that you could hear their pickaxes on the track, and, faintly down the wind, the murmur of their voices.

It was, now that he thought about it, a mighty queer place to build a church.

"Say," he said to the driver. "Has that church always been there?"

"Far's I know," The Weasel said, indifferently.

"I mean was the railroad built before the church?"

"Sure."

"Why would anybody put a church by a railroad track?"

The Weasel's eyes came at him sideways. "Wasn't you born in this town?"

"Sure."

"Ain't that church always been there?"

"Yes. But I've been away from here for a long time." The driver's beady little eyes stayed on his, making him feel the necessity for further explanation. "I just never thought about it before. The church was always there as far back as I can remember and I suppose I took it for granted. You know. It was there, and I never thought about things like that. Looking at it just now it struck me as a strange place for a church."

The Weasel nodded. "Know what you mean. After you ain't seen something for a while you see things in it you didn't know was there. Happens to everybody."

He backed the car into the road that led to the town. Then he glanced at Johnnie in the mirror and said: "You musta forgot Lennox don't like Catholics much. That was the only piece of land they could buy. When the railroad went through, a lot of Irish come here and laid track and stuff like that. Then they wanted a church, and this here piece of land by the tracks was the only piece for sale in the whole town. So that's where they built her."

"Can't they buy land now?"

"Oh, I wouldn't say that." The Weasel grinned. "But somehow there ain't never been none for sale on the main street where the Episcopals and the Congregationals got their churches."

It was like a faint cloud over the sun, so that you saw houses and trees in the distance, not clearly but blurred a little, darkened where they had been bright; like fog over a curve in a road when you wanted to see it whole and couldn't; because for the first time it occurred to Johnnie that perhaps nothing was ever the same, certainly not exactly as you had remembered it. Not that the thing itself changed, but that you changed, and therefore you could no longer find what you thought was there.

He had seen that church there by the track for years and accepted its position, never questioned why it was there because he had looked at it with a boy's eyes. And the eyes of a boy did not see what a man's eyes saw. So, of course, there would be other things about Lennox that he had either forgotten or had never really seen.

He began to remember all the things he had disliked about the town; it was not what the driver had said that brought them back, because he had not approved or disapproved of the location of the small, humble-looking church with its tombstones clustered about it. But the sly, satisfied smile that still lingered on his face was like a wink, a nudge in the ribs.

Thus he began to remember the gossip that went on in the postoffice, the general store, the drugstore, outside the churches after the service on Sundays. The smile on the face of the little man driving the car was typical of the town's smugness, its satisfaction with itself, its sly poking fun at others.

He shifted his feet on the floor of the car. They were turning into the main street; and this was not the way he had planned to view it, with his mind only half on it because he was upset and vaguely uneasy. Instead of enjoying the sight of this familiar street, he was remembering that he had wanted to leave the town that first year he and Glory were married. But she had objected.

And he was wanting the same thing now; because the town—and this little man represented it and what came out of his mouth was the thinking of the town—the town wasn't big enough to hold him any more. He wanted to live some place where when you got off a train the taxi-driver repeated the address out of the corner of his mouth; and didn't know who you were, let alone that your mother had been expecting you; and really didn't give a damn except whether or not you could pay the fare.

It had all gone sour on him. Less than five minutes ago he had been standing in the door of the train, holding on to the impatience that had built up in him as he came East across the country, boxing it in; and even at that, when the train finally slowed down at the curve in the track and he actually saw the grimy little station, he had all he could do to keep from jumping off before the train stopped moving. His mind had been filled with Glory, not the goddam town, because that was something else again. Sure he wanted to see the town, but it was Glory he couldn't wait to get to. He had forced himself to stand still, close to the door, looking out, watching the countryside slow down, the houses become not just houses but individual buildings that he knew and recognized.

The town stinks, he thought. At least it's not what you remembered. And that isn't quite accurate. It is simply that you had forgotten the things you did not like about the town. You glossed them over and prettied them up and fondled them for four long years, until what you finally held was not this town.

Had he done that with Glory? No. He couldn't have because she kept sending him snapshots and she was just the same—slender and bright-haired and smiling. No. He hadn't done that with Glory. Of course there would be some things he had forgotten about her because they had only been married a year when he went in the army—but those would be unimportant little things.

And having reassured himself about Glory, he turned his attention to the street. He lowered the car window and sniffed the air. Yes, they were burning leaves. He couldn't tell exactly where, but he could smell that old familiar, smoky, pungent odor. And it pushed his distaste for the town far back in his mind. And he thought, If I were a dog my hide would twitch with the pleasure of it, the smell of it.

Because I'm home and it's the time of year when to smell this air is like drinking old wine—smooth and mellow; and after sipping it you feel the blood going a little faster through your veins and you feel warm. He forgot about the town and the little man who was driving the car.

There were leaves caught in the picket fences in front of the ancient houses that lined the street. He watched the wind blow them along the ground. And he imagined that under the wheeze of the taxi motor he could hear the faint, dry sound of the leaves. And he thought, Oh Christ, stinking town or not, I'm so glad to be home that it hurts!

"Town looks just the same, don't she?" said the driver.

"Yes, it does." He squirmed as he said it because the guy must have been studying him in the mirror and seen how he was drooling over the place. Who the hell is he, anyway, he wondered, and felt an active dislike for him because of his sharp rat's face, his way of sitting at the wheel, humped over, almost as though he were deformed. "I don't remember you," he said. "Doesn't Crandall have the taxi any more?"

"Sure. But business got so good, what with the gas rationing and no tires and all, that he expanded and hired me."

"You live in Lennox?" he asked. They were passing the post-office and he turned his head for another look at it. He used to ride up from the Point on his bicycle to get the mail on Saturdays. Miss Blandess always looked at him over the top of her glasses, turned away, searched carefully through a box marked "R" and said either: "No mail for Roane," or, "Mail for Roane. Two letters."

Then the driver said: "Yeah. But I was born in Westville. Lived in all these towns 'round here. Know 'em by heart. You'd be surprised how much you get to know about a town driving taxi in it."

"I guess so," Johnnie said. He hoped the guy wouldn't go into the detail of what he knew about Lennox; and he was sorry he had started him talking, but he couldn't stand having him pry into his mind the way he must have been doing. "What's your name?" he asked.

"Tom Walker. But there ain't three people 'round here who remembers it. Mostly they call me The Weasel."

Studying his profile, Johnnie thought it would be pointless to ask why, because the answer was there in the sharp face, the small, close-together, beady eyes; and in his sly way of looking at you so that you weren't quite aware of it at first, but before you knew it his glance was inside you, feeling its way around.

As they approached the Town Hall, The Weasel put the brakes on, slowing the car to a crawl. He lowered the window next to him and spit.

"Ah!" he said in disgust. "Missed it! There's a hollow in the road I aim at every time I go by. Been doing it ever since they locked me up in the town jail for two nights. They said I was drunk and I wasn't."

Then he glanced at the Town Hall and waved his hand at a man who was coming out of the door. Johnnie followed his glance and saw the dark figure of a man standing at the top of the long flight of steps that led to the street.

The wide columns on the building reached straight up to the roof and in the sunlight the branches of the trees made a moving pattern on its white painted front. The man was silhouetted there as though he were posing in front of a backdrop in the theater.

In spite of the sunlight, Johnnie got the feeling of darkness, for the man's clothes were dark, his figure was heavy; the shoulders thick and the legs slightly bowed.

"Good old Ed," The Weasel said, waving again. "You remember him?"

"Sure. He sold us a car once." Johnnie saw Ed lift his hand in salute and the gesture and the man's figure reminded him of something. It was a fleeting, momentary impression that he could not place.

He reached back into his memory of Ed Barrell—nothing there like this. There were images of Ed in a derby hat and a suit with the pants pressed to a razor's edge, selling cars; taking prospective customers for long rides through back roads to prove how sweetly the new six-cylinder jobs took to a bumpy road.

There was Ed come on suddenly because his car was pulled around a curve and half-hidden by a clump of bushes so that all Johnnie saw was these same powerful shoulders and the back of the gray fedora he wore on his days off. And Ed was kissing somebody else's wife with a kind of male powerfulness, a drive and an urge that Johnnie could see and feel and understand just in the glimpse of the forward thrust of Ed's shoulders. The sight of his shoulders lifted like that made him know for the first time what it would be like to hold a woman close in his arms, making him aware of his own maleness because Ed at that moment was like a tomcat walking stiff-legged toward a female—ready, waiting, hungry.

No, it wasn't anywhere in his memories of Ed that he had seen this gesture before. It didn't have anything to do with Ed. There was someone, some place, some photograph in a newspaper, some gesture he'd seen in a newsreel—he tried to trace it through his mind. Of course, he had it now—it was a newsreel showing Mussolini on the balcony of some place or other in Italy. That was what Ed had reminded him of standing at the top of those stairs—the same bull chest, round head, and gesture of the hand. The impression was heightened because Ed was standing on those steps and wearing dark clothing.

"Good old Ed," The Weasel repeated as the car picked up speed. "He's still screwing all the women in town."

It was a statement of fact that needed no answer. So Johnnie let it ride. And then he was conscious of a pinprick of uneasiness because The Weasel gave him one of those sly, sharp looks in the mirror, then turned his head to look at him.

And as The Weasel's short neck turned between his humped-over shoulders, Johnnie decided he was looking to see what knowledge he, Johnnie, had that would make him react to the statement. And the only reason a man would react to a statement like that would be if he knew that his wife was one of Ed's women.

In spite of himself, he examined the idea, and then dismissed it as being utterly ridiculous. Yet if that wasn't it, why had The Weasel taken his eyes off the road to look at him?

He must expect me to say something or my expression to change. But why? What's it to me if Ed is still the town bull? It doesn't concern me one way or the other. Ed was short and bow-legged. Everybody in town knew he had a weakness for women. It was a town joke. It had nothing to do with him.

Yet he straightened up in the car seat and said, "Yeah?" and when The Weasel did not answer he said, fishing, "He doesn't look like much. Wonder what the women see in him."

The Weasel smiled. "You never can tell about women. Not being one I couldn't say. I guess after they been married awhile they get kind of restless. It ain't what they expected. Kind of monotonous, especially since the movies show 'em how it could be. Mebbe Ed shows 'em how it could be different. Gives 'em a little excitement."

Monotonous, get restless, not what they expected. His mind echoed the words. How did he know the same thing hadn't happened to Glory? God knows you couldn't really prove anything by her letters; because if you looked at them sharply, trying to analyze them, they didn't say anything. She never said anything really personal.

She wrote that she missed him and that the weather was cold

or the weather was hot or that it had rained or snowed; and that she liked living with his mother or that the young couple, who were occupying the small house where she and Johnnie had lived when they were first married, had taken down the screens or put up the screens or picked the chrysanthemums or had not picked them; or that the porch furniture had been left out on the lawn and she was afraid the rain would rust it.

"You want to stop by the grocery store?" The Weasel said innocently, slowing the car down.

"No," he said roughly. This was like being poked at with a stick, herded along in a given direction that you had not chosen. Maybe there wasn't any connection between the little guy's having talked about Ed's performance with women and then about married women getting bored, and then asking if he wanted to stop by Perkins' store to see Glory. But it certainly seemed to him that there was.

Besides, he had not planned on seeing Glory in the store with half the town smirking and grinning when he held her close to him. Much as he wanted to see her, ached to see her, he had decided weeks ago that he would wait until she came home from work. He had no intention of spreading his emotions out in front of the town. No, he'd wait until she got home tonight just as he'd planned. He had waited this long, a few more hours would not matter.

He stared out of the window in an effort to build up a wall of silence between him and The Weasel. Thus he obtained a long, sweeping view of the town green: the Congregational Church on one side, the drugstore across the street from it; and the big expanse of lawn in between. The white urn was still in the center of the green and there were scraggly geraniums in it, or at least he assumed they were geraniums. Every Hallowe'en he used to turn the urn over, he and five or six other boys, just for the fun of it.

And the Congregational deacons—fat men in heavy overcoats—lurked behind the elm trees hellbent on catching them. And, of course, outwitting the deacons was what made the fun.

A bulky, slow-moving figure, clad in a long black cape, paused in front of the church. He recognized Mrs. Gramby and was pleased, because seeing her again, even from a car window, was like rediscovering a half-forgotten landmark. She looked almost the same as when he had left, except that she moved more slowly, leaned more heavily on her cane.

"Folks been betting she'll hit the ninety-year mark," The Weasel offered. "But I dunno. Her waterworks are pretty well shot to hell and her false teeth slip and she can't get none that will stay in her mouth."

Listening to The Weasel was like having a dirty hand paw through your personal belongings, leaving them in confusion; and so soiled that after the first look you were disgusted and tempted to throw them away, for they had changed. Just now he had neatly destroyed his pleasure at the sight of Mrs. Gramby, for he painted a dismal picture in which she smelt of urine and her false teeth clicked when she talked.

But, he thought, The Weasel speaks for Lennox. This statement represents Lennox, though it issued from the tough, lopsided mouth of this wizened little man. And he damned the town as a place where the state of an old woman's kidneys was avidly discussed in kitchens and bedrooms, in the postoffice, in the drugstore.

He didn't have to live here. He and Glory could leave any time, live in a city—a big city. And he said to himself, I hope this little bastard driving this rattling car will keep quiet from here on in. I want to think. I don't want him sticking his mouth into my mind.

The Weasel kept stealing sly glances at him in the mirror.

And during one of those seconds when The Weasel's eyes were on him and not on the road, a black cat emerged from the undergrowth near the river and ran directly in front of the car.

Johnnie's first view of the cat was of a streak of blackness which he identified as a cat, crouched low, its belly almost touching the ground. He felt the car lurch and sway; and knew that The Weasel was frightened and had pulled the wheel sharply to the left instead of to the right. Then the car went over a soft, slight obstruction.

"God damn!" The Weasel said. "I hit him."

The Weasel's eyes sought the mirror and Johnnie knew when he'd located the cat because he blinked. And though Johnnie didn't want to, he turned around and looked back.

The cat was flattened in the road, smashed into flat, black fur and dark red blood. The blotches of blood seemed to increase in size as he looked.

The Weasel frowned and Johnnie looked away from him. This was an omen of evil. Having a cat cross the road was bad enough, but it had to be a black cat that chose the moment of his arrival to run from one side of the road to the other. And then they had to kill the damn cat.

"Guess it's bad luck," The Weasel said softly. "Sorry. Especially when you're just coming home and all."

"It's all right. Doesn't mean anything," he said quickly. Knowing that it did mean something, knowing, too, that he wished to Christ he'd never got in the damn taxi with this wizened little man. It was childish to have wanted to walk in the house unannounced, to come on his mother suddenly when she wasn't expecting him. If he had telephoned her, she would have met him at the station. But no, he had to do it this way.

When The Weasel stopped the car in front of the house, Johnnie paid him, dragged the barracks bag from the back of the car. He watched the taxi until it disappeared around the curve in the road. This was a hell of a note. He was suddenly afraid. Because that rat-faced little man had managed to make him see that nothing ever was the same; nothing ever could be the same—either on the surface or deep underneath.

3

THERE WAS A NAGGING, PERSISTENT wind blowing from the northeast—a wind that carried the damp cold of the sea with it. Johnnie Roane felt suddenly cold, and turned the collar of his field jacket up around his neck. He shivered as he looked at the house where he was born, the house where he had spent most of his life, because he could not rid himself of the fear that enveloped him.

He stared at the house, searching it for known, familiar details. It appeared to be unchanged. The clapboards were painted white and the blinds dark green. He remembered when the big-paned modern windows were put in, for his mother said the small panes of glass in the old windows were a nuisance to wash.

The sight of the house was reassuring. There was nothing about it that surprised him unpleasantly. He felt easier in his mind; and some of the fear drifted away.

He glanced toward the garage. The doors were open and he could see the back of the car—same license numbers as when he left: RR15. But instead of 1942 he knew the markers read 1946, though he could not read the small figures of the year at this distance.

Four years was a long time out of a man's life. It left him with the curious feeling of having been cut off, pinched off in the middle like a rubber tube so that the flow of living was rudely and abruptly stopped. Now that the constriction had been removed, he was a little dizzy. This house had stood here while he was gone and people had lived in it; people who were his family; they had known experiences completely different from the ones he had known and they had changed in countless subtle ways just as he, too, had changed.

Then he thrust his doubts and fears behind him and faced the wind—felt it sharp and cold against his face. He lifted the barracks bag to his shoulder and started walking up the path in a long, swinging stride. He headed for the front door, changed his mind, and turned instead into the narrow path that led to the back of the house, to the kitchen.

As he turned the corner of the house, he said to himself, You think too much, Bud. You always have and it ain't healthy. Because it occurred to him that he was, in a sense, walking around the side of this house with a thousand other guys—none of them the first ones home from the war; certainly not the last ones. Other soldiers had returned home before them—still others would come after them, six months or a year later. He wondered if, as they walked around the side of other small houses in other small towns or thrust their keys into the locks of the doors of city apartment houses, they, too, paused for a moment because horrid little fears left them feeling cold and slightly apprehensive.

He heard the clink of silver, the rattle of dishes. He identified the sounds as he approached the kitchen door. He knew that his mother had finished eating her lunch, that it was hot in the kitchen and that she had opened the kitchen door. There were quick footsteps inside the kitchen. He put the barracks bag on the ground, mounted the steps, knocked at the door.

His mother's voice said, "Who is it?"

He didn't answer. Instead he rapped again; and his mother said, "What is it?"

He stood away from the screen door, flat against the side of the house. Kid stuff. But he couldn't help it. He wanted to see her face, caught unaware in just this fashion.

The quick footsteps neared the door. "Who is it?" she said.

"Grocery man," he said gruffly.

"What?" She opened the door and saw him. For a moment she didn't move, and then she said, "Oh!" and her breath came out in a sigh. And then she said, "Johnnie! Oh, Johnnie!"

All the color went out of her face. She started fingering a corner of the apron she was wearing as though the feel of the material would convince her that this was reality; as though she needed to know there were kitchen aprons in the same world where when you opened a screen door and looked out you beheld your only son. She looked down at the apron—quickly—as if she needed further evidence and found it in the blue-and-white print of the percale and the red of the rick-rack braid.

She dropped the corner of the apron and came out on the porch. "Johnnie," she said again, and touched the sleeve of his jacket. "Oh, Johnnie, you're home."

He hugged her and then pushed her a little away from him to look at her. She was stouter; the gray in her hair was more pronounced; but her eyes were just as he had remembered them—dark brown with a glow in their depths; and her mouth was generous and somehow as friendly as her eyes. The lines from her nose to her mouth had deepened, but the quirk at the corners of her mouth was the same—it suggested laughter.

"They sure fed you civilians good," he said, grinning.

"It's this old corset," she said. "If I'd known exactly when you were coming I would have—"

"Put on the new one? Your best one?"

"Of course," she said, and ignored the laughter in his eyes.

She turned toward the kitchen and held the screen door open wide. And as he watched her he thought, She's holding it open for you, Bud, because as far as she is concerned you represent all the king's horses and all the king's men.

But all she said was, "Let's go inside. And I'll fix you something to eat."

While his mother was frying bacon and scrambling eggs, he looked at the kitchen. It was exactly as he had remembered it: the big black iron stove still looked all wrong in the same room with the modern white-enamel sink; and the round oak table took up too much space in the middle of the floor.

The sharp edge of his dislike for the town blurred and softened; for none of this had changed—the kitchen, the car in the garage, the river off there behind the hedge of privet in back of the house, his mother's eyes and mouth.

His mother said, "You've grown so." He thought he saw a faint flicker of dismay in her eyes, but he was not certain.

"Yeah?"

She turned away from the stove to look at him. "You're a man," she said. "It doesn't seem possible anybody could have grown that much."

"I was a man when I left."

"Oh, no," she said. "You were only a boy. Twenty-two. Why, at that age you didn't even have your full growth. You were nothing but arms and legs."

"I was married. So I must have been a man."

The fork she was holding in her hand slid to the floor because she made a sudden startled movement. "You didn't stop by the store to see Glory?" she asked. "She doesn't know you're here?"

"I thought I'd wait until she came home. Sort of surprise her."

It was going to be tough to wait, tougher than he'd realized. But he'd manage to get through the next few hours.

"She might not want to be surprised," Mrs. Roane said. "You know women like to get dressed up for their menfolks. Not just by dressing up their clothes, but dressing up their minds, too. Why don't you call up the store and let her know you're here?"

"No," he said stubbornly. "I want to do it this way. I want to see her walk in the door and come in the house not knowing I'm here."

They were, finally, alone in the room; in the bedroom he had slept in as a boy—a room strangely familiar and yet at the same time unfamiliar.

He stood with his hand on the door, listening to the soft murmur of the voices of his mother and father drifting down the hall. Very soon his mother would be breathing evenly, gently; and there would be the sound of his father's snoring—a regular, not unpleasant sound. His father would sigh in his sleep and then snort, loudly, and turn over and the bedsprings would creak. His mother would say, "Jonathan. Are you all right? Jonathan . . . Jonathan . . ."

He closed the door quietly, took his hand away from the knob, turned toward Glory. He couldn't help staring at her. He had been doing it ever since she came home from work. She had run up the back steps; her footsteps light, quick. When she entered the kitchen, she brought a rush of sweet, cold air in with her; and it seemed to him that the early fall dusk was wrapped about her, enveloping her with a soft, mysterious glow that shimmered deep down in her eyes and clung to the edges of her hair.

His mother and Glory had done most of the talking, for he couldn't find words for what he wanted to say. When his father came home, they ate supper and afterward listened to the radio. His father had smoked a pipe and asked endless questions.

He had answered his father's questions, sensibly, he hoped. But while he talked he could not take his eyes away from Glory because she was more delicately beautiful than he had remembered. The one thing he had wanted was to be alone with her, here in this room.

Now that they were here and alone, he felt awkward, self-conscious.

"Glory," he said softly.

She was taking the bedspread off the bed, folding it up, and she turned toward him with the crinkled cotton spread in her arms. "Yes?" she said.

"I love you," he said, walking toward her. He held her close to him, squeezing her tight in his arms.

"You're wrinkling the spread," she protested.

"The hell with the spread," he said. He took it away from her and put it on the back of the Windsor chair near the bed.

When he turned toward her again, doubt made him pause. She was looking at him warily, as though she were half-afraid and afraid that her fear would show. Then he was holding her in his arms again, burying his face in her hair; started pushing her slowly toward the bed.

"Oh, darling," he said. "I love you, love you, love you." He held her closer, kissing her.

"You're rumpling my dress," she said.

"Well, take it off." He made a gesture as though he were going to help her, and she drew away from him. "Come on, take it off," he repeated.

She unfastened the belt of her dress, commenced to roll it up. He watched her fingers as they wound the belt neatly, tightly. There was something wrong. How could she stand there concentrating on the winding of a belt?

He sat down in the chair near the bed, fumbled with his shoelaces, knotting them up as he tried to unfasten them; and cursed under his breath. His fingers caught in the buttonholes of his shirt. He paused in his hurried undressing to wonder what kept her standing there—so unmoved, so unexcited as she wound the belt with neat, sure hands.

Perhaps she was embarrassed, but that was not possible. They were not a pair of awkward honeymooners, just married, half-afraid of each other. If he stopped staring at her, she might lose the self-consciousness or whatever it was that prevented her from undressing. He did not look in her direction again until he had turned back the covers on the bed.

She was still standing by the bureau, tugging at the belt, pulling it into a smaller, tighter circle. He was unreasonably angry at the sight.

"Are you going to stand there all night fooling with that damn belt?" he asked.

"Of course not," she said calmly.

That was all she said. She made no move to undress. Finally he took the belt out of her hands. "You want me to help you?" he asked.

"No," she said, not looking at him. She walked away from him, opened the closet door, took a long silky housecoat from a hanger, reached up on a shelf for a pair of slippers. Then she recrossed the room and pulled a thin flimsy nightgown from one of the bureau drawers.

"Hey," he said. "You don't need the nightgown."

She walked toward the door and then opened it.

"Where are you going?" he asked, surprised.

"To the bathroom."

He lay down in the black walnut bed and stared up at the carved grapes on the high headboard. He distinctly remembered when his mother bought this bed for him. He was fifteen and growing fast and she said he needed a man-sized bed. She had found this huge affair at an auction sale and had been furious because his father had said, "Enough to give the boy nightmares. I bet whole families have died in that bed."

It seemed strange to be lying in it again. Only of course he wouldn't be alone. Glory would be here beside him. He had forgotten how black and gloomy the bed was. The wood of the headboard was so dark and the headboard was so high that when you looked up at it, it was like looking at a wall you had to climb—a high black wall, unscalable because the darkness of its surface discouraged you, broke down your belief in yourself before you could get started.

What the devil was Glory doing in the bathroom? He listened for the sound of water running from the tap. Nothing. He found himself staring at the figured wallpaper. It was full of fancy gold flowers, repeated again and again. If you looked at it long enough you'd get dizzy.

If he had to use this room again he would change the wallpaper. Queer that Glory hadn't done it. As a matter of fact there was nothing in the room to indicate she had been occupying it. No books. No newspapers. No magazines. The pictures on the walls were the ones he had hung there years ago.

But wait, the mirror over the chest of drawers was a new addition. It used to hang in their living room. He remembered when she bought it at Malley's in New Haven and came lugging it home on the bus because she couldn't wait for the store to deliver it.

Now that he thought about it, she had never been able to wait for anything she really wanted. She had to possess the object she wanted, then and there, at the very second she conceived a desire for it. Why, then, was she deferring this moment of reunion, putting it off—

The door opened and Glory came into the room. The housecoat she wore was made of taffeta. It was a pale blue-green in color—the color of the sea, he thought; and her hair, long, the ends of it touching her shoulders, is as bright as the sun against that bluish-green material.

The hem of the housecoat swept across the wide floor boards, making a faint, rustling sound as she walked toward him. And he thought of many things, all at once: that the floor boards were as old as the house and that his mother had said they would outlast any new hardwood floors; and how he used to wax them and hated the job; and that Glory at that moment of entering the room appeared taller than she really was; and he wished she had not put on this long trailing thing called a housecoat; and at the same time he was glad that she was wearing it because its color made her as tantalizing as she had been in his dreams of her.

She slipped out of the housecoat and he saw that her breasts, her small waist, the long lovely legs, were partially revealed, partially concealed, by the thin material of the nightgown.

When she lay down beside him, he leaned toward her, saying, "Oh, Glory . . . Glory . . . Glory . . ."

He put his arm around her waist and the softness of the delicate gown and of her body made him aware of how big and clumsy his hands were—the skin toughened from handling metal and tools and being soaked with the oil and grease of motors. He buried his head between her breasts and he thought, This is all there is in the world of any importance—this outlasts everything else—this is warm and alive—this gives back to you some of what you lost—this makes you forget wars and rumors of wars—

She moved under his arm and pushed his head away. "Don't," she said. "You're hurting me."

"I'm sorry." He reached for her hand and kissed the hollow in the palm. "I love you so," he said softly. "There aren't any words for it. I've missed you so. I used to dream about you at night—about lying in bed beside you. But I always woke up alone in some godforsaken place. It seemed as though the dream would never come true. That I wouldn't live that long. And I still can't quite believe that I'm here and that you're real—"

He stopped talking and kissed her throat, her eyelids, her mouth. He felt her pull away from him and ignored the motion because he was filled with a sudden urgent desire that blacked out everything except the fact that she was there in his arms.

She was lying flat on her back, staring up at the ceiling. The delicate, rose-colored nightgown was rumpled about her and she lay motionless, not speaking.

It took a few minutes for him to realize what it meant. And he thought, This is what rape is like—to hold a woman close to you, and force your body on hers, ignoring her protests. For she had protested, by pulling away from him, by the final shrinking submission, by this silent withdrawal. He was so hellbent on having what he wanted that he had turned a deaf ear, a sightless and unheeding eye.

"Glory," he said gently, "what's the matter?"

"I don't know," she said. "I don't know. But I can't bear to have you touch me any more."

You spent four years in Africa, in England, in France, grubbing around in the insides of airplane engines and then they shipped you to an air base on a godforsaken island. Finally you came home. And your wife told you she couldn't bear to have you touch her any more.

At the time she told you, she was wearing a flimsy nightgown, designed by someone who had never been in a war, but who knew that wars were won and lost in bedrooms because if the top general's wife turned away from him because she couldn't bear to have him touch her any more, why, the final outcome of a war in China or Africa or Indonesia or some other place might suffer a sea change.

Yeah, he thought, the guys or dames who dream up this silky come-on bedroom stuff know what they're doing. They were called Victory nightgowns, according to some pictures he had seen in *Life* magazine. Victory, yeah. Oh, yeah, Victory. What was a victory worth, what did it cost, and whose was it, anyway? Certainly not his. Technical Sergeant Johnnie Roane. He came, he saw, he conquered. Came, saw, conquered—and went down to defeat.

"Well," he said hesitantly. "Why? I mean what's wrong with me?"

"There isn't anything wrong with you. It's me. And I don't know why."

"Is there—" He started and stopped because he felt like a fool. This was what they asked in moving pictures and in plays, in magazines and in books whenever the story involved a man and a woman. It was always the same question—banal, meaningless, pointless. Because the answer did not and could not explain anything—whether it was "yes" or "no" it still wouldn't explain anything.

"Is there somebody else?" he said doggedly.

She was still lying on her back, looking up at the ceiling. She didn't turn her head to look at him, she made no attempt to answer him.

She is so beautiful, he thought, so beautiful and so remote and so completely lost to me. He didn't know why, probably never would know why. But he had to know why.

He grabbed her by the throat, shook her. "Is there somebody else?" he repeated.

"Don't. You're hurting me," her voice was muffled, half strangled.

"Is there somebody else? Is that it?" His hands tightened about her throat. It seemed to be his own throat squeezed between violent, angry hands, for his voice was hoarse, half-strangled, too. "Is that it?" he said. "Is that it?" And he shook her again.

He heard her scream. It was such a thin, weak sound that it frightened him. His hands fell away from her throat. The scream gained in volume, slowly, perceptibly, until it filled the room.

"Ah, don't," he said. There was terror in the sound that issued from her throat. Probably every frightened woman in the world had made a sound like this—a gurgling, terrified, unbearable noise that beat about your eardrums, that made you wince away from its high pitch.

Under the high-pitched sound that was filling the room, he could hear footsteps coming swiftly up the hall. Either his father or his mother was coming, perhaps both of them. He covered his face with his hands.

There was a knock on the door. He couldn't move. There was no way of explaining a thing like this. He glanced at Glory. The Victory nightgown was rumpled about her body. Her throat bore the clear imprint of his hands.

He made himself get out of bed; reached for his shorts. He was aware that Glory had stopped screaming, though the sound still echoed in his ears. The knock on the door was repeated. This time it was demanding, insistent. He started for the door, got as far as the foot of the bed.

He saw, with surprise, that Glory had moved quickly. She was walking toward the door, had, in that quick movement, straightened the gown about her, shoved her feet in the furry slippers by the bed.

"Yes?" she said, not opening the door.

"Is there—" His father's voice faltered, hesitated, stopped. Then it started again and this time it was strong and clear. "Is there anything wrong?"

"Oh, no," Glory said. She patted her hair in place with a

swift motion of her hands. Then she opened the door just wide enough so that his father could catch a glimpse of her in the delicate rose-colored gown. From the sound of her voice she was smiling. The draft from the hall lifted the folds of the gown about her feet.

"I'm sorry if I disturbed you," she said. "The window came down on my hand and I thought—" Her voice grew fainter. "I thought there was blood on it."

He listened to her, amazed. She should have been an actress, he thought bitterly. And how quickly she could think, and how quickly, lie. His father and mother knew she was terrified by the sight of blood—a nameless, horrid kind of fear that set her to screaming and fainting. He never had known why—something that had happened to her when she was a kid and it was so long ago that she herself had forgotten how and when it began.

"Is it hurt badly?" His father's voice was gentle, concerned.

"Oh, no," she said quickly. "It wasn't hurt. I got frightened and screamed before I knew whether I'd broken the skin or not. See?" She thrust a hand through the cautious crack of the door.

Then his father said, "It is all right, Johnnie?"

"Sure," he said. He took a deep breath. "It's okay," he said.

His father's footsteps started back down the hall. Glory closed the door. He couldn't bring himself to look at her. He ought, he supposed, to be grateful to her. Because of her his mother and father no longer thought he had turned murderous on his first night at home.

There was an uneasy silence in the bedroom that Mrs. Roane had shared with Mr. Roane for some twenty-eight years.

Finally Mrs. Roane turned her head toward Mr. Roane and said, "Jonathan, I don't believe her. It was something else."

"Why?" said Mr. Roane.

"Because those windows—those windows don't slip down

suddenly like the old-fashioned ones. They've got chains on them. And they stay put. The man who put them in said those chains would outlast the house."

Mrs. Roane waited for a reply. Then she put her hand on Mr. Roane's arm because she was afraid that in another minute he'd be snoring. She said, "Jonathan, you don't think—"

"I don't know," he said. He sounded confused, uneasy. "I don't know," he repeated.

4

HE SAT ON THE EDGE of the bed, hunched over, his chin on his hands, staring at the floor. What happens next? he thought. What do you do now?

Something soft touched his bare feet—a thing soft as the wing of a butterfly. Glory had come to stand in front of him. The thin nightgown was brushing against his feet.

"I'm sorry, Johnnie," she said. "Honest. I don't know what made me say I didn't want you to touch me any more. I guess I was tired. That's all it was. Honest."

He looked at her doubtfully, wanting to believe her. She worked in the general store, stood on her feet all day, waiting on customers, checking the orders, answering the telephone—more than enough to make a woman tired. But not that tired. He had been gone four years and—

"You sure there isn't anybody else?"

"Of course not," she said quickly. "How could there be? There aren't any young single men left in Lennox. The ones who went off to war got married before they left. There's nobody around but old men and wrecks of young ones—the ones who came back without arms or legs."

She was obviously waiting for him to say that he believed her. But how could he? Hadn't he just heard her tell his father a swift, smooth lie?

The edge of the nightgown moved gently over the top of his foot. He got up, walked to the window, and looked out. It was a dark night, no stars in sight. A black curtain seemed to have dropped down over the town; if he reached his hand up far enough he could touch it. The wind was coming straight from the northeast—a cold, strong wind. It would rain tonight.

He got into bed and watched Glory as she climbed in on the other side. She reached up a bare and beautiful arm and turned the light out. In the sudden darkness he kept seeing her arm as it reached for the light—white, slender; the fingernails were lacquered a deep red that caught the light.

He wondered if anyone, anywhere, any time, had looked forward to something, waited for it, dreamed over it, shaping and reshaping it in his mind, and then had found the reality exactly like the dream. He doubted it. Reality always ate the living heart out of a dream.

Glory moved closer to him. Her body was warm, soft. How did his feel to her—hard, unyielding? And he thought, What do you talk about when the lights are out, what do you talk about in a pitch-dark room, what do you talk about with only the wind moving in the room, what do you talk about after you throttle your wife, after you choke her in a fit of rage?

"I had forgotten how tall you are, Johnnie. And your shoulders got broader while you were away," Glory said.

"Yeah?" So that's what you talk about.

Once again he saw Ed standing on the Town Hall steps—a dark, broad-shouldered figure, slightly bowlegged. He was one of the few healthy males left in the town. Or was he healthy? Wasn't he supposed to have something wrong with his heart?

Why was he thinking about Ed Barrell? Glory had said that

he, Johnnie, had grown taller. And his shoulders were broader. His mind had developed some kind of squirming, eel-like quality. When she said "tall," his mind said "short." When she said "shoulders broader," his mind twisted and turned and came up with Ed Barrell—squat, shoulders too thick, chest too wide, bull-chested. Town Bull.

What do you say lying in a black walnut bed when the lights are out?

"I saw Ed Barrell today," Johnnie said. Glory didn't move. The rhythm of her breathing stayed even, slow.

"Yes?" she said.

So he had to continue. "And I saw Mrs. Gramby, too: I didn't see either of them to speak to. Just caught glimpses of them from the taxi window."

This time she made an impatient movement, her breathing quickened. "That old woman!" she said. "She makes me sick. Momma can't stand her either."

At first he did not understand what she meant, for he thought she was talking about his mother; and he knew that his mother liked Mrs. Gramby. Then he remembered that Glory always referred to his mother as Mother Roane.

"Your mother?" he said. "What's your mother got to do with Mrs. Gramby?" So this is what you talked about.

"Momma lives with her. Didn't I tell you? Of course I did. I *knew* you never half-read my letters."

"I did read them," he said indignantly. "I read them five and six times. And kept them tied up in bundles. On Sundays I'd go over them one at a time." He paused, remembering. In the barracks on Sundays, he wore a pair of olive-drab shorts. And all around him were other guys in shorts—reading letters, writing letters, cursing, talking, dreaming, as they fingered those pieces of paper—white, pale blue, pale pink, gray. Some of the letters were typed, some written in neat careful hands, some like

Glory's in writing that looked young—big letters, wide space between the lines.

The olive-drab shorts and the bundles of letters were symbols of the war. He found himself thinking of peace in terms of the day when he would wear white shorts, underwear that he bought and paid for himself because it happened to be the kind he wanted to wear. And when that day came, he and Glory would be together. He would no longer have to pore over a bundle of old letters; re-reading them like a drowning man clinging to a bit of driftwood.

"You never said anything about your mother living with Mrs. Gramby."

"I did, too. I know I did. I wrote and told you all about the wedding. It was in the Congregational Church and I wore a new print dress that Momma made for me. It was two years ago in the spring. Momma wore a dark gray gabardine suit and a small hat made of violets. Not real violets. Cloth ones. But they looked real."

"I remember that part," he said hastily. "But—"

"Momma married Mearns Gramby. Mrs. Gramby's son. She lives in the Gramby House."

"Oh, yes," he said. She had written many times about the Grambys. It hadn't meant anything. Mrs. Gramby had taken on a dimness, a fading quality so that he had difficulty figuring out who Glory was writing about. He had been hungry for news of Glory—what she was thinking about, whether she missed him, if she dreamed about him and how often. Instead, she talked of the Gramby House. It seemed to run through her thoughts like a connecting thread—but he never could figure out what it connected with.

"Does your mother still sew?" he asked, abruptly.

"Sew?" Glory said. There was indignation in her voice. "Of

course not. Why should she? She's Mrs. Mearns Gramby now. What would she be sewing for?"

The muscles of his face relaxed and he almost smiled. Glory sounded as though she had said, "Her Majesty, Queen of the Belgians or the English or the something or other. What would Her Majesty be doing sewing for a living?"

She's an awful little snob, he thought. He reached out his hand toward her, remembering how he had teased her about being a snob when they were first married; and he intended to remind her of it. He touched her shoulder. It was bare except for the bit of lace which formed the strap of the Victory nightgown. She moved away from him in a quick withdrawal that left his hand in contact with the edge of the pillow.

He knew then that she had been telling the truth when she said that she could not bear to have him touch her any more. She might be tired, she might have aching feet and legs, and her mind could be fagged out from checking grocery lists, but that would not explain why she had just recoiled from the touch of his hand—a hand extended on impulse.

Glory said: "Women aren't made the same as men. They don't enjoy sexual intercourse."

Oh, damn-it-to-hell, he thought, why does she keep trying to fix up the unfixable? Why do I care? Why don't I get up tomorrow morning and leave her? What makes me want her? Why should the way her face is shaped, the color of her hair, the way she walks—why should these things enchant me?

The rain began—so gentle at first it was a mere whisper of sound against the windows. It grew slowly in intensity until it was a downpour. As he lay there in the dark, listening to the beat of the rain against the windows, he remembered how he had dreamed of talking to Glory, yearned to talk to her; to tell her of his urge to live in a city; the urge to paint.

Just before he went to sleep he thought, Who could it be? Is it Ed Barrell? Could I tell by looking at him if he's the one?

When he woke up the next morning, it was still raining. The room was full of wind and the dampness of the rain. He glanced at Glory while he dressed. Her hair was all about her face; curling over the pillow.

As he looked at her, he felt a quick, hot desire well up in him. He wanted to wake her up and make love to her. Instead he finished dressing. Then he went out of the room, closing the door softly behind him.

5

UPSTAIRS IN THE FRONT BEDROOM in the Roane house, a window shade flapped back and forth in the wind. The sound awakened Glory. She sat up in bed and with a sudden, jerky movement, thrust one arm forward, as though to ward off a blow. She thought Johnnie had made a violent, threatening gesture toward her while she slept.

Then she saw that he was no longer lying beside her in the walnut bed. He was not in the room at all; and his clothing was gone—the clumsy army shoes, and the uniform that had been draped over the back of the Windsor chair. The angry, slapping sound that had wakened her was simply the wind blowing the shade, in and out of the window.

I am shivering, she thought, because I am cold; and because of the damp air in the room, the endless dripping of the rain; but most of all because I am afraid, afraid of Johnnie.

Why couldn't things have stayed the way they were? Other mornings she had drifted awake, emerging from layers of sleep, slowly, luxuriously. After she was fully awake, she would lie motionless, relaxed, her eyes closed, thinking about Ed. Her thoughts were always the same: that today something wonderful was going to happen; that today she would find out what it would be like to have him make love to her.

She got out of bed, shut the window with a bang, and stood in front of it, listening. The rain was making an unpleasant sound like a hand tapping on the glass.

"Why didn't Johnnie close it when he got up?" she thought. The curtains were wet. There was a pool of water on the wide floor boards under the window.

Then she remembered and felt her throat with careful fingers. It was sore to the touch. Undoubtedly the imprint of his hands showed clear on the skin. His hands had been like an iron band, cutting off her breath, squeezing it back inside her throat. Thinking about it was like having the nightmare memory of a dream come suddenly alive in broad daylight.

She crossed the room and looked at herself in the mirror over the chest of drawers. Yes, you could see where his hands had been. The skin was red, angry-looking. Those red places would become purplish bruises and anyone who saw them would know that someone had tried to choke her.

I'll tie a scarf around my neck—a white one and wrap it high about my throat and the marks won't show. The salesmen who came in the store would think it was a new style.

She dressed quickly, putting on a skirt, a dark green sweater. When she fastened the scarf around her throat, she looked in the mirror and frowned. She would have to wear the scarf for several days. Eventually there would be a comment or a question. A customer would lean over the bread counter and say, "S'matter, you got a sore throat?" and then grin, and continue, "Johnnie musta been playin' rough on his first night home." It would be half joke, half conjecture.

Ah, yes, Johnnie, she thought. He's downstairs now, eating his breakfast, waiting for me. And I don't want to face him. Not today. Not tomorrow. Not ever.

Last night when he said he had seen Ed, she almost stopped breathing. How had he known there was something between her and Ed?

There wasn't—yet. Right now it looked as though there never would be. She evidently didn't attract Ed the way other women did. The men who patronized Perkins' store were always dropping sly hints about his weakness for married women.

They had made her curious. When he came in the store, she made it a point to wait on him, deliberately overlooking customers who had arrived ahead of him; greeting him with a special smile; brushing against him when she helped him select the ripest oranges, the heaviest head of cabbage. For the last month or so he had been bringing her home from work, three or four nights a week.

The first time Mother Roane saw her getting out of Ed's car there was a faint astonishment in her face and then a wave of hot red color suffused her neck, her cheeks.

After that, whenever Ed brought her home, Mother Roane was always hovering near the front gate. Her face was expressionless, her eyes calm, friendly. "Hello, Ed," she'd say. "Nice of you to bring Glory home. Save her that long walk."

Mother Roane's easy acceptance of Glory's presence in Ed's car managed to destroy the feeling of intimacy she and Ed had built up. He would shift his cigar from one side of his mouth to the other, push his hat farther back on his head, pull it forward, shove it back again and start talking about the flowers growing just inside the fence.

"Your roses sure are big. The white ones are new, huh?"

Mother Roane talked about fertilizers and sprays and the best time of year for pruning as though she took it for granted Ed had an honest, active interest in roses.

Glory began to feel as though she were being spied on, as though Johnnie himself were leaning over the front gate, just behind his mother, watching her step out of Ed's car. It made her uncomfortable. She told Ed that it would be better if he let her out of the car at the first curve in the River Road, well out of sight of the house.

It had made a little difference. She felt free and Ed must have, too, because he began taking her for rides, long rides through the back roads. He would park the car at a spot where there was a nice view, on the crest of a hill, or by some small, aimless stream. But he never made love to her, though his eyes lingered on her face—bold, hot, calculating—as though he were estimating her, conjecturing about her.

When she returned from those rides she had a breathless, excited feeling, as though she were on the verge of discovering some important and hitherto hidden secret about herself.

She rarely thought about Johnnie. She didn't want to. When she first married him she had found his eager devotion a pleasant thing. He listened when she talked. He never flatly contradicted her or threatened her. Whereas Momma had been very free with her hands when she got mad and was completely absorbed in herself as well.

But after six months of Johnnie's adoration, she was fed up. She did not see how she could go on cleaning house and washing clothes and cooking meals, year after year. At the end of the year she was so bored it frightened her. Sometimes she quarreled with Johnnie just to break the monotony of their existence. He was almost as bad as Momma about small extravagances and pinched pennies because he wanted to go to college.

Then Johnnie went into the army. She got a job in Perkins' store and she was free for the first time in her life. Momma had no control over her and Johnnie, who had bottled her up in the little white house, with dishes and laundry and cooking, was gone.

She hadn't missed him either. It was more a feeling of relief than anything else. Before she married him she had worked in the cold cream factory in Westville, but Momma took money from her, for board and room and electric light; and made her pay part of the phone bill and somehow managed to leave her with only a few paltry dollars out of her pay envelope every week.

The money she earned at Perkins' was her own to spend on clothes, and movies and trips to the hairdresser. Mother Roane wouldn't take anything for board and room. She said she was only too glad to have Glory with her; it made her feel as though some part of Johnnie was in the house.

Perkins' store was full of life and movement. Salesmen and farmers and truck-drivers came and went all day long. They liked to talk to her, to tease her. They called her Morning Glory and Angel Face and Glory Hallelujah, and leaned over the counters to touch her hand and smile into her eyes.

It was a whirlpool of activity after the quiet, dull, back-water life she'd led with Johnnie. His letters never failed to startle her. He took it for granted that she was interested in his hopes and dreams. But she wasn't.

He wrote about cities, the ones he had seen, the ones he wanted to see and to live in. Some fellow in his outfit was an artist and was teaching him to paint. The letters made her uncomfortable with their lengthy descriptions of cities and of painters; and running through them like a refrain was a demanding love that cried out for fulfillment.

She answered him briefly, for she doubted whether he knew what he wanted—he was one of those people who liked to write letters. But she knew what she wanted. She did not intend to return to a life of cooking and cleaning in that small frame house of theirs. Neither did she intend to live in a city. She would be lost in a city—just another pretty girl in a world full of pretty girls. Perkins' store offered more excitement than the biggest city in the country. She was the prettiest girl for miles around and all the men who came in the store paid homage to her.

Ed came in the store every day. And always there were the tales about him, whetting her curiosity. Just last week a farmer with a feed bag on his shoulder paused on his way out of the store to say, "Old Whoosis better watch his wife. She's out there talkin' to Ed," and the store echoed to the rafters with the guffaws of the other men.

She looked out of the front window and sure enough Ed was leaning against the side of a car, talking to the woman who sat behind the wheel. And watching the sudden brightening of the woman's eyes she had a sudden savage impulse to hurl something out of the window, something that would destroy the woman's face, dull the sparkle of her eyes.

That was the day she admitted to herself that she had fallen in love with Ed, that she had been dressing especially for him, thinking, Will it be today? Will he say something today that will show he wants me?

Mother Roane would glance at the new hairstyle or the new dress or the high-heeled sandals and say, "I like to see a girl keep herself pretty for her husband." Or, "Johnnie would love to see you in that new brown suit."

She couldn't decide whether or not these comments of Mother Roane's were a deliberate and pointed way of reminding her that she was still married to Johnnie.

She hadn't known which day he would return. When The Weasel stopped in the store, yesterday, and told her that Johnnie had come home, she felt as though she had been backed into a corner by a violent hand.

And I've got to go downstairs and face him. I can't hide away from him by staying in this room. If I don't hurry, I'll be late for work. Ed always comes in the store early in the morning and I wouldn't want to miss him. It's a mess, all of it, any way you look at it. I don't want Johnnie and I haven't got Ed and may never have him.

She hesitated with her hand on the knob of the door, thinking, I'm not ready to face him this morning any more than I was ready to face him last night. He can see all of this in my eyes and I am afraid of him because of it.

She went down the stairs, reluctantly. She had to put on a performance, an act; pretend that she was overjoyed because he had returned. She had to do it because it was what was expected of her; and she felt as though she were walking a tight rope, liable at any moment to lose the delicate balance that kept her aloft.

Just before she entered the kitchen, she took a deep breath. "Hello," she said brightly. "It's a nice morning for ducks, isn't it?"

Johnnie was not in the kitchen. Mother Roane was sitting by the window, her hands hovering about a mending basket that she held in her lap. She was staring out at the cove.

Glory, looking at her, thought, She can't see anything out of those windows the way they're steamed up and with all that rain sluicing against the outside of the panes. She might as well be trying to look through cardboard—gray, thick, impenetrable. But she keeps her head averted, pretending that she sees the cove, because, for some reason, she does not want to look at me.

Then Mrs. Roane turned her head, smiled gently, and said, "Hello, Glory. It looks like an all-day storm, doesn't it?"

"Yes, it does." She took a quick look at the table. There was only one place set. "Johnnie had his breakfast?"

"Yes. He came down early," Mother Roane gave Glory a quiet, appraising look. "He went out for a walk," she said. "I fixed lunch for him to take with him."

"A walk? A walk on a day like this? Why he must be—" She swallowed the word "crazy" and said hastily, "Why would he go walking in all this rain?"

"He said he wanted to look at the town. He hasn't seen it for quite a while." Mrs. Roane picked up a sock, thrust a darning needle in one side of a gaping hole in the heel.

Glory watched the needle go back and forth in the heel of the sock. This is an act she's putting on for me, she thought. The calm, quiet mother act. She's pretending there's nothing unusual about Johnnie dashing out of the house before I'm up, to go mooning about in the rain.

"Did Johnnie eat much breakfast?" she asked.

Mrs. Roane looked up, nodded her head. Glory stared at her, frowning, because she was thinking, I'm too worried and frightened to eat, but he ate like a horse, gulping down eggs and bacon and oatmeal. His mother is peaceful, contented, too, as she sits darning that sock, weaving the needle in and out through that gaping hole. They are heartless, both of them.

"I thought he might have been too upset to eat—upset about last night," Glory said pointedly.

"Oh, I don't think so," Mrs. Roane said easily. "He knows how you are about the sight of blood. When he came down this morning he said he wouldn't wake you up, that you needed to sleep, because you were so frightened when the window came down on your hand." She paused and then said, "Is it better this morning?"

"It's all right," Glory said. She walked over to the stove, poured a cup of coffee. She kept her back turned toward Mother Roane. There wasn't the faintest suggestion of a bruise on her hand.

Mother Roane didn't believe that business about the window coming down on her hand. The lack of belief was in her voice, in her eyes. She knows there's something wrong between me and Johnnie. She's going to take sides with him against me. I would like to tell her the truth, tell her that her precious son tried to choke me to death. I'm cornered here in this house with him demanding a response I can't give him, with her looking on, showing her disapproval, feeling sorry for him. And then there's Ed—Ed who I want and haven't got and may never get.

Glory sat down at the round table in the center of the kitchen, shoved the knife and fork aside, took a sip of coffee.

"There's orange juice in the icebox," Mother Roane said.

"I don't feel like drinking it."

"Is that all the breakfast you're going to eat? Just coffee?"

"I'm not hungry," Glory said. "Besides, I'm late."

Why can't she leave me alone? It doesn't seem possible that in a room as big as this kitchen anybody could feel so crowded. It's the way she looks at me, as though I had committed a crime, but she has to be patient and put up with me because I'm not quite right in the head.

Glory glanced at the clock. She *was* late. It was ten after eight and she was due at the store at eight-thirty. But Mother Roane obviously did not intend to drive her to work. She wasn't dressed to go out—thin house dress, last summer's canvas sandals on her feet.

I won't ask her to take me. If she's mean enough to let me walk in this pouring rain, why, I'll just go ahead and walk and get soaking wet. Perhaps I'll get pneumonia and die and then I won't have to put up with that patient look on her face and have Johnnie staring at me, feel his murderous hands about my throat, or have to sit waiting, with my tongue hanging out, for Ed to make up his mind about me.

Mrs. Roane put the mending basket on the window sill. "I thought this was your day off," she said. "That's why I didn't get dressed. It won't take me a minute to get my things on and I'll drive you up to the store."

"Why, it *is* my day off," Glory said, surprised. "I forgot about it. Isn't that funny? I never forgot about it before."

The whole day is wrong, she thought. Part of what's wrong with it is this rain dripping from the roof, streaming down the windows; and the rest of what's wrong with it is that I usually go to Sarah Lou to have my hair done on Tuesday afternoons—and then, afterward, for a ride with Ed.

"Did Johnnie know it was my day off?" she asked.

"No, he didn't," Mrs. Roane said. "In fact, I didn't think about it myself until after he went out. He got to talking and I almost forgot to give him his toast. He was telling me how New York looked yesterday morning. He changed trains there. Had to go from one station to another, in a taxi. He wants to live there. I guess I forgot everything just listening to him."

Glory could see them—Johnnie and his mother, sitting at the table, talking, talking, talking. Johnnie's face must have been alive and eager. He probably waved his hands in the air, gestured with his fork, forgot to eat and then suddenly remembered and shoved too-big mouthfuls in his mouth. His mother must have leaned halfway across the table, smiling at him the way she had smiled last night: as though he was something special that had unexpectedly been given to her, something she had been wanting all her life and finally got and couldn't quite believe it.

They had forgotten that Johnnie had a wife—a wife left alone upstairs; shut up in a dreary bedroom where the wind and the rain blew in through an open window; a wife whose throat was sore to the touch because Johnnie had squeezed it between his big, hard hands. She had been left alone to eat her heart out while they sat down here snug and secure and intimate in this big warm kitchen. She was suddenly jealous of their contentment, of their happiness in each other.

"New York?" she said quickly. "We're not going to live in New York. We talked about it upstairs last night, in the big walnut bed—" She gestured toward the ceiling, establishing her relationship with Johnnie, underlining the intimacy his mother hadn't been able to share, never would be able to share. "We're going to move back into our own house just as soon as the people who are in it now can find some other place to live."

Mrs. Roane went on talking just as though Glory had not spoken. "He's wanted to live in a big city like New York ever since he was a little boy."

If Johnnie went to New York she didn't have to go with him. She could stay in Lennox, be near Ed, go on working in the store. But Mother Roane was saying something else.

"Johnnie says he wants to be an artist. That's what he's going to do—study to be a painter."

"An artist?" Glory said sharply. "A painter?" She stared at Mother Roane, her eyes following the slow in-and-out movement of the darning needle, thinking. Then his letters did mean something, he was always writing about painters. "He doesn't know anything about painting. The only thing he knows is machines and engines—the insides of cars. How could he be a painter?"

"He wants to learn. Some boy he met in the army was an artist. And Johnnie said that knowing this artist helped him decide that was what he was going to do. Besides, he was always drawing, even as a child."

"It's absolutely crazy," Glory said. "He can't earn a living doing that. Does he think I'm going to support him while he fools around with paints?"

"Oh, no. You see the Government arranges it so that he can study anything he wants. They pay for it."

"That money isn't enough to live on," Glory said impatiently. And all the time she was thinking, Everybody but me. All of them get what they want but me. He gets New York and painting and she gets her son back from the war—that's what she wanted. I'm the one that everything goes wrong for. She's happy; he's happy. I won't have it. It isn't fair.

"Where's he going to study painting? Here in Lennox? Is he going to take lessons from Spatter Bronson who does the walls and ceilings of the houses all over town?"

"He said he was going to live in New York," Mrs. Roane said. She looked up from her darning. "I suppose that's where he's going to study."

"But I'm not going to live there. I'm going to stay here. All of my friends are here. Momma lives here—"

She got up from the table, walked up and down the room, slowly at first, then faster and faster. Never once have I had a single thing I ever really wanted; when I married him I thought I would be free and he built a cage around me and stood in the door of it, admiring me; and it was a cage as tight and narrow as the one Momma kept me in. When he left I was happy, happier than I've ever been. Now he's back again, intent on smothering the life out of me with his unwanted love. Just his presence in the town will push Ed farther away from me, will scare him off.

Anger and frustration made her shout, "Why didn't he tell me? Why did he tell you and then go off for the day? Just as though he didn't want to see me."

"He didn't know it was your day off. You forgot it yourself. So did I." Mother Roane's voice was gentle, conciliatory. "I don't think he meant to tell me. He got to talking and couldn't seem to stop. Just as though a lot of things that had been shut up inside him suddenly pushed their way out. He had to tell somebody. And last night—" She turned her attention to the sock in her hands. The darning needle went back and forth—steadily, slowly; the unfinished sentence was left suspended in the air.

Last night. Last night, Glory thought. I don't want to remember last night. I don't want to remember anything. I want to be let alone; to start out fresh with no memories and go on from there; I want to live my life in my own way. I wish last night had never come.

Why had Mother Roane said that, anyway? Glory stared at her, trying to read her thoughts. But a woman with sewing or knitting in her hands is unreadable; with eyes, hands, mind concentrated like that, it's impossible to tell what her thoughts are. Momma was the same way once she got a needle in her hands.

"I think I'll spend the day with Momma," she said abruptly. "If Johnnie comes home any time soon, tell him I'm at the Grambys'." She went out of the kitchen, slamming the door behind her.

6

THAT MORNING THE TOWN WAS all gray gloom. It seemed to have withdrawn deep inside itself as though reluctant to face a day so dark, so dominated by wind and rain. Leaves were blown down from the trees; and the tall grass in the meadows that edged the town moved back and forth, now upright, now bending, so that the grass seemed to shiver and recoil under the impact of the wind.

The storm made Glory restless. She spent the morning trying to decide whether she should keep her regular weekly appointment with the hairdresser. If she kept it, she knew that afterward she would go for a ride with Ed.

The sound of the rain beating against the bedroom windows made her uneasy. She went into Mother Roane's room at the back of the house and stood staring out at the cove. She caught sudden glimpses of it through the rain-streaked windows. It was black, sullen, bordered by a ripple of white foam that gnawed restlessly at the edges of the marsh. The foam retreated and then returned, retreated and then returned; and as she watched it she got the feeling that she could hear it snarl because it could not get free of the marsh that confined it.

The same restless irritability and frustration were inside of her. On a day like this, she thought, I can't get Ed out of my mind. I keep seeing him as he drives his car, his hands caressing the wheel, his eyes half-closed as he looks at me. I want to hear his voice in my ear, saying that he loves me.

If Johnnie went to New York, she could stay in Lennox, go on working at the store. She could get a divorce from Johnnie, marry Ed. But Ed had a wife, a wife who had been in a tubercular sanatorium for years. He could get a divorce from her. But could he? And did he want to?

Suppose he wouldn't get a divorce, did she have the courage to face the town, to become "that Roane woman" who lives with Ed Barrell? No. Well, they could go somewhere else to live. But the store—she didn't want to give up working in the store. It was all she'd ever known of excitement and fun.

As she went out of Mother Roane's room, she thought, Ed hasn't said he wants you. He's never even put his arm around you. What makes you waste your time planning a future that includes him?

She washed stockings and underwear in the bathroom sink, then ironed three blouses and a dress—working quickly, trying to keep from thinking as she moved the iron back and forth.

It was afternoon before she went downstairs to call Sarah Lou. She canceled the appointment.

Mother Roane was in the kitchen, and hearing her at the telephone said, "I fixed lunch for you, dear. Nice soup and a custard and some cookies."

"No, thanks," Glory said curtly. "I'm going to Momma's now. I'm awfully late because I stopped to wash and iron."

When she left the house, the rain had dwindled to a fine mist. As she neared the center of town, the sun came out. Gray wind clouds scudded across the sky, for the wind persisted in spite of the pale, undecided sunlight. The church, the drugstore, even the trees, might have been cut out of cardboard, she thought, for the sun was not strong enough to cast shadows from the buildings, to give a look of glowing life to the grass and trees. She shivered and walked faster because she got the feeling that some spirit of evil was hovering over the town, had come between it and the sun.

Then she caught sight of the Gramby House and began to walk more slowly, eyeing the white shutters, the ruffled curtains, the small-paned windows. Some day this sleek and polished house would belong to Momma from its huge chimneys and gray slate roof right down to the last pinkish brick of which it was built. The thought never failed to give her a little thrill of pleasure.

The window shades were drawn to the same point, midway, all over the house. You could only have that kind of exactness in a house where there was a maid. And a box hedge required a gardener. She opened the gate, paused on the flagstone walk to admire the shiny dark green leaves of the hedge.

Mrs. Gramby's gardener, known in the town as The Portegee, was down on his hands and knees, covering the hedge with long boards. He was fastening them down securely, driving the supports into the ground with repeated blows of a hammer. One side of the hedge was completely concealed.

"You must be expecting a bad storm," she said.

He glanced up at her and grunted. She got a glimpse of his swarthy face, of the fierce mustachios that curled about his mouth, of the turquoise earring in his ear, and then he bent his head, went on working. No manners at all, she thought. Well, one of these days this place would belong to Momma. Momma couldn't live forever and then it would be hers. She'd change a good many things, for she wouldn't have any surly help like The Portegee and Neola.

On second thought she'd keep him. He was supposed to be

a very fine gardener. He grew strawberries and grapes in the greenhouse in winter; and tea roses and daffodils. Yes, she'd keep him on and explain to her friends. "Oh, Portulacca's impossible. Gruff and cross as can be. But the best gardener in the state. We're always winning prizes in the flower shows because of him."

So she smiled at him and said sweetly, "I think the storm's over. You'll have done all that work for nothing."

He straightened up, touched his cap. She thought he was going to say something, for he took the corncob pipe out of his mouth, held it in his hand for a moment, as though he was clearing the way for words. Then he thrust it in the opposite corner of his mouth with a ramming motion. This gesture gave her the feeling that he had spoken, had agreed with her, but that some inner shyness prevented him from putting his agreement into words.

As she walked up the path she heard him clear his throat and she turned around, thinking he was about to speak. Instead he spat a stream of nicotine-colored saliva over the hedge, in the direction from which she had come.

Damn you, she thought. One of these days this place will be mine. Then we'll see who you'll spit at.

As she started up the front steps, Neola opened the door.

"Helloa, Neola," Glory said, thinking, You go with the house, too—dark uniform, ruffled cap, and all. When Mrs. Gramby dies you or someone very like you will bring me my breakfast in the morning.

"Good afternoon."

"Is Momma home?"

"She went out early this morning, Mrs. Roane. If you'll step inside I'll find out whether she's returned."

All of them—Neola, The Portegee, Mrs. Gramby—acted as though Momma was an undesirable paying guest. It was a rotten ugly trick and they did it all the time. Whenever she came here, they pretended that they didn't have the faintest idea whether Momma was in the house or out of it.

"Is that you, Gloria?" Mrs. Gramby's voice reached into the hall—firm, loud, untouched by age.

"Yes, ma'am," Glory said. She wished she hadn't said "ma'am." It sounded humble—like a servant. But the old lady's voice frightened her; it always had.

She entered the living room, reluctantly. The tomcats glared at her—one on the sofa, one on a chair near the fireplace, one on Mrs. Gramby's lap. There was a fire burning feebly in the fireplace—a stingy small fire that could not possibly dispel the chill in the room.

"Your mother's upstairs," Mrs. Gramby said. "She'll be down shortly. Won't you sit down while you're waiting? Oh, no, not there! Leon III takes his nap there and the minute you sit down he'll be in your lap."

Glory selected a hard straight chair in the middle of the room. When Momma got the house, the first thing they'd do would be to remove that horribly alive-looking portrait of the late Mr. Gramby that hung over the mantel. No matter where she sat, he always seemed to be staring at her, and she half-expected to hear him say, "What are you doing in my house?" Had he looked like that when he was alive—his eyes staring so insolently, his lower lip protruding?

"I hear Johnnie's back home," Mrs. Gramby said.

"Yes, ma'am. He came yesterday."

"I think I saw him in Mr. Weasel's taxi."

"He told me he saw you," Glory said. And that he had seen Ed Barrell. She jerked her mind away from the thought of Ed. What would happen if she got up and poked the fire? The room was cold. She wished Momma would hurry up and come downstairs. In any other house in town, one would say, "I'll go up to her room," and walk briskly up the long curving staircase.

But not here. There was a rigid formality in this house. Mrs. Gramby maintained it. Right after Momma had married Mearns Gramby and come here to live, she, Glory, had rung the front doorbell, opened the door, and started up the stairs.

Mrs. Gramby had come into the hall, leaning heavily on her cane. "Kindly go in the living room and sit down. I do not permit that kind of running around in my house. Neola will tell your mother that you are here. If your mother wants you in her room, she will take you there herself."

The old lady had made no effort to be friendly. She limped back to the living room, sat down in a wing chair, the same one she was sitting in now, picked up a book, and read it, turning the pages slowly, as completely absorbed as though she had been alone in the room.

Where was Momma, anyway? This waiting was unbearable. The cats kept blinking their eyes, sneaking glances at her. No one save a horrible old woman like Mrs. Gramby would want to own three striped tiger cats and name all of them Leon. The late Mr. Gramby had owned three such cats, and each time one died Mrs. Gramby searched the countryside for a striped tom to take its place.

The doorbell rang. She wanted to get up and look out the front window, see who it was, for few callers came here. But she didn't want Mrs. Gramby to say, "Sit down. I don't allow people to peer out of the windows in my house." So she sat motionless, listening to Neola's footsteps as she walked up the hall toward the door.

Mrs. Gramby said, "That must be Mr. Weasel."

Neola came to the door. "The driver's here," she said. "Shall I tell him you're not going?"

"Oh, no, don't tell him that. I'm going as usual. The rain has let up. Will you call Mrs. Roane and tell her we're on our way to pick her up?"

When Neola re-entered the room, she was carrying a long black cape, a high-crowned felt hat, and a man's umbrella. Mrs. Gramby stood up and Neola draped the cape around her shoulders; pulled the hat firmly over her white hair; and then handed her a pair of black kid gloves.

Glory went to the window to watch the old lady's slow progress down the front steps. She took the steps one at a time, pausing in between and pretending that the pauses were necessary in order that she might pull the gloves over her swollen finger joints. But she's actually pausing because her joints are stiff and full of aches and pains, Glory thought. You can tell by the way she walks. I wonder how old she is; and I'd say just from looking at her that she couldn't last much longer.

The Weasel held one of the old lady's arms. Neola gripped her firmly on the other side. When they reached the flagstone walk, wind got caught in the folds of the cape; and Glory, watching it billow away from Mrs. Gramby's body, thought, She's like a monstrous bird, flapping its big black wings as it walks awkwardly along the ground.

Mrs. Gramby paused on the sidewalk to speak to The Portegee. He took his cap off while he talked to her. He talks to her. I bet she tells him to spit at other people.

She drew away from the window lest Mrs. Gramby turn around and see her looking out. With her gone I have the whole run of the house, she thought. I can pick up a fold of the drapery to examine the material, I can stare at myself in the mirrors upstairs and downstairs, I can open that drawer in the little table by her chair and see what she keeps in it. When she's here, even if she isn't in the same room with you, she seems to be watching,

watching the house; it's so real, like she was right there, that I hardly dare ask Momma about the weather.

She risked another glance out of the window, and saw The Weasel's car bend under Mrs. Gramby's weight. I bet she's all of two hundred pounds, short like she is and wide. They ought to put her on a diet. Momma says she eats like a pig.

As soon as the car pulls out of sight, I'll go upstairs and find Momma. The Weasel was helping Neola push Mrs. Gramby into the car—it looked like an elephant's behind they were working on, pushing and pulling and a heave-ho, boys. There. They had her in.

But Neola wasn't going. She leaned into the car, tucking a robe around Mrs. Gramby's legs, making no effort to get in herself. Perhaps she was going to get in on the other side. Neola's presence in the house would be as inhibiting as Mrs. Gramby's.

The Portegee was studying Neola's rear with an intensity that was laughable. So that's how it is. He's in love with her or at least he'd like to get close to her as she leans over. Even with that bulky brown raincoat around her, you could see that Neola's legs and bottom were very shapely. If Neola was white and didn't have that dead-pan expression on her face, she wouldn't be bad-looking. Not anything to rave about, but she'd get by in a crowd.

No. Neola wasn't going. She slammed the car door, waved her hand. The car pulled off and Glory saw a kid-gloved hand waving at the window. Then they were gone.

The Portegee was talking to Neola. She wished she could hear what they were saying. He had his pipe in his hand and he smiled, suddenly. His teeth were white, evenly spaced. His face grew lighter in color just because of the smile; and the fierce mustachios moved up higher until they practically waved under his ears.

Neola's face, too, was alight with laughter. Then she tossed her head, tried to look cross and couldn't, for she kept laughing. But she walked away from The Portegee, mincing along.

From where Glory stood she could see the swaying of Neola's body under the raincoat, and from the way The Portegee was staring he must be getting an eyeful from the rear. And as she watched their faces she thought, bitterly, The whole town is happy, everybody but me. They have the things they want—all of them.

When Neola opened the door, Glory was sitting near the fireplace.

"Neola," she said, "can't something be done to make this fire burn?"

"There's a poker in the corner. If you stir the fire a little, it'll burn more briskly. But we don't like much heat in here. It's bad for Mrs. Gramby." Neola spoke quickly, from the hall, and disappeared.

Mrs. Gramby had gone out, so it didn't matter whether the room was warm, and Glory poked the fire, piled logs on it, and watched with satisfaction as a brisk, curling flame crept between the logs. The first thing Momma should do after Mrs. Gramby died was to fire Neola.

One of the cats jumped down from the sofa, landing on the floor with a thump that startled her. She'd get rid of those devilish cats, too. They were always making sudden, uncanny movements. It was easy to believe that this one had read her thoughts and was protesting against change of any kind.

Footsteps, sounds on the stairs. She couldn't tell whether they were Momma's or not—the stairs were too heavily carpeted for anyone to be able to identify a footstep.

Then her mother came into the room and said, "Hello, Glory. I waited until Mrs. Gramby went out before I came down. I didn't feel like being bothered with her today."

"Hello, Lil," Glory said. Momma looked thinner in the face. I wonder if I can talk to her, not about Ed, of course, but about Johnnie and me—and oh, I don't know, lots of things. We've never done much intimate talking, but, today, a cold, raw windy day like this, with a fire in the fireplace and just the two of us alone here, perhaps today we can really talk.

"On rainy days this place gets on my nerves. Storms upset the cats and they roam all over the house." Lil twisted her hands in a nervous gesture. "Sometimes I wake up at night and there's one of them in my room, on the foot of the bed. Staring at me. Their eyes are yellow in the dark."

"Let's not talk about them," Glory said quickly—"Not here in front of them."

Lil said sharply, "I never heard such nonsense. Why not?"

"They keep looking at us as though they understood what we said."

Lil gave Glory a disgusted look, glanced at the cats, and then walked over to the fireplace, held her hands out toward the fire. But Glory noticed that as she went on talking, she lowered her voice and did not look toward the cats.

"Mearns insists we have to keep our bedroom door open at night so the cats can have free run of the house. He likes to wake up in the morning and find one of them on his bed. They've been coming in his room ever since he was a little boy and he says he can't shut them out now."

They always ended up talking about the cats, the house, and old Mrs. Gramby. Today wasn't any different. Now that Momma had started she would go on for hours. And I've simply got to make myself remember to call her Lil instead of Momma, otherwise she'll get mad. Though why her being married to Mearns should mean I have to call her by her first name I've never been able to understand.

"Well, anyway, Mrs. Gramby can't live forever. Then you can change all this." Glory waved toward the cats, the room.

"Yes," her mother said thoughtfully. "But sometimes I wonder. She's never sick. It looks as though she had made up her mind not to die."

"Johnnie's home," Glory said abruptly.

"Her diabetes doesn't seem to bother her much," Lil said. "Doctor Williams says he's established a beautiful balance between all that food she eats and the insulin she takes. She eats like a horse, you know. The last time the doctor was here he said she was good for at least twenty more years."

"Johnnie came home yesterday," Glory repeated.

"Yes, I know," her mother said impatiently. "Can you imagine me going through twenty years of this—insolent servants, treated like a roomer who hasn't paid her rent, listening to Mearns and that old woman while they talk politics, politics, always politics?"

"Well, it won't be for long."

"Doctor Williams said twenty years. I asked him."

"You asked him?" Glory stared at her mother, surprised.

"Don't look at me like that. I told him that Mrs. Gramby's death would be a terrible blow to Mearns and me. I said that I wanted to know when to expect it so I could prepare Mearns for it." She stopped talking for a moment; then she said, "I don't like Doctor Williams. I never did like him."

"Why?"

"He's so abrupt and he's got such a rude way of talking. When I asked him about Mrs. Gramby he said, 'Well, Lil, offhand I'd say you had about twenty years in which to prepare Mearns for his mother's death. Yes, just about twenty years. And if I were you I'd take up my sewing again while I waited so I wouldn't get bored while I prepared Mearns' mind.' If she lives that long she'd be a hundred and something. Who ever heard of such a thing?"

"I don't see anything rude about that," Glory said. "You didn't fool him any. He knows you want Mrs. Gramby to hurry up and go. He comes here to see her all the time. He's got eyes. Why wouldn't he know that you don't like the cats and that Mrs. Gramby won't let you change anything in the house? I don't know why you asked how much longer she was going to live."

"Who said I wanted her to hurry up and go?"

Her mother's voice was shrill, angry, and Glory couldn't for the life of her see why it should be. "You did," she said. "You just said it looked like she'd made up her mind not to die." She and Momma always managed to get a stupid argument started. Momma would say something and then turn right around and pretend she hadn't said it and argue about it. She had come here for understanding and sympathy and instead she and Momma were going to have a fight. She could see it coming, for Momma's lips were set in a thin, narrow line that made her whole face look pinched. In a minute she'd be saying every mean thing she could think of.

"You can pretend you don't want that old woman to die. But I do," Glory said fiercely. "I want to be somebody here in Lennox. I want to live in this house some day and have parties and dances here—in the Gramby House—and be waited on—"

Neola was all the way in the room, carrying a tea tray before Glory saw her. She heard every word I said. She couldn't help it the way I was shouting. She closed her eyes, hearing her own words, going over them: "You can pretend you don't want that old woman to die. But I do—" Why didn't Momma say something, turn the whole thing into some kind of joke, fix it up?

Neola said, "Mrs. Gramby ordered tea for you." Her voice

was matter-of-fact, her face expressionless. She put the tray down on a low table in front of the fireplace.

Lil said, "Neola's getting a divorce." Her voice was smooth, silky.

"Really, Neola?" Glory said. This led somewhere, but she didn't know exactly where.

"That's right," Neola said. She was going out of the room. She was ignoring them.

"Who ever heard of a nigger divorce?" her mother said softly.

Neola stopped in the doorway, turned around slowly and stared at Lil, at Glory. Her face was expressionless, but her eyes blazed with contempt. She went out of the room without saying anything.

"You shouldn't have said that, Momma."

"Don't call me 'Momma.' I can't bear it!" Lil said sharply. Then in a quieter voice she said, "Come and get your tea. Will you have lemon or milk?"

"Just lemon. No sugar. I have to watch my hips." And instantly she thought of Ed, heard him say, "Hips? You haven't any hips." She was standing quite close to him in the store, handing him a loaf of cake. He drew away from her and his eyes were bold and hot, lingering on her face, her breasts, her thighs. She had caught her breath as she waited for his next words, thinking, It will be now, here in the store, that I will hear him say he loves me. But he hadn't. He paid for his purchases, went out of the store. That was all.

There was a moment of silence while Lil poured tea and Glory said quickly, "Momma—I mean—Lil, I want to talk to you."

Lil's eyes stayed on the cup and saucer she was holding in her hand. She ignored the urgency in Glory's voice. "These are Minton, you know." She touched the cup lightly with her forefinger. "They've been in the family for years." She leaned back in the chair, sipped the tea, and then smiled as though pleased with herself. "Why did you say I shouldn't have said that to Neola?"

"Didn't you see how she looked at us—as though we were dirt? She was mad all the way through."

"I said it to make her mad. 'Mrs. Gramby ordered tea!' Did you notice she never says 'ma'am' to me? Never calls me Mrs. Gramby? Neither does that damn Portegee. He won't even touch his cap to me. And as for Cook—"

Lil paused, took a deep breath, and put the delicate china cup down on the table. Glory watched her, thinking, There must be some way to catch her attention. She can't go on forever talking about her own troubles.

Lil was mimicking Cook, talking quickly, not pausing for breath. "All I did was go in the kitchen and he screamed at me—not even a foot—not ever—so long as you're in this house—not even a foot do you put in my kitchen. I take a knife and slit your long neck. Put one of those long feet inside the door and I take the knife—so—I sever the long thin neck—so—"

Glory said, "You told me that before," and sighed. She wasn't interested in the Grambys' cook. She had seen him time and again, waddling up the main street, market basket over his arm, bright yellow gloves covering his fat hands. He had come in the store once, and leaned over the vegetable counter, glared at her, at the vegetables, the other clerks, and sniffed, "Vegetables not fresh," and had never come in again.

"A nasty foreigner talking to me like that! I can't even walk by the kitchen without his screaming at me. But Neola and The Portegee can go in there whenever they please." Lil sighed. "This is an awful way to have to live."

"Listen, Lil," Glory said firmly. "Johnnie came home yesterday. Home from the army," she added because Momma had the most disconcerting way of forgetting things that didn't directly involve her. "He wants to go live in New York and be a painter."

"A painter?" Lil said, surprised. "I didn't know he could draw."

"That's just it. He can't. That's why the whole thing is so absolutely crazy." I'll tell her slowly, all of it, not about Ed, but that I can't bear Johnnie any more.

"Can't you stop him?"

"I suppose so. But if I'm going to get New York out of his mind, I'd have to be awfully nice to him. And right now I don't feel like being friends with him."

"If you don't want him to go to New York, you'll have to stir yourself to keep him here. It won't hurt you to be friendly. If he goes and you stay here in Lennox, you'll have to support yourself." Lil's eyes flickered, the lines about her mouth deepened. "I couldn't help you any, you know. Mearns gives me money now and then. Enough for cigarettes and stockings and that's all. You couldn't depend on me for anything."

Glory, listening to her and watching her pour herself a second cup of tea, thought, Why did I come? She's always been like this, talking about herself; everything for her is food and clothing and shelter. Yet I had hoped the wind and the rain, the bleakness of the day, might turn her mood into a generous one. Somewhere in the back of my mind I could hear her saying, "Let Johnnie go to New York by himself if that's what he wants. You come live with me. This is a big roomy house. You won't have to worry about a thing. Mearns and I will look after you."

The wind and the rain had merely served to deepen Momma's discontent with her own lot. I wonder if I'll have those same long lines about my mouth when I'm her age.

"I guess I'd better be going," Glory said finally.

"I'm glad you came. You haven't been in to see me for weeks." Lil put the teacup down, hurriedly, and stood up as though she were relieved the conversation had ended. "Wait, I'll ring for Neola."

They're so damn formal here, Glory thought, as she waited

for Neola to get her raincoat from the closet under the stairs. Unless someone sees you in and sees you out, you might lurk under the sofa, waiting for an opportunity to steal their damn teacups.

"Good-bye," her mother said sweetly. "Be sure and give my love to Johnnie."

Glory went down the steps, keeping a wary eye out for The Portegee. She planned to look straight at him and then deliberately turn her head. But he wasn't anywhere in sight.

When she reached the walk she looked back at the house. It had a friendly air despite its size. Once those awful people—Neola, The Portegee, and Mrs. Gramby—were out of it, she and Momma would redecorate it from top to bottom. Mearns wouldn't object, and even if he did Momma could manage him; after all, he had married Momma when he was the most eligible bachelor in the state. If and when his mother ever died, this would be a very pleasant house in which to live.

7

WIND BLOWING STRAIGHT FROM THE northeast twisted the skirt of Glory's raincoat about her legs, whistled in her ears, as she walked up the street.

The sun, she noticed with regret, was only a faint yellow blur, very nearly obscured by the dark gray wind clouds—a sure sign there would be more rain before night. The thought of rain was as depressing and irritating as the talk she'd had with Momma. Yes, irritating was the right word. She and Momma had always irritated each other.

Queer that they should look so much alike, wear the same size clothes, have hair the same color—only Momma, of course, kept hers that reddish-yellow color with the stuff she bought at the drugstore. But with those curls piled on top of her head she looked quite young. If it weren't for the deep lines around her mouth and the hardness of her eyes Momma could pass for thirtyish. We look alike, but there's no love lost between us.

Momma had perfected the knack of withdrawing from other people's problems. She remembered the sudden, shrinking dismay she had felt right after she married Johnnie. They were leaving the parsonage and she had turned to Momma for comfort, for reassurance. She was afraid of Johnnie; not for the same reasons she was afraid of him now. She had wanted to marry him, but when the brief ceremony ended, she knew a moment of panic, brought on by fear of the future, fear of the tall gangling boy walking beside her, fear of those strange life-death words, "Till death do us part."

She had turned to Momma, reaching, groping for her, out of this half-blind fear. Momma had pecked at her cheek with cold lips and said in her ear: "You're settled and safe now. I won't have to think about you any more. I can put my mind on myself," and then moved swiftly away from the little group standing on the parsonage steps.

What was it like? Oh, like expecting to find a strong hand which would help you down from a high and lonely place; and then, just as you reached for it, the hand was withdrawn—deliberately, coolly.

But that is always happening to me, she thought. The hand is always withdrawn or someone blocks the way to it: Johnnie or Mother Roane or Momma. Even Ed, Ed, who will only touch me with his eyes.

She paused at a corner where the Post Road was bisected by a black macadam road. The black road led to Ed's filling station and she wished she dared follow it. The rest of the afternoon would be long, dull. It hung ahead of her—hour after hour of sheer unbroken time. Tonight she would eat supper in the kitchen with Johnnie and his mother and father. They would hang on Johnnie's every word, their eyes would hover about him. Then later she and Johnnie would be alone again, upstairs in the big walnut bed. And he would make love to her. I can't bear it, she thought. I just can't.

By this time, too, there must be a murmur, a thread of talk about her and Ed, running through the town. Sooner or later Johnnie would hear that Ed brought her home from work, picked her up at the hairdresser's. The knowledge would fill him with that same hot anger that had burned in him last night.

But it was all so innocent, so harmless—so damn meaningless.

"What do you do on your afternoons off?" Ed had asked.

"Go to the hairdresser's mostly," she had said and waited to see what he would suggest. Perhaps it would be a trip to New Haven to the movies, or to New London—or perhaps they would eat dinner in one of those roadhouses where they served broiled lobster and the waiters wore evening clothes and there was a dance orchestra. The cars parked in front of the place would all be new and shiny like Ed's, and when she got out of Ed's car people would stare, and there would be a man just inside the door who would lead them to a special table near the front.

"What time you get through?"

"About four o'clock."

"I'll stop by and pick you up."

So on her day off, late in the afternoon, when she had finished at the hairdresser's, she went for even longer rides with him. He owned the only new car in the town, delivered just about six months ago. The car ran smoothly on its fat new tires, engine softly purring as the car skimmed over the bumpy back roads.

If she didn't show up today, Ed would know why or he would think he knew why. He must know that Johnnie was home, everyone seemed to know it, and he would think that Johnnie's return had brought their rides to an abrupt end.

The New London bus came around the curve, far down the road. That's an omen, she thought, a sign, that I ought to meet Ed. She stepped out into the road, signaled the driver to stop. She got on the bus and said, "The head of the street. Near the hairdresser's."

She sat midway in the bus. There must be some way of making Ed declare himself today. This was nonsense, these drives, this talk about the weather. Passengers got on and off the bus. A group of women carrying shopping bags boarded it in front of one of the chain stores.

"You girls musta bought the place out," the driver said.

The women grinned at him and the driver got out of his seat, lifted the heaviest of their bundles inside for them.

Glory eyed the women who got on, thinking, A few more years and that's the way Johnnie will have me looking. I'll have four or five children and never quite enough money to go all the way around. I'll be riding buses to get to the markets where the food is cheapest; and wearing a house dress under a winter coat; and I'll put on wrinkled cotton stockings in order to save my best ones for Sundays; and carry a cloth knitting bag instead of a pocketbook. I'll start for home at this hour of the day so's to have the supper ready for Johnnie and he'll wolf it down and grunt and reach for the newspaper. Then he'll take his shoes off and sit sprawled in a chair half-asleep until time to go to bed.

She forced herself to stop thinking of life in terms of Johnnie. And she became aware of the smell of heat from the engine, of the choking fumes from the exhaust, and of the sharp, cold wind coming through the cracks under the windows of the bus.

At the town pump the driver slowed down and then brought the bus to a dead stop. An old shepherd dog was crossing the street. Glory recognized the dog as being one that belonged to Perkins. Almost every day she caught glimpses of him, for he wandered about the town, moving slowly, cautiously.

But this time she got a good look at him, for he turned his head toward the bus. His eyes were rheumy, the pupils blurred and vague. Most of his hair was gone, revealing great patches of scabious skin; what remained of his hair was tangled and matted about his haunches.

When the bus started off again, she was grateful for the harsh grating sound of the gears, for it rubbed out the sound of the sharp outcry that had welled up inside her and had finally issued from her lips. The sight of the blind old dog and the shabby housewives with their bundles of food had outraged her, making her shout a defiance against time, against the gray gloom of the day, against the thought of old age, and against death itself.

She got off the bus in front of the hairdresser's, thinking, I've been cheated too long. I've never had anything I really wanted, and if I don't hurry up and get it I'll be too late.

Ed's car was drawn discreetly off the road, just a little beyond the hairdresser's. She could see the back of his head, the gray fedora tilted so far back it would drop off if he moved his head even as much as a millionth of an inch.

As she walked toward the car, she thought, Today. I can feel it in my bones. It's going to be today. Something's going to happen today.

Ed headed the car toward Essex, taking the back road through the woods.

"The rain's let up," he said.

"Yes." Is that what he was going to talk about—the weather? "It's a little colder out," she said. If it had to be the weather, then she would talk about it, too. "When I woke up I thought we were in for an all-day rain."

She unbuttoned the collar of her raincoat. It was cold outside, but it was warm in the car. He had all the windows closed. She took the coat off, folded it up, and held it on her lap.

The dark green sweater she was wearing hugged her breasts and Ed stared at them until she began to get the feeling he had touched her with his hands.

"It's a shame to have a Lana Turner like you wasted in this town," he said softly, and then looked away from her.

She felt as though she were on the edge of making a tremendous discovery—a discovery that would reveal a secret, exciting reason for her existence. And once she found it, her whole body would quicken with life, the blood would flow faster and faster through her veins just as it was doing now.

"I suppose you say that to all the girls."

"I've never seen any others of whom it would be true. You ought to wear sweaters all the time."

Somehow he always managed to evade the truly personal note. Now that business about the sweaters really didn't mean anything. Because she was certain his eyes were telling her something far more important. There must be some way she could get his mouth to say what his eyes were saying.

She moved a little closer to him.

The car went smoothly, quickly, over the road. She watched his hands on the wheel as he turned into the narrow lane that led to the hill called Obit's Heights. Would this day end like all the other days? If so, then they would park at the very crest of the hill, and look out over the river, the Sound. They would stare at a train slowing for the bridge, then watch the smoke from its engine until the smoke blended with the clouds in the sky and disappeared. He would glance at her, sigh, step on the starter, turn and twist the wheel until he got the car headed back down the hill. That would be all.

They reached the summit of the hill.

"Obit's Heights is a queer name for this place," Ed said. He parked the car neatly—close enough to the edge so that you couldn't see any land through the windshield, nothing but water.

"It's an Indian name," Glory said. "Obit was a chief who lived up here. There's some kind of story about him. He threw his daughter down into the river from here or something." She frowned, trying to remember. "Either that or she ran away in a canoe. And Obit threw himself in the river."

How had they started talking about a long-dead Indian chief? She changed the subject abruptly. "I may go to New York to live," she said.

He did care, she thought. He had been looking at the river and he turned toward her quickly.

"Why would you do that?" he asked.

"I may have to. Honest. Johnnie wants to live there."

He knows Johnnie's home. He isn't asking when he got here or anything. He knows that Johnnie came yesterday, that this is my day off, and that I came for the ride anyway. It ought to mean something to him.

"You can't leave Lennox," he said. "You can't—"

Then he was holding her in his arms. Why hadn't she thought of threatening to go away long before this? She waited for him to kiss her and her breath caught in her throat. Suppose it wasn't—

Only it was. She put her arms around his neck, drawing him closer, thinking, I'm alive now at this moment for the first time. She wanted to cry, to sing, to laugh. This was what she had been waiting for and wanting, without knowing it. When his mouth drew away from her mouth, his hands away from her body, she made a small protesting sound, clasped her hands tighter about his neck, strained closer to him.

He pushed her away, turned his head to look behind him, and frowned at what he saw.

She turned, too. Why hadn't they heard the wheeze of the town taxi climbing the hill? For it was there behind them. And The Weasel had the look of a squirrel busily hoarding nuts for the winter. He was grinning at her, at Ed, his sly little eyes moving back and forth.

Mother Roane and Mrs. Gramby were in the back seat. And she stared at them, dismayed; thinking, I must have looked like a dog dragging itself along the ground, so filled with desire I was crazy, and had to be satisfied, rubbing myself against Ed, burying myself in him.

Why did they have to pick this view to look at? Damn them. It'll be all over town tomorrow. They would chew it and rechew it, at the railroad station, in the drugstore, at the postoffice. The harpies at the Red Cross meeting would whisper it to each other and then aloud they'd say, "And that poor boy just home from the army the day before."

The women sitting in the taxi wouldn't tell—not Mrs. Roane and Mrs. Gramby, sitting there on the back seat of the taxi, with their faces blank with surprise, their faces falling apart from surprise. They were getting their faces together now—almost had them together. They were beginning to act as though nothing had happened. They were pretending to look at the river, the bridge, the sky.

It would be The Weasel who would pass the word around. He would tell all of his passengers, out of the side of his mouth, and his eyes would watch their reaction in the mirror. He would help the story to go swiftly, in and out of the grocery store, the filling stations, the boat docks.

When he got through talking, everyone would know. Momma would be mad as hell. They might even fire her at Perkins' store. And Johnnie—

Mrs. Gramby was leaning toward The Weasel. She must have told him to drive on, because he turned the car around.

Glory watched the town taxi as it went down the hill. Neither Mrs. Roane nor Mrs. Gramby looked back. They were sitting up very straight and stiff in the back seat, apparently not talking.

Ed patted her hand. "I guess it looked kind of funny to them, us being up here. I'm sorry it happened like this, Glory," he said gently.

She waited for him to continue. He was going to say something else. He had to. She held her breath while she waited.

"Whyn't you come up to my place some time soon?" he said. "I've got a little place—a cabin up in the woods."

"Okay," she said. She watched his hands on the wheel as he turned the car around.

"I'll stop by some night and pick you up when you get through work."

And Johnnie, she thought. Johnnie would know, too. Mother Roane wouldn't tell him. The town would tell him. The town would let him know what they thought of her. Fear set her to shivering and even as she shivered she was conjecturing what it would be like to be alone with Ed in the cabin in the woods.

"I'll come soon," she said.

She half-closed her eyes as the car went down the hill and through the wood. But Johnnie, she thought, what of Johnnie? She would have to fool Johnnie, fool Mother Roane, lead both of them to believe that anything they heard wasn't true. It was the only way.

"I'll come soon," she repeated softly. "Honest." And then she added, "Is it on a hill?"

"What?"

"The cabin. Is it on a hill?

"Yes. And there's a brook near it and a lot of trees. You'll like the place. You wait and see."

She could see herself standing on the hilltop, outside the cabin, the wind blowing through her hair. She and Ed would have hold of each other's hands and the sun would be on their faces. It would be like a movie. And she and Ed would go inside and there would be a fireplace, a big cobblestone one, with a chimney that reached up and up to the rafters. They would lie close to each other, near the hearth, so they could watch the flames licking up the chimney as Ingrid Bergman and Cary Grant did in that last picture—or was it Jennifer Jones?

The car slowed down, turned into the River Road.

"Let me out here," she said.

8

AS THE TOWN TAXI CRAWLED down the hill that is known as Obit's Heights, it swayed violently on the curves. When The Weasel turned into the main road, the motor stalled. He stepped on the starter and the car jerked forward, throwing Mrs. Roane against Mrs. Gramby.

"I'm sorry," Mrs. Roane said and pulled back into her corner of the car.

"That's all right," Mrs. Gramby said. This was the first time either of them had spoken since she had told The Weasel to take them home.

Mrs. Gramby moved closer to Mrs. Roane. It was, she decided, the only way to indicate her sympathy, for she could not discuss Gloria in front of Mr. Weasel. She could not discuss her anyway. There was nothing to say about her.

She made her voice gentle, lowering its pitch, as she talked. "The town changes, doesn't it? I can remember when there were more trees, fewer people, no cars. It was a simpler life in those days. People knew each other better, trusted each other more."

"Yes," Mrs. Roane said. Her lips were drawn together in a thin, tight line.

Probably to keep them from trembling, Mrs. Gramby thought. I won't say anything else right now.

She did not speak again until the car had gone through the Essex woods, crossed the overhead bridge above the railroad tracks. A train pulled in at the station. They turned their heads to look at it, turned their attention back to the road when the car entered the main street.

It is better for her to talk than to keep silent. She is thinking of her son. She is afraid. And so am I. Why did he have to marry that empty-headed girl? And my son, my son had to marry Gloria's mother.

They were passing the town green when she said softly, "Sheep used to graze here. In those days everyone went to church on Sunday. I think that was a good thing—getting dressed in your cleanest clothes, your best clothes, and then spending an hour or so in a place of worship. It was refreshment for the spirit. You listened to the old hymns and they were majestic. You heard the Word of God read by a man whose voice invested those familiar words and phrases with a special beauty."

"Yes," Mrs. Roane said. She turned her face toward Mrs. Gramby and went on talking, slowly, carefully. "Johnnie wants to live in New York. He wants to study painting."

Good, Mrs. Gramby thought, she's talking. She hasn't heard a word I said, but the sound of my voice must have soothed her a little, eased some of the pain in her heart.

"That's only natural. Young men want to explore the world. Especially the young men who are born in small towns. Whether Johnnie becomes a painter is not really important."

"He's always wanted to live in a city. Ever since he was a little boy. Cities seem to have a special fascination for him."

"Many young men are attracted by cities. They have an urge to conquer the world. Sometimes the world of a small town offers them enough challenge. More frequently it does not, and so they go elsewhere."

Mearns had wanted that, too. But she would not let him go. When he finished Yale he talked of living in Chicago or San Francisco—some Western city. He said the East was too old, too worn out, too familiar. But she had urged him to stay in his father's law firm in New Haven. She had made it impossible for him to leave, binding him closer and closer to her.

And all because she had been terrified lest he marry some cheap impossible young girl. She had sought and found flaws in all the girls he had ever talked about. Then she had frightened them away, flaunting her jewels and her house in their faces; bullying them by her arrogant manner; staring them out of countenance when he brought them home to dinner. When they had gone, those girls he had brought home for her approval, she had laughed at them, using her malicious wit to make them ridiculous in his eyes.

Then at forty-seven he had married Lillian—a hard, shallow woman with an acquisitive, seeking mouth, a woman who dyed her hair and starved herself in order to stay slender.

Nothing worse could have happened to him. The name would die out. Lillian was too old to have children.

She had been guilty of an enormous crime in keeping him here in Lennox. She should have let him go. But he was her only child and she was not a young woman when he was born. So she had stood guard over him, believing that she could keep him safe because she was stronger than he.

The name of Gramby had once stood for something. Mearns, too, in a sense, had brought honor to it. The name would disappear, lost down the reaches of time. No heirs, no issue, the line ended. It was almost gone now, for the name meant nothing—just an old, diabetic woman and a house made of pink brick and a middle-aged man who was addicted to vitamin pills and mouth washes.

That last part wasn't fair to Mearns. He should be described as the last of a long and honorable and distinguished family. But he—she sighed deeply—he was married to a self-seeking, almost but not quite vicious, middle-aged woman.

She patted Mrs. Roane's knee. "You help Johnnie get to a city."

"His father will oppose him. He wants him to stay here and carry on the business."

"I know. But Mr. Roane will not protest too much if he sees you are in favor of Johnnie's going away."

When Mrs. Gramby spoke again there was a note of urgency in her voice. "Johnnie is young and strong. He will starve in New York while he tries to paint. But at his age there are many things more important than food. Many, many things. You urge him on, push him toward New York. The sharp pangs of hunger there will make him far happier than three bountiful meals a day here in Lennox."

"I guess you're right."

The Weasel brought the car to a jerky stop in front of Mrs. Roane's house. And under the asthmatic wheeze of the motor, Mrs. Gramby heard her whisper, "I am afraid."

The Weasel glanced at her curiously and Mrs. Gramby wondered if he had heard the whispered words. Then he got out of the car, held the door open for Mrs. Roane. He braced his body in order to hold the door steady against the impact of the wind.

"The wind seems stronger," Mrs. Gramby said mildly when he got back inside the car.

"Yeah," The Weasel said. "Blowin' up for a real storm." Then he muttered half under his breath, "In more ways than one."

"Please don't mumble," she said sharply. "What did you say, Mr. Weasel?"

"It looks like it was going to be a real storm," he repeated, eyeing her in the mirror.

"Yes," she said. "Yes, it does." She repeated the words absently, for she was trying to decide whether she should ask Mr. Weasel who that man was. She had seen him so many mornings when she walked up to the postoffice. He was always in the vicinity of the Town Hall, lolling against the railing, standing on the steps, just emerging from the basement. Finally her curiosity got the better of her.

"Who was that man with young Johnnie Roane's wife?" she asked.

"Name of Barrell. Ed Barrell. Good old Ed."

"What does he do?"

"Runs a filling station. You know, a gas station." The Weasel shot an occasional hasty glance at the road ahead of him, but for the most part he kept his eyes on the mirror, studying Mrs. Gramby's face. "He—er—" He frowned, scratched his head, finally said quickly, "Well, he kind of makes it his business to sort of make love to the females here in town. Got quite a reputation for it."

It was a changed world, she thought with distaste. There had been a time when a young married woman would not have spent so much as a moment in the company of the town rake. But this girl, this Gloria, had got into his car, driven to a lonely hillside with him and there welcomed and responded to his gross lovemaking.

During the course of the years—not all at once, but slowly and surely—the line between good and evil had been rubbed out. It was once so sharp and clear one did not cross it no matter what the push and pull of one's emotions. And so if one were charitable one would say that Gloria was not to be condemned. Instead of a sharp line of demarcation between right and wrong, Gloria and her generation had found only the vague blur made by erasures—it was all that remained of a moral code after the impact of two world wars.

But I am not charitable. Wars can come and wars can go but by my standards she is a harlot. Didn't she think about Johnnie, at all? Couldn't she control herself? The boy had barely got home. And my son had to marry the mother of an unprincipled creature like that! The mother and the daughter look exactly alike—but please God they are not wholly alike. Mearns deserves better than that.

She stopped thinking about Gloria because, as they drove past the postoffice, she saw Rosenberg, the young Jewish lawyer. He was coming out of the door—a slender, erect figure, somehow lonely. She turned her head for a second look at him. He might be an island, set apart, a good distance from the mainland, out of reach of it.

His face reminded her of someone, but she could not remember who it was, though she was certain that at some time she had known a thin, sensitive face exactly like his. And she thought with irritation that this constant forgetting people and faces was one of the most unpleasant symptoms of old age.

The men standing in front of the postoffice looked past the young lawyer. One of them nodded. None of them, as far as she could see, actually spoke to him. They turned their heads, watching him walk down the street. One man gestured toward his back and the others shook their heads in disapproval.

When the town was younger, when she was growing up, a man was judged solely by his actions; not prejudged because he was born in Russia or in Poland. She felt vaguely sorry for the young man and yet she was certain he would thrust her pity away if he knew of its existence. Those idlers, standing in front of the postoffice, who had stared at him without speaking, had been thinking, "No Jews. They would ruin the town." Ruin it for what? For whom? The houses were of no great value.

"They got Jews moving into the old Bristow place," The Weasel said.

She glanced at the back of his head, and then looked out of the car window. Mr. Weasel had an uncanny and disconcerting way of following one's train of thoughts. She had often wondered how he managed it.

"They will enjoy living there. It is a very pleasant house," she said.

"You ain't got no feeling about them?"

"About whom?"

"Jews."

"Why, no, Mr. Weasel," she said. She started to let it go at that and then decided she ought to make an effort to explain exactly how she felt and why.

"When you get to be as old as I am, you don't have 'feelings' about who buys a house or a piece of land. You have lived long enough to know that it does not matter. 'When it is morning think thou shalt not come to the even; and when even come, be not bold to promise thyself the morning.'"

"That's very interestin'," The Weasel said politely. "But I don't see what it's got to do with Jews. Now you take that Jew lawyer—he don't get no business from here in Lennox, but he gets just enough cases trickling in from other towns to keep him here. What's he want to come here for? Why don't he stay where he was? Next thing he'll have all his relations here. I ain't got anything personal against him, but I just don't see it."

"I assume he came here because he wanted to live here. And he stays here for the same reason that you and I stay. We like the place. The Jew, as you call him, is a man like yourself. With the same desires, the same weaknesses," she said severely.

Then her voice lost its firmness. She murmured half to herself, "Subject to the same diseases, healed by the same means, warmed and cooled by the same winter and summer."

Ah, me, she thought, I am always slipping down by-paths into the past. Just then I was not here in this rattling car. I was in New York, on my honeymoon, seeing *The Merchant of Venice* for the first time. And Mr. Gramby was holding my hand, caressing it, and whispering that he loved me.

She tightened her grip on the late Mr. Gramby's silver-handled umbrella and said: "Mr. Weasel, I am an old woman—full of aches and pains. I would give anything I have to be young again, to have a strong responsive body. I would rather be that young Jewish lawyer, Rosenberg, than myself—old and tired and worn-out. There is a whole world ahead of him. Some of it sweet and full of love, some of it bitter and full of hate. But if I were given the chance I would change places with him—now, at this moment."

Yes, she thought, I would rather be any of them, the young lawyer or that other young man, that young Johnnie Roane, who has a harlot for a wife.

It began to rain again. Big, hard drops hit the windshield. The drops slowly decreased in size, but they came down faster and faster until a curtain of water shut out the street, the trees, the houses.

What would this day be like for that boy, just home from the army? The rain and the wind would encompass him, shut him in with his disillusion. He might have found life more bearable if the sun had been out, clear and hot. There were hope and promise to be found in sunlight. But sun or rain didn't really matter. The trouble was that people made such muddles of their lives.

There was always the one mistake, the one fatal error, that led straight to disaster. Johnnie Roane, for example, should never have fallen in love with that girl, let alone married her.

And I, she thought, if I could have foreseen what the intensity of my love for Mearns would finally lead to, I would have acted differently. It is sheer folly to try to control the destiny of another human. But you had to know that while you were still young and strong, while life still bubbled through you. I am too old now to let Mearns go. Besides, it is too late. I have succeeded in binding him to me. He would be lost without me.

If she had the chance, if she were younger, she would push Mearns out of her life. Birds had better sense about such things than humans. As soon as the fledglings could use their wings, the parent bird deserted them.

The regrets of an old woman are stupid, dull, she thought. And yet if she were thirty-five, able to walk swiftly, instead of hitching along in this slow, painful, lopsided fashion, she would try to show the town how impossible it is to control the earth, to arbitrarily decide who is to own it.

As I get older, I keep going back to the past, comparing it with the present; making myself unhappy by remembering it as a more gracious time in which to have lived. There is no going back. I live now in this century, in this day.

Just as The Weasel drove up in front of the Gramby House, Neola emerged from the front door, carrying an umbrella which she tried to hold over Mrs. Gramby's head. But Mrs. Gramby waved her away. Once out of the taxi, she unfurled the late Mr. Gramby's oversize umbrella and, holding it over her head, walked slowly up the flagstone path. When she reached the steps, she allowed Neola and The Weasel to help her. She went up the steps, slowly, leaning her weight against them, pausing now and then to catch her breath.

At the door she turned to The Weasel and said: "That was a pleasant ride, Mr. Weasel. I'll be going again next week. And I wish you would think about this: 'There is no man without fault, no man without a burden, no man sufficient to himself, no man wise enough to himself.'"

"Yes'm," The Weasel said meekly.

9

AFTER THE WEASEL LEFT MRS. Gramby, he came into the drugstore. His greasy cap was shoved far back on his head, its position giving him a jaunty, devil-may-care appearance. I was standing behind the cigar counter and he walked over to me, leaned on the case, establishing himself comfortably.

I knew he wanted to impart a particularly choice tidbit in the way of news, for his eyes kept darting about, looking at me, at the shelves behind me, at the cash register, out toward the back room—literally looking everywhere at once.

"How's tricks, Doc?" he said.

"Fine. How's tricks with you?"

"Hunky-dory. Absolutely hunky-dory," he said, grinning. "I just left old Mrs. Gramby off at her house. She's been out for her weekly ride with Mrs. Roane—Johnnie's mother."

"Is that so?" I said. And I moved away from the cigar counter, away from The Weasel.

There are magazine racks built into the wall on each side of the front door. I walked over to these racks, opened a bundle of new magazines that lay close by on the floor, and began taking the old issues of the magazines out of the racks, replacing them with the new ones.

In doing this, I was deliberately ruining The Weasel's performance. He prefers to have your undivided attention when he talks, so that he can observe the expression on your face and thus determine whether his words are pricking the bubble of some cherished illusion of yours.

He had said, "Mrs. Roane—Johnnie's mother," so I knew that whatever he was about to tell me concerned Johnnie. The Weasel never blurts out a bit of gossip. He is something of a showman. He sets the stage before he tells a story, carefully identifying the characters, in order to sharpen the appetite of his listener.

He followed me over to the door, and standing close beside me, he cleared his throat several times—deliberately, self-consciously. I would not look at him. I walked around him to select magazines from the bundle on the floor; once I stepped on his foot and I kept bumping into him and saying, "Excuse me," or "I'm sorry."

I did not want to hear what The Weasel had to tell me about Johnnie Roane. Johnnie had been in the store, that morning, rather early, when it was pouring rain. Water sluiced off his sou'wester, ran down his raincoat, dripped into his shoes, forming a pool of water that spread and widened where he stood. His face was too old and too disillusioned for so young a man. I had thought about him, off and on, during the day. And now, late on a rainy, windy afternoon, I could not bear to hear The Weasel's explanation of Johnnie's lost and hopeless look. For as the story emerged from The Weasel's cynical, lopsided mouth, it would become ugly, common.

But The Weasel is not easily discouraged. He stayed close beside me, frowning as he watched me work. When he saw that I was not going to stop rearranging magazines to listen to him, he told me that he had seen Ed Barrell making love to Glory Roane.

"So close together you couldn't get a straw between 'em," he said and giggled. "You shoulda seen old lady Gramby and Mrs. Roane! I thought their eyes would fall right out of their heads onto the floor of the taxi."

"That doesn't mean anything," I said.

"I suppose Ed and Glory went up on Obit's Heights just to look at the view. Good old Ed don't take no women nowhere just to look at a view unless it's a view of his—"

"Watch your tongue," I said. "I never could bear to hear a pot call a kettle black. Come to think of it what were you doing up on Obit's Heights?"

"Who—me?" he said. He grinned at me with such absolute delight that I regretted having asked him the question, regretted having turned around to look at him.

"Oh," he said, "I knew Johnnie had just come home from the war yesterday. I wanted to find out whether Glory was going to keep her regular date with Ed in spite of Johnnie's being back. I've been seeing her on Tuesdays, coming out of the hairdresser's, falling all over herself to get in Ed's car. So when I went to take old lady Gramby out for her ride, I started trying to figure out where Ed and Glory would be apt to go."

"What do you care where they go? What's it to you?" I said irritably.

He ignored my question, went on talking. "So I put myself in Ed's shoes. And I says to myself, now if I was going to try to lay some other feller's wife, where would I go? Then it come to me. Just like that," he snapped his fingers. "I'd pick Obit's Heights. It's a nice private place this time of year, a secret place. Not a soul around. So I says to Mrs. Gramby, you ain't seen the river from up there at the Heights for a long time. She and Johnnie's mother thinks that's a fine idea. So I drive 'em down to Clinton first so the old lady can go in the bank and count her pearls. Then we go up Obit's. And sure enough I flushed Glory and Ed—just like they was a coupla partridges."

When he finished talking, he laughed. His laughter has no humor in it, no warmth. It is an unpleasant, gritty sound that issues from his throat; and it has the same effect on the ear as the sound of a file being drawn back and forth across a fingernail.

The harsh rasp of his laughter filled the store. It seemed to point up the phrases he had used as he talked: gone to the bank to count her pearls, home from the war yesterday, falling all over herself to get in his car; couldn't get a straw between them; thought their eyes would fall out on the floor of the taxi.

I could fairly see Mrs. Gramby in the bank at Clinton with her safe-deposit box open in front of her. I could hear the rustle of paper as she fingered through the stocks and bonds and the old letters; could see her face light up as she gazed at a pin or a ring, reliving the past as she examined it.

And Johnnie Roane—home from the war. What a way to put it! Home, once a place to play in, warm and secure; home, now become a place cold and insecure, a place of defeat, because Ed Barrell was making love to Glory.

I could see Glory, hurrying, hurrying to get into Ed's car, day after day, could see her hair in the sunlight on clear warm days, could see the ever-present hunger in her eyes. Ed and Glory had found a secret place, a place where wind and rain could not reach them. But The Weasel came following after, tracking them down, until he found that secret place. I saw Mrs. Gramby and Mrs. Roane, sitting on the back seat of the taxi, staring at Ed and Glory, staring until their eyes fell out of the sockets and rolled on the floor of the taxi—startled eyes, frightened eyes.

The Weasel's words had evoked a picture of raw hurt and

pain and secret, furtive love. Now he was putting a frame around it—a frame of laughter.

I could not bear the sound of his laughter.

"For the love of God," I said, "can't you stop making that noise?"

He gave a hitch to his trousers, tightened his belt. He looked at me out of the corner of his eyes, furtively, and then looked away. "What's the matter?" he said coolly. "There ain't no law that I ever heard of about a man laughing if he feels like it." But he stopped laughing.

"No," I said rudely, "there isn't. But there isn't any law that says I have to listen to you while you laugh."

Then on a sudden impulse I said, "Don't tell anyone else what you told me. It will only make trouble all the way around."

"Trouble?" he said innocently. "What kind of trouble? You've got me wrong. I ain't making any trouble. If there's trouble being made, it's Glory and Ed who're making it. Not me. It ain't going to make a particle of difference whether I tell what I seen or whether I don't."

He selected two comic books from the magazine rack, paid for them and left, saying, "Guess I'll run along. I got a lot of things to do before the night's over."

After I finished rearranging the magazines, I went into the back room and sat down in a chair by the window. As I watched the top branches of the big elms sway back and forth in the wind, I wondered what the things were that The Weasel had to do before the night was over. Surely one of his self-appointed tasks would be to let Johnnie Roane know that Ed had been making love to Glory.

Conveying that bit of information seemed to me a waste of The Weasel's time and energy. The expression on Johnnie's face, when he was in the store in the morning, suggested that he already knew about Glory and Ed, either because someone had told him or because he had sensed it.

I have known Johnnie all his life. I watched him grow up and pass from the penny-candy stage, to the nickel-bar stage, to the coca-cola-drinking stage, and then on to the first package of cigarettes bought self-consciously and smoked with caution. As far as I know, he has never reached that jumping-off point, that peculiarly final adult stage: the bromo-seltzer-first-thing-in-the-morning.

I remember when his mother and father were courting. His mother was a waitress at the railroad-station restaurant; and his father was a stonemason and contractor—an apprentice, just learning the trade.

His father bought beribboned boxes of candy from me. And at Christmas one year he spent almost an hour selecting an enameled dresser set and matching manicure set—an elaborate affair decorated with hand-painted roses. I was fairly certain that he would be getting married soon. And I was right.

The day Johnnie was born, his father came into the store to give me a cigar. He was strutting about like a rooster, walking up and down and talking, and waving his hands in excited gestures that were completely foreign to him—all because he had a son.

Not too long after that, Mrs. Roane wheeled Johnnie up from the Point in the baby carriage. Her cheeks were red and she was breathing hard from the exertion, the long walk. She came into the store, holding him in her arms, and sat down to rest awhile, and as she sat there holding him, she talked to him in a soft murmur, then looked embarrassed. I took hold of one of his small, perfect hands to show her that I understood. He was smooth-cheeked and innocent of eye, a pleasure to look at, and at the same time, wonderful and miraculous—all infants are like that before the world toughens and hardens and coarsens them.

He grew like a weed. In no time at all he was tall enough and strong enough and old enough to mow lawns; and he used to run errands for me after school. He was always buying pencils and paper and every spare moment he was sketching—the inside of the store, the fountain, the back room, or the trees across the street. When he wasn't doing that, he was reading. I never saw a boy who read so much and so swiftly and with such concentration.

I always thought he would become an artist. But—he fell in love with Glory and married her. He went to work in his father's contracting business. Then later, he went off to war.

I am very fond of him. Yet when he came into the store this morning, having been gone for four years, I was at a loss as to what to say to him. What I finally said was as banal and ordinary and commonplace as though he were a casual acquaintance and not a boy I had known from birth. I could not find the words with which to tell him how much I had missed him and how overjoyed I was that he was home again—safe and sound.

"Glad to see you home again," I said when I shook hands with him. He was so tall I had to look up at him; and I looked straight into his eyes. They had the same blank expression you see in the eyes of a person suffering from shock.

About a year ago there was an auto accident out in front of the store. An open roadster ran head-on into Spatter Bronson's little car. The folks in the roadster seemed to be all right and, at first glance, Spatter was okay. But when you looked in his eyes you knew that there was something terribly wrong with him because his eyes were blank, suggesting that whatever fluid had given them life and expression had been drained out of them. Johnnie's eyes were like that.

So I found myself saying, "Glad to see you back, Johnnie," twice in succession.

"Thanks," he said. "I'll have a pack of Camels."

"It's kind of wet for a walk."

"Well—yes. But I wanted to look at the town. I haven't seen it for a long time."

"It's just about the same. The changes are buried deep, way under the surface, and it takes a long time for them to crack the crust."

"Maybe so," he said.

After he left I looked at the puddle of water on the floor where he had been standing. The seventeen cents I had rung up on the cash register and the wet place on the floor were the only evidence that he'd been there. I got the mop and wiped up the floor, and I couldn't help thinking that most of us don't leave much more than that behind us—a few cents more or less that goes to our relatives, if any; and a puddle that has to be mopped up, a puddle in the form of worn-out clothes and furniture.

Normally I am not given to dwelling on death and the general futility of life; but that steady, slanting rain and the damp cold that came with the wind depressed me. Then, too, Johnnie Roane carried with him a quality of gloom, so deep, so dark, that it was contagious.

I found it easy to think of Glory with contempt. Yet I could not help wondering if she would have remained faithful to Johnnie if there had been no war to interrupt the normal course of their life together. Under other circumstances she might have remained one of those pretty, more or less useless girls who get married and cook unappetizing meals and keep a house middling clean and middling dirty; and then later on have children, not because they want them but by accident—born of a moment of careless, lazy passion.

And yet I am not certain that it would have made any difference if he had stayed at home. Perhaps it was inevitable that Glory should eye some other man and sooner or later get to imagining what he would be like in bed.

I do not know her quite as well as I know Johnnie. She was born and grew up in the next town—Westville. She came to Lennox to go to high school because the town fathers in Westville have never seen fit to put a high school in their town—possibly because they are afraid of too much education.

When Glory reached high-school age, she came into the store almost every day with a crowd of young boys and girls. Right after school lets out the front door opens wide and they burst into the store, laughing and kicking up their heels like young colts. At first glance the girls are all plaited skirts and long bare legs and flying hair and high, chirruping voices saying, "Two cherry cokes, please, Mr. Fraser. I'll start off with two."

The first time Glory came into the store I noticed her, separated her from the others. She wore the same type of plaited skirt and white blouse and bracelet loaded with charms that tinkled every time she moved her arm; and carried her books in a strap which she swung back and forth—just like the rest of them.

The resemblance ended there. For she had the most amazing eyes I have ever seen. They seemed to blaze in her face; due partly to the color—they were a deep violet-blue—but due mostly to the way she looked at things. It was as though she tried to see all of a thing at once, devouring it, because she was impelled to decide then and there, in that first hungry glance, whether it was something she would want and had to have; or whether it was undesirable, completely worthless, and therefore to be discarded, quickly.

As I sat there by the window, thinking about Johnnie Roane and his wife, Glory, the daylight faded, died. In the growing darkness the store was filled with shadows. Wind rattled the windowpanes. Rain hit the glass so hard it sounded as though someone were standing outside, throwing pebbles against the windows.

I knew I ought to get up and turn the lights on in the store.

But I didn't. I continued to sit there, thinking of Johnnie—of the blank look in his eyes, of the gloom that hung about him like a mantle. And of Ed Barrell, who had a weak heart and was no longer young, so he wasn't drafted.

Even now I am not certain that I understand him, or understand any of the men like him, who pursue women. His wife had been in a tubercular sanatorium for twenty years or more and during those years he took to hunting females as though they were big game.

He used to come into the store, late in the afternoon, almost every day. He would lean against the counters, puffing clouds of smoke from his cigar and eyeing the women who came in and out. During the summer he would show up two or three times a day. If some of those summer women came in wearing shorts that came halfway up their buttocks, Ed fairly quivered like a hound that has got the scent.

If there were no customers around, he would sit down at a table in the fountain room and leaf through the pages of some magazine like *The Fighter* and spin yarns about the days when he was a professional boxer. Sometimes he went into the telephone booth, and stayed there as much as a half-hour, whispering obscenities to some woman over the phone. If I was in the back room putting up prescriptions, I could hear every word he said. When he came out he would be laughing, softly, under his breath.

When he left I would take the flit gun and spray the booth, for he left a strong, unaired smell behind him—compounded of gasoline and motor oil and the strong, rank smell of the cheap cigars he smoked; and something else as well, the sour smell of lechery, for it would be impossible to convince me that he did not carry the odor of that about with him, too.

That last thought brought me out of my chair. I turned on

all the lights. The ceiling light in the back room, the small lamp on the prescription counter, lights at the soda fountain, in the store proper, window lights, everything—I set the place to blazing with lights.

But the light didn't help. No customers came into the store. It was too windy out, too wet. Everyone with sense was home. I began to feel that even the company of a female would be desirable and I went to the front door, in search of Banana, my yellow cat.

While I stood there a car went by; its headlights made the black macadam road gleam. After the car passed, the street was totally dark, for the lights in the houses were mere pinpricks, obscured by the driving rain.

Banana answered with that soft mewing she makes when she hears her name. I returned to the back room and sat down by the window; and she followed me in there, walked in and out between my legs, purring.

As I sat there I began thinking about the day the war with the Japanese ended. When you look back on some important, historic day, you never remember it whole, exactly as it was; you remember only some small and inconsequential part of it.

On that afternoon of which I speak, there was only one customer in the store—a young woman, a stranger. She bought a magazine and a couple of newspapers.

The radio was turned on in the back room. When I handed her change from the five-dollar bill she had given me, I had my ear cocked for an announcement. For two days there had been a whole series of false alarms about the surrender. During the afternoon messages kept coming through to stand by for official word from the White House.

She was putting the change in her pocketbook when I heard the official announcement. And I said, "The war's over."

She looked at me, tried to say something. When she opened her mouth, no words came out. She tried twice and finally she whispered, "Is it true?"

"Sure," I said. "Just came over the radio."

I left her standing at the counter and walked to the front of the store because the bell on the Episcopal Church had started to ring—a silvery, sweet sound, seeming to float over the tops of the elm trees. I wondered why the bell on the Congregational Church wasn't sounding and as I looked out the front door I saw the minister running into the church. He pulled the bell rope himself; I could see him exerting all his strength on it.

I forgot the woman was still in the store because the deep tones of the Congregational bell were mixing and blending with the Episcopal bell and I gave myself up to listening. Only once before had I ever heard those bells sounding at the same time. That was the day when the First World War ended—that war which was supposed to be the last war, and wasn't.

Under this blending of the bells, I heard another sound, right there in the store. I turned around. The woman was standing next to me, leaning against the door jamb. She was crying. But she was not making the loud, blubbering sound one usually associates with weeping. Her eyes were full of tears, washed in them, floating in them. They ran down her face, streaking her powder, her rouge, blurring the mascara on her eyelashes. The sound I had heard was the soft quickness of her breathing.

She began to crumple, to slide down toward the floor. I tried to hold her up and she kept on sliding down and trying to pull herself back up. I got her braced against the magazine racks and patted her on the shoulder.

"Is it true?" she said again.

"Yes. It's true. The war's over," I said, as though I were unaware that this was the second time she had asked me.

Then she said something I couldn't understand. She saw that

I couldn't make sense out of her words and she straightened up and took a deep breath, making a sound that was part moan, part sigh. And what she finally said was this, "I ought to be in St. Louis. I ought to be in St. Louis."

Cars were racing up and down the main street, swerving in and out, tires screaming, the engines roaring. The people in the cars were cheering and waving at each other; sounding their horns, long and loud. And what with the continuous ringing of the church bells and the swift-moving cars, the town was full of a nervous excitement.

I cannot remember a single word of all the speeches that were made on the radio that night, for the only really vivid memory I have of that day the Japs surrendered is of that woman, a stranger, her make-up ruined from tears, saying in a strangled voice, "I ought to be in St. Louis."

The woman who had said she ought to be in St. Louis kept mixing with my thoughts of Johnnie Roane. I suppose all of us have some St. Louis we ache to be in, a St. Louis that is the shape and form of our dreams, our desires.

But it seemed to me that the St. Louis that Johnnie Roane wanted so desperately to be in was completely unattainable. For he had put his heart and soul in Glory's hands—and that was a mighty unsafe place for a human heart to rest.

10

THE WEASEL TURNED THE TOWN taxi around in front of the drugstore. As he drove through Whippoorwill Lane, he stole occasional glances at himself in the mirror over the windshield. He had no passengers, so he talked to himself.

When he crossed the Post Road he said, "Have to get some gas before I go up to the station." Then he winked at the mirror and murmured, "Good old Ed."

He wished he could see Lil's face when she heard about Glory carrying on with Ed Barrell. She would be good and mad. First chance he got he'd needle her about it. After Lil got herself married to Mearns Gramby, she began acting like she'd never known anyone as common as a taxi-driver.

But he never intended to let her forget that they were born in the same town. When he went to get Mearns to take him to the New Haven train, Lil came to the front door. If it was a nice morning she'd walk down the path to the gate, holding on to Mearns' arm, leaning up against him, acting young and kittenish, talking baby talk to him. At the gate she'd kiss him and wave good-bye to him.

As they came down the walk, he stared at them, shifting

his gaze from Lil to Mearns and back again to Lil. By the time Mearns got into the car his face was bright red and he couldn't seem to stop clearing his throat.

He would wait until Mearns was all the way in the taxi before leaning out to say loudly, "How are you, Lil?"

Lil's head would jerk back just like she was a horse being pulled up short by a hard-handed rider; and her mouth would twist as though it hurt her when she finally said, "Good morning."

He laughed, remembering the day he ran into her in the drugstore. He'd needled her good that day.

"Hello, Lil," he'd said. "Getting some hair coloring?" Looking at her blond curls and letting her see that he knew they came out of a bottle.

Doc Fraser was handing her a package of cigarettes and she clawed them out of his hand, her long red fingernails biting into the cellophane wrapper.

"I'm Mrs. Gramby," she said. "I wish you'd remember that."

"Mrs. Gramby?" he said. And he had made his voice innocent, a little stupid. "There's only one Mrs. Gramby in this town and that's the old lady. You're 'Lil' to me and everybody else."

A muscle in her cheek started to twitch and he watched it and then he said: "You ain't forgot we went to school together, have you? What would I be getting formal with an old friend for? Why, I remember when you used to wet your pants in the first grade, Lil."

Doc Fraser looked like he wanted to laugh, but he remembered his dignity and, though a smile almost parted his lips, he clamped his mouth together in a straight line and stopped looking at Lil's face and acted as though something about the church spire had attracted his attention.

Lil flounced out of the drugstore and he followed close behind her as far as the door, and just as she went down the steps he had said, loud enough for her to hear, "Meaner'n cat turd and barley." She turned around and glared at him, but she couldn't prove he was talking about her, so after that one nasty look she went on up the street.

They were a stuck-up bunch of bastards—the Grambys. Except, of course, the old lady. She was okay. Every time she called him Mr. Weasel he wanted to laugh. It was funny how somebody as nice as she was had managed to give birth to a piece of horse like Mearns. He got in the taxi every day in the week and never opened his mouth until he got to the station. Year in and year out all he said was, "Thanks. I'll see you tonight."

He'd read the paper all the way to the train. Every morning they went by the drugstore and got a *Times* before they headed for the station. And it was the same thing at night. When Mearns got off the New York express about six, he'd ride home in silence, reading a *Sun* that he bought in New Haven.

When Mearns got out of the car in front of the Gramby House, he said, "Thanks. See you in the morning."

He'd never been able to needle him. But I'd like to get him good, just once, watch his face go to pieces. Pompous bastard. He lowered the car window and spit. Wind blew the saliva back against his hand. He wiped it off on the side of his coat.

"It's my own spit, ain't it?" he said defensively and glared at the mirror.

When he drove into Ed's filling station, he noticed with pleasure that there wasn't a car in sight except for Ed's car, parked close to the building. He could see Ed inside. The lights were on and Ed had his feet on top of the desk, his hat on the back of his head. The man who worked for Ed musta gone home. He wasn't anywhere in sight.

"I bet Ed's feeling good. Got some young, tender female flesh practically in his hand."

He drew the taxi close to one of the gas tanks and sounded

his horn. Ed acted like he didn't want to get up from behind the desk, so he sounded the horn again and Ed reached for a raincoat.

"Do him good to get wet. He's been sitting in there dry as a toad and other folks been out in the wind and the rain."

"Fill her up," he said cheerfully when Ed emerged scowling, trying to hold his raincoat together.

Ed got the gas in the car in a hurry. The Weasel handed him a five-dollar bill, thinking, Wonder what the hell women see in him. He's got bowlegs and his face ain't exactly handsome. Always looks like he needed a shave. "Here y'are," he said aloud. "I'll come in for the change. Save you the trouble of coming out in the rain again."

The Weasel followed Ed inside the building. He noticed that the small kerosene stove in the far corner of the room was lit.

"See you got a fire going," he said. He stood close to the desk, eyeing Ed as he reached into the desk drawer for the metal box where the change was kept.

"Yeah. It's damp and cold in here when it rains."

Ed wouldn't look right at him. He was working a cigar around in his mouth, and he kept his eyes on the dollar bills as he counted them into The Weasel's outstretched hand.

"How's your wife, Ed?"

"About the same."

"She don't ever get no worse or no better, does she?" The Weasel said. He sat down on a chair near the window. "Might as well pass the time of day with you for a while. It'll be another hour or so before a train is due. Things are slow right now. Only train passenger I had yesterday was young Johnnie Roane—just home from the war. We get just about one fare off'n each train."

Ed said nothing. He laid the cigar down in an ash tray and picked up a toothpick.

The Weasel's gaze shifted from Ed to the rain beating against the one big window. "This kind of weather must be tough on the t.b.," he paused, and then said softly, "I remember your wife when she was a kid in Westville, wearing her hair down her back in long curls. Funny she ended up in a t.b. place."

"How's the old car holding up?" Ed said abruptly. He got up from the desk and went over to the window.

"Pretty good. Old Mrs. Gramby likes to ride in it. Told me when she got in it this afternoon that it suited her good because she and the car seen their best days long ago. Don't see why a nice old lady like that had to get a daughter-in-law like she's got. You know—Glory's mother—Lil. Cheap people." And he thought, yeah, good old Ed, no matter which way you try to steer, I can bring you right back to what I saw you doing this afternoon up there on Obit's.

Ed moved away from the window, sat down behind the desk and shoved the cash box aside. He's going to pretend he's got a lot of work to do, The Weasel thought, as he watched him pull a ledger out from the desk drawer.

"Lil always was a bitch," The Weasel said absent-mindedly. Ed was moving the cash box again, taking his wallet out. He seemed to be checking the contents of his wallet and the cash box, and then writing figures down in the ledger.

"Guess there's a lot of work connected with running a fill."

Ed grunted by way of reply. "But I suppose you don't let that interfere none with your private business," The Weasel said slyly.

A long red moving van pulled in near the gas tanks. The Weasel grinned because Ed jumped up from the desk, grabbed his raincoat, and hurried out of the building. He's so glad to get away from me I bet he feels like giving that van free gas.

He stood up in order to watch Ed from the window. The instant Ed was out of the door, he slowed down. The van sounded its horn—loud, insistent, impatient. Got a beller like a bull, he thought admiringly. But good old Ed wasn't hurrying any. He don't care how long that van stays because he thinks maybe I'll get tired of waiting and go home.

I bet he checks their tires and their oil and wipes the windshield and puts in water just to keep from having to come back and talk to me.

He turned his attention to the desk, walked over to it. Good old Ed left all his money out he was in such a hurry. Must be about twenty dollars. He fingered through the crumpled bills, keeping one eye on the window.

Ed was talking to the driver of the van, hadn't even started to put gas in yet. He was good for at least fifteen minutes out there in the pouring rain. The Weasel turned back to the desk. Jesus! Ed was in such a hurry to get away from me he left his wallet right there in plain sight, forgot to put it back in his pocket.

He must have had it a long time, too. Kind of worn around the edges. Got thirty bucks in it. There's his driving license. Fifty-five. I'd 'a' said he was still in his forties. All that screwing he does musta preserved him. Got his lodge card and here's the bill from the state sanatorium for the t.b.'s where his wife is, marked paid; and a couple of bills from the oil company also marked paid; a cleaner's ticket for a suit. A couple of ticket stubs for a movie over in New Haven; wonder who he took with him.

None of it very interesting. He started to put the wallet down and then he saw there was a leather flap that concealed another section. Jesus, he thought, and felt a little thrill of wonder go through him. Because he was holding in his hand a picture of old Stone's wife and a picture of that Bates girl, the one who was in high school. Snapshots of them and neither one of them had a thing on—just as naked as the day they were born. How in the name of God had good old Ed got those pictures and who developed them? He wouldn't dare take 'em any place in Lennox to be printed.

He glanced hastily out of the window. Ed had the hood of the van lifted; he was looking at the engine. The driver of the van got out and he looked at the engine, too. They'll both have nice wet behinds before they get through, wonder what cock-and-bull story Ed told the driver to get him out of the van.

There was a folded piece of paper in the wallet—right in back of where the pictures were. It was stuck to the leather. He worked it out gingerly, wondering what it was, for the edges of the paper were slightly discolored, suggesting it had been there for months without being unfolded.

It was a letter. He read it through twice, frowning. Who in hell had written it and why had Ed kept it? He must have thought it was important enough to save and he carried it around with him all the time. He read it through again: "Darling Ed: I think I can meet you at the usual place on Saturday. Petey is going away for the weekend. Your own Kittikins."

In the upper corner in the same handwriting it said October 1, 1945. He turned it over; but the back was blank, offering no clue to the writer. It was a sheet of double-fold paper. The letter was on the first inner fold. He tore it off and replaced the blank sheet in the wallet. If Ed looked in there and didn't actually take the piece of paper out and examine it, he would never know that the written-on part was gone.

He placed the wallet on the desk and went to stand near the window. Ed was screwing the gasoline cap on the truck. Then he picked up the water bucket and filled the water tank.

I ought to be able to smell out who wrote him that letter, The Weasel thought. I wasn't born here in Lennox, but I know as much about this town as anyone else.

He took a last look at the letter before putting it in his pants pocket. The dame who wrote it musta been in the habit of meeting Ed somewhere. She musta been married because if she was single she wouldn't write about arranging to meet him because some other man was going away.

Ed had kept it so it musta been important. Perhaps it was from one of those naked women. No, first place, the Bates girl wasn't married. She could meet him any time, any place she pleased. Old Stone and his wife moved away two or three years ago. Besides, Stone's wife didn't give a damn who knew she rode around with Ed and that she went up to his place in the woods all the time. She wouldn't send Ed no letters saying she thought she could meet him somewhere. She'd just go ahead and meet him and dare old Stone to do anything about it.

Besides, Stone's first name wasn't Petey, it was Joshua. Folks in town used to snicker about it—Joshua Stone Is All Alone. Kids coming from school used to sing it in front of his house when they went by and the old man would come running out, leaning on his cane, hollering and screaming and swearing he was going to call a state cop if they didn't go away.

When Ed opened the door, The Weasel was at the window, watching the big red van pull away.

"Big truck, ain't it?" he said.

Ed said, "Mmmmm." He started to take his slicker off, and then he looked at the desk, at the wallet, and glanced at The Weasel out of the corner of his eyes.

The Weasel watched him as he approached the desk. He picked the wallet up, glanced inside it, pretending to be looking at the bills and all the time he was furtively lifting the flap that formed the secret pocket, verifying its contents.

"Forgot I left this in here," he said, and put the wallet in his pocket. Then he took his raincoat off and draped it on a hook.

"Where was that truck from?" The Weasel asked.

"Providence."

He wondered if there was any way he could let Ed know he'd seen those snapshots and then decided, no, it was too dangerous. Ed would start looking for the letter and of course discover that the important part of it was gone.

"Well, guess I'll be shoving off," he said. "You sure gave that truck the works." He moved slowly toward the door. "What 'smatter, didn't you want to talk to me?"

"The guy's going to Florida. He wanted everything checked—tires, gas, oil, water."

"Oh. Somehow I got the feeling you suggested it to him. But that's okay. I know when I'm not wanted. Lots of folks don't and they have to get hit over the head before they find out. But not me. I can always tell when my company ain't wanted."

"So long," Ed said. He didn't look at The Weasel.

The Weasel opened the door, paused on the threshold to watch the rain. Then, turning up his coat collar, he started out the door, grinning, and said, "Now you take a young feller like that Johnnie Roane. The only way he's going to learn when he ain't wanted is by getting hit over the head with a meat axe."

He was soaking wet when he reached the taxi. He got inside and slammed the door, then peered toward the building. Too bad I can't see Ed's face, but I give him a coupla good ones, he thought with satisfaction.

At the railroad station he parked the taxi under the sign that said: Crandall Taxi No Parking In This Area. And then ran, hunched-over, a small gnomelike figure, toward the protection of the platform roof.

Once inside the station he nodded to the ticket-seller, thinking, That's just where he belongs; for the grated window made the ticket-seller look as though he were in a cage.

He sat down behind a desk which was placed cater-corner in the dusty waiting room. If I put my mind to it, he thought, I can figure who Kittikins is. He fingered the telephone, stared vacantly at the sign on it: "This telephone for taxi calls only—no private outgoing calls permitted." Old Crandall oughtta take that sign and stick it up his what's-his-name. I ain't never called anybody up on this phone and he knows it.

Glory couldn't have written the letter. She and Ed hadn't started carrying on until just lately. Too bad I can't go around town collecting women's handwriting. I could find out that way. On the other hand, it might not have been written by a female in Lennox, coulda been some lonesome female in New Haven. But I got the feeling it's somebody right here in the town.

He'd just have to sit and wait and see what he could find out. Trouble was there wasn't any men named Peter, here in Lennox, whose wives could have wrote it. There was old Pete O'Connell, who had never married and lived by himself in a shack down near the boat dock and nursed a bottle night and day; he never had a woman that anybody ever heard of, a bottle seemed to do him just as well. There was Pete Frankel the butcher. He had a sour-faced fat wife and three skinny kids. But she wasn't the type. She was too stingy even to buy handkerchiefs to blow the snot out of the kids' noses. She wouldn't be meeting a man anywhere. Besides, what man would want her? Ed Barrell never picked no ugly women to fool around with and Frankel's wife was all loose fat and flabby breasts and frowsy hair. No, she hadn't written the letter.

He sighed, admitting defeat. And in sudden irritation he tore old Crandall's sign off the telephone and pulled it apart. He scattered the bits of paper on the floor, thinking, That'll give Crandall something to get mad over.

Then he walked over to the ticket window, peered through the wicket. Limpy, the ticket-seller, was listening to the radio.

"Heard your wife ain't so well," The Weasel said.

"Nothing the matter with her that I know of," Limpy said defensively.

"No? Well, mebbe there ain't, but she was buying a bottle of Lydia Pinkham's down in the drugstore yesterday afternoon."

Limpy fiddled with the dial of the radio, turning it quickly so that there was a sudden blare and then an equally sudden dying-away of music, of voices. "She's all right," he said, and tuned in a news broadcast.

"Saw Glory Roane, young Johnnie Roane's wife this afternoon, up on Obit's, with Ed Barrell."

"Yeah?" Limpy's voice sounded interested.

The Weasel pretended to listen to the news coming in over the radio. "So they've settled the auto strike, huh? About time. Most of the cars in town are falling to pieces. Except Ed's."

"What was Ed doing up on Obit with Glory Roane?" Limpy asked cautiously.

The Weasel waited until he saw a gleam of impatience in Limpy's eyes, then he said, slowly: "Well, I guess they figured they was minding their own business. But there was a lot of other folks' business mixed up in it. I had old lady Gramby and Johnnie Roane's mother in the taxi. And when I drove 'em up the hill, Glory was kissing Ed, hugging him so close you couldn't get a basting thread between 'em."

He watched Limpy's face as he talked. Limpy was thinking about his wife and the time she ran off with the tailor; and returned, reluctantly, some months later, only because the tailor got tired of her.

"Good old Ed," The Weasel said softly. Limpy wouldn't find a radio broadcast very interesting. From now until the station closed for the night, he would be worrying about his wife. It was going to be a rainy night, too. Dark came early when it rained like this—a dark, rainy night.

"Say," Limpy said hesitantly, "what do women take Lydia Pinkham's for?"

"I don't know exactly. Some say for female trouble. I always figured it was to bring their passion back." He shoved his cap far back on his head. "It's probably just as good for men as it is for women. You oughtta try it some time, Limpy," he said gently, watching Limpy's facial muscles quiver.

Then he walked over to the desk, sat down, and started humming to himself. Petey, he thought, some guy whose wife was messing around with Ed Barrell. Just about this time last year. Must be a guy who lived right here in Lennox. It had to be or all the fun would be gone out of it.

He stared at the gray walls of the waiting room, at the faded posters, at the train schedules chalked up on the blackboard near the door. Finally his gaze fastened on a picture of a mammoth engine heading into a long stretch of track. "Use the railroads for pleasure, for safety, for speed." He read the words on the poster aloud, softly, absent-mindedly.

Whoever she was she thought she was safe. Wonder what made Ed keep that letter. He probably don't run with her no more and he's keeping the letter as a reminder, sort of like money in the bank, just in case he ever needed it.

Use Ed Barrell for pleasure, for safety, for speed. He laughed gently. He'd always wanted to find a nickname for Ed. Speed. Next time he saw him he'd call him Speed. Then after a while he'd call him Pleasure and then finally take to calling him Safety. Then he'd let him know it came off a railroad poster. "Ed Barrell for pleasure, for safety, for speed."

Taking the bottle of ink and the pen from the top of the desk, he walked over to the poster. He carefully inked out the words "the railroads" and scrawled Ed Barrell in big printed letters and then filled the letters with ink so that they stood out, sharp and clear.

11

IN THE ROANES' HOUSE THERE was a white linen cloth on the round table in the dining room. Johnnie saw, with surprise, that the table was set with his mother's wedding-present china—the company dishes, easily recognizable because he had tried, with some degree of success, to scrape the gold band off one of the plates when he was about eight years old.

A special occasion, very special, indeed, he thought. The overhead lamp was lit. It had been lowered and the round fringed shade was quite close to the table, concentrating a pool of pinkish light on the thin water glasses, the big dinner napkins.

The light shining through the big rose-colored shade enlivened the room, the table. It changed the color of things. His father's shirt-sleeves were not white; they were a delicate blush color. His mother's face was rosy, young, and the gray in her hair was not discernible; her eyes glowed like jewels in the lamplight. He stole a cautious glance at Glory, who was sitting beside him. Her hair was like—He forced himself to look away, for under the rose-colored light her hair flamed and shimmered, reflecting the light.

Mr. Roane bowed his head, started an impromptu blessing,

long, involved, covering the past and the present, touching on the future. After the first five minutes Johnnie stopped listening, began to think of Glory. He had thought about her all that day as he walked about the town in the rain.

She had been uppermost in his mind when he stopped in the drugstore to buy a package of cigarettes, early in the morning. Pop Fraser had taken one long look at his face and then Pop shifted his eyes to the church across the way and kept them there.

After he left the drugstore, he sought shelter from the rain. So he had sat on the church steps, smoking, telling himself that Glory was tired last night, that was all, everything would be okay tonight. It had to be. Rain, dripping from the eaves, sliding down the Doric columns, monotonous, depressing, denied the conclusion he had reached. But he could no more stop his thoughts than he could stop the perpetual drip of the rain, the blowing of the wind.

He had no proof of Glory's infidelity. Yet he had sat there convincing himself that it was true; then, that it was not true.

Finally the sight of the green across the way set him to thinking of himself as a boy, walking past this church, a skinny, long-legged kid, wrapped in dreams, a kid who read too much. When he was nine he climbed an apple tree and misjudged the strength of a branch, and he fell and broke both legs. He had to stay in bed for weeks. Thus he made the discovery that inside the pages of a book he could escape from the bed, from the cast, from the room. He could go anywhere, any time, without having to pay the fare, without bothering to ask permission. And he had read too much from there on in.

All through high school he had read omnivorously, swallowing books whole. The librarian used to look at him, a vague puzzlement in her eyes, when he handed her five, six, seven books at a time. She always said the same thing, "Do you really read all these?" And he would nod and flee the place quickly, so that he could get inside the greatest number of books in the shortest possible time.

Was there a purpose behind it all? You were once young and then you grew up, fought in a war. Did all this happen so that, finally, you would sit for a while on the steps of a church and think about your wife, doubting her?

He had stared at Whippoorwill Lane, the short street that went past the drugstore. Whippoorwill Lane ended at the Post Road and on the other side of the Post Road was a black macadam road which led to Ed Barrell's filling station. Yes, all roads lead to Rome. Rome is a filling station. Rome is Ed Barrell and his bowlegs and his bulging chest and his leaky heart.

And as he sat there on the steps, he began to toy with the thought of killing Ed. He clenched and unclenched his hands, for he ached to twist them about the man's thick throat.

When he realized what he was doing, he got up and walked on, doggedly, slowly. He had walked about the town all day. Rain squished in his shoes, ran down his collar. And still he walked, up past the postoffice, to the railroad station, and beyond, as far as Rabbit's Brook and then back again. He sat on the old millstone and munched a sandwich. It was afternoon then and the rain had become a ghost of itself—a mist, fine, foglike.

When he left the millstone, he went down to the old boat dock. And always, as he walked, he thought of Glory, remembering things about her. When they were first married, if he got angry because she had bought some foolish, extravagant dress instead of paying the grocery bill, she would sit on his lap and say, "Oh, Johnnie, I love you so—honest—I love you so—"

The faint sweet smell of her hair would be in his nose, dispelling his anger. And he remembered that he had thought, All men have a fetish, some one thing about a woman that casts a spell about them, holding them enraptured. If he had a fetish, then it was Glory's hair. It was like a net, a gleaming net, spread wide to hold his heart.

Finally he had sat on a bench in the old shed at one end of the dock. One side of the shed was open, facing the sea. The water was as gray as the sky, as gray as his thoughts. The only sounds were the gulls screaming and quarreling and the lap of the water against the piling. He had gone to sleep there and awakened to find he was cold, his legs stiff.

His father's voice droned on. This blessing tonight was longer than the ones Pop used to say at Thanksgiving and at Christmas. He stole a glance at Glory. Her head was bowed. He could not see her face. The edges of her hair gleamed in the roseate light. He found himself wanting to touch her hair just as he had done on that day when he proposed to her. That same feeling of hurry, of doubt, was in him now. Would he know ecstasy tonight as he had known it then? But first there had been the doubt.

It was a Sunday afternoon. He and Glory were on the back porch at her mother's house, sitting in the glider. Glory's hair against the green cushions was bright and warm and glistening.

"I love you," he had said. He swallowed twice, quickly, aware of a faintly acid taste far back in his throat. Then he said, "Let's get married. Will you?"

She had laughed at him. He had expected anything—surprise, perhaps fright, possibly a halting acceptance—but not laughter. He was half-suffocated with embarrassment, wordless with embarrassment. It sharpened all his senses so that he became suddenly aware of the squeaking sound the glider made as she sent it back and forth with a slight motion of her foot; aware, too, of the roar of traffic—continuous, far-off on the Post Road—and the clack of a lawnmower next door; and aware of the long sweet line of her throat and of the gentle tremor of her body as laughter ran through her.

He remembered thinking, Time will obliterate the memory of this moment. Why doesn't it hasten? Somebody, please, make the clocks tick faster so that I can forget this.

Then she said, "Oh, Johnnie, I thought you'd never ask me." Her laughter was a soft, lovely, rippling sound. She said again, "I thought you'd never ask me. Honest."

He hugged her and he felt slightly dizzy, for his emotions had changed so swiftly: doubt and despair to ecstasy, too fast, too sudden, no transition stage. Yes, he had hugged her and then touched her hair and he could have sworn that it was warm.

Something else had happened. The screen door opened. And her mother came out of the house. "What's going on here?" she demanded. Her voice was ugly, frightening.

He started to get up and Glory pulled him back, holding his arm in a firm grip.

"I won't have it," her mother had said, glaring at him. "You needn't think you're going to get a free lay—"

He had made a strangled sound in his throat, too astonished to reply.

Glory said calmly, "Oh, shut up. We're going to be married."

Then Lil, Glory's mother, said: "That's fine. You're a nice boy, Johnnie. I've always liked you. Congratulations." And she shook hands with him and, though her hand was cold to the touch and though she quickly removed it from contact with his hand, her voice was sweet and soft.

He had never liked Glory's mother since then. He and Glory used to call her Ole Lightnin'—half in earnest, half in jest. They had stayed as far away from her as they could get.

He was so engrossed in his thoughts that he did not hear his father say, "Amen."

Glory touched his arm. "Johnnie," she said softly, "the blessing's over."

He lifted his head, murmured, "I'm sorry."

The blessing had not only ended, but his mother was explaining why they were eating in the dining room, why this was not "supper" but a regular dinner, complete to dessert and coffee bubbling in the percolator on the sideboard.

"This is the home-coming dinner," she said while she carved the roast. "For Johnnie. So of course we couldn't eat in the kitchen."

"The fatted calf?" Mr. Roane said.

"The fatted calf and the brass band and the keys of the city," she answered, smiling.

She's smiling because she wants me to think she's joking, Johnnie thought. Only she isn't joking. She means it. This roast, with its bubbling juices and its crisp, crackling, browned outside fat, and the roasted potatoes lined up around it on the platter represent the keys to the city and something more; the something more pushed down, until it runs over. Oh, hell, there is no way I could ever begin to live up to what both of them think I am. What would it do to them if I should throttle that thick-throated bastard with my bare hands, squeezing his bull neck until his life escaped gasping from his throat? Absalom, my son, my son, is a murderer; the warrior home from the seas to throttle, to kill; the warrior turned strangler—

There was such animation in Glory's face he couldn't take his eyes away from her. She wasn't avoiding his glance either. She was finding excuses to touch his hand; each time she passed a plate down the table her hand lingered against his.

"What did you do all day, Johnnie?" she asked.

"Walked. In the rain." He paused. "And thought about you."

"The town looks just the same, doesn't it?" Mrs. Roane said.

"Sure. A little down-at-the-heels, but nothing that a dash of paint wouldn't fix up. Too bad there isn't a special paint that could be used on aging humans to fix them right up."

Glory said, "You say the funniest things." And giggled.

He stared at her in surprise and then went on talking. "But on the whole I would say the town of Lennox is largely unchanged." He put a forkful of food in his mouth, chewed it with deliberation before he spoke again. "The Weasel asked me the same thing."

"The Weasel?" Mrs. Roane and Glory said it together, at the same moment, and then looked at each other warily.

"Great minds," his father said. "Same thought at the same moment."

His mother and Glory laughed politely, self-consciously, and both of them looked a question at Johnnie.

"The Weasel drove me home from the station yesterday," he explained. "That was almost the first thing he said, 'Town looks the same, don't she?'"

"Oh," Glory said. "I thought first you might have—run into him—somewhere today—while you were out walking."

He frowned as he listened to her, because there were pauses between the phrases, as though she had been running and lost her breath. Not quite that, but as though she had been walking fast for a long time so that when she spoke she had to stop between phrases until the quickened pace of her breathing slacked off, and thus there was a jerkiness to her speech.

"Uh-huh," he said finally. "But the town really doesn't change."

"Oh, I think it does," Mrs. Roane said. "It's different in a lot of ways. The Parker House that used to be there by the old dock was torn down years ago. The Hartford boat doesn't run any more. I remember when the fancy ladies and their gentlemen used to come up from New York on that boat in order to spend the weekend at the Parker House."

"We've got roadside inns and constellations and automobiles instead," Mr. Roane said. "I don't think it makes much difference. People just get around a little faster than they used to. I can't see that that's changed 'em any or changed the town, for that matter. People are still getting born into this world the same way they always have. They still get married and sooner or later they die and some of 'em take the dying hard and some of 'em take it easy just the way they always did."

"But the fancy ladies and the New York sports aren't around any more," Mrs. Roane said. There was a curious insistence in her voice.

"They call 'em by another name these days. I don't see any difference in a pro—"

"Now, Jonathan—" Mrs. Roane interrupted.

"Well, anyway, I remember when one of those fancy ladies was murdered." Mr. Roane laid down his knife and fork, leaned back in his chair. "The town was crawling with New York reporters. They held the trial up at the Town Hall. Stinky Sanders was the janitor in those days. And he made a small fortune charging people a dollar apiece to get inside. And most folks have such a crying need to feed themselves on other folks' troubles and sins that Stinky didn't have to do a lick of work for two years after that trial was held. He charged two bucks for front-row seats. Quite a number of the fancy ladies had to testify and everybody wanted to get a good look at 'em."

"Almost all those fancy ladies ended up like that," Mrs. Roane said. "I think that's why so few girls in Lennox used to get in trouble back in those days. They could see for themselves what could and did happen. Nowadays it's not so easy for a girl to see that. I blame the movies more than anything else. They make it easy for a girl to believe that somewhere there's a beautiful carefree life if they could just find it. Lots of them start looking for it without stopping to figure out how much it costs."

Johnnie was uneasily aware that something had gone wrong.

His mother never talked in this fashion. When she finished, there was a long, awkward silence. Then Glory and his mother started to chatter like magpies.

He listened to their voices as they spoke of the storm, of the strong wind that kept blowing from the northeast, of the best way to make coffee, whether to use a percolator or a drip pot, and he got the feeling that they were talking *at* each other, moving carefully around a fuse that was set and ready to go off; neither of them willing to acknowledge the presence of an explosive, but nevertheless edging cautiously around it.

"How was your ride?" Mr. Roane said.

He interrupted their talk so abruptly that Johnnie decided that Pop, too, had sensed a strangeness in this sudden perpetual chattering of the two women.

"Ride?" Mrs. Roane said blankly.

"Didn't you and Mrs. Gramby go for a ride today? It's Tuesday, isn't it?"

"Yes, yes, of course," Mrs. Roane said hastily. "I don't know where my mind was. It was a nice ride."

"Where did you go?"

"We just rode around. Over to Clinton and through the back roads. It was beginning to rain again just before I got home."

"How about you, Glory? What did you do today?" Mr. Roane asked.

"Johnnie went for a walk," Glory said, and Johnnie noticed that same evasive expression was back in her eyes again. Then she added quickly, "I forgot this was my day off and when I came downstairs this morning he'd gone out."

"I forgot it, too," Mrs. Roane said.

"This was your day off?" Johnnie asked. He wanted to ask her what she had done all day, and didn't. Because he didn't want to know it if she had been absorbed in some special project of her own, content without him, while he tramped doggedly through the rain, killing time, trying to persuade himself that all was well between them, and then, finally, ended up sleeping on a hard wooden bench in a deserted shed at the boat dock.

Glory said: "Yes. And I felt just awful when I remembered it and found you had gone. Honest. I couldn't think what I used to do on the other days when I was off. So I spent most of the day with Momma."

His mother said, "Glory, will you get the dessert? And I'll pour the coffee."

He watched Glory as she handed the best china plates around—the plates with pictures of wild geese flying, wings spread wide. The thick pieces of apple pie obscured the geese, but he knew they were there because he could see the tips of their wings. The first ambitious piece of drawing he'd ever attempted had been a copy of those geese.

"I used to wake up at night to find I'd been dreaming about apple pie—apple pie that looked like this." He glanced down at the plate in front of him. "And just before I could get a piece in my mouth, I always woke up."

"I thought you used to dream about me," Glory said softly.

"I did," he said, and then paused, startled, because if she meant what she said, then—"I always dreamed about you," he said quickly. "The apple-pie dream came about once a month. You were constant, steady, with me all the time." Like a net, he thought, a golden net spread wide for to hold my heart. Because as she stood beside him, he caught the faint sweet smell of her hair.

Then she sat down and smiled at him, looking directly into his eyes without evasion. And he thought, Oh, God, somehow—and I don't know how it happened and I don't much care—but somehow everything is all right because she's looking at me the way she used to. He had to turn his head away from her because he knew if he kept on looking at her, he would start making love to her then and there in the dining room.

When they finished eating, he and Glory washed the dishes, firmly disregarding his mother's protests. She hovered near them in the kitchen and then she left them alone, for she had been unable to get them away from the sink.

"Johnnie," Glory said, "I'll be so glad when we get back in our own house."

"Sure," he said carefully. New York? he thought. If it had to be Lennox with Glory, Glory with the sleeves of a green sweater rolled up to her elbows and hands plunged deep in a dishpan, with her hair catching and holding the light; Glory with an apron tied about her waist, the bow at the back somehow making her waist very small, so very small, and showing up how gently and sweetly her bottom curved—or New York without her, then, ah, yes, it would be Lennox and the small white house and the contracting business.

Perhaps some time, later, some months or years later, he might get the other thing, but the chances are you won't, son. You'll be here for the rest of your natural. You take what you can get and you say thank you prettily and you do not examine it with a frown. You want Glory, you have never known why Glory and not some other woman; you have her, you do not know why she is suddenly yours again; but having her means Lennox. So you forget you ever heard of a paintbrush or a drawing pencil or a place known in some circles as Manhattan Island and in other circles as Good Old New York, Little Old New York, city of hope, city of death.

"I love your mother," Glory said, smiling. "But every woman wants her own house. It makes a difference."

"Yeah, I guess it does. When can we get our own place back?"

"Oh, Johnnie! You mean you want to? You'll stay in Lennox?" She turned toward him.

"If that's what you want," he said quietly.

She wiped her hands on a towel which hung on the rack near the sink. Before he quite realized what she was going to do, she had put both arms around his neck and was kissing him—his mouth, his eyes, his nose. The hunger and the pain and the despair which had been in him vanished at the touch of her arms. He hugged her so close to him that he could feel her heart beating next to his and as he kissed her a part of his mind kept saying, This only, only this, and he thrust one of his hands into the soft silkiness of her hair, twisting and turning his hand, getting it inextricably entangled in the brightness of her hair.

The door between the kitchen and the dining room opened suddenly and the sound made them draw away from each other. It was his mother who entered the room. She was carrying a tray full of coffee cups. "Oh," she faltered, "I'm sorry. I forgot to take these off the table."

The expression in her eyes puzzled him. Was it bewilderment, surprise? No. Besides, why should she be surprised to find him kissing Glory? Soft brown eyes—the eyes that belonged to his mother—some expression he had seen before but not in her eyes. Ah, yes. It was pain. The red setter run over by a car, the rabbit caught in a snare, the old man whose joints were misshapen from arthritis, Pop Fraser's eyes this morning when he had looked up at him over the top of his glasses and then looked away—pain. That was it. Why?

Glory said, "We're going to move into our own house just as soon as the people who are in it now can find themselves a place to live."

She sounded triumphant. She seemed to glow with triumph. He supposed it meant a lot to a woman, having a place of her own. Until this moment he had not realized how much it meant; the thought of going into her own home had transformed Glory.

"It's hard to find places to live. It may take quite a while before they find something," his mother said.

"Oh, I'll help them. I'll find them a place. Don't you worry about that," Glory said. She took hold of Johnnie's arm and squeezed it, laughed up into his eyes, put her head on his shoulder.

"Isn't she beautiful, Ma? Isn't she?" Johnnie said, looking down at Glory.

"Yes," Mrs. Roane said. "Yes, indeed." And she went out of the room quickly.

That night Glory slept in his arms, curled close to him. He woke up once and listened to the rain and she was still there, not withdrawn, not moving away, so close it was as though she had become part of him. The beat of the rain against the windows was a pleasant sound. He wondered idly why he thought so—roof over your head, woman in your arms, warm in bed, so you enjoy the rain and hope to hell that half the poor unfortunate bastards in the world who are womanless are out in it, getting soaked to the innermost corner of their lousy hides. The wind, the damp cold, Ed Barrell, could no longer touch him now. Nothing could touch him now because he had Glory. Just before he went back to sleep, he decided that he had never lost her anywhere except in his imagination.

12

THAT NIGHT THE DRUGSTORE STAYED empty, deserted. Finally I turned off most of the lights—two of the ceiling lights near the back of the store and the ones in the fountain room.

It seemed to me a lonesome, discouraged kind of night, highly unsuitable for reading or serious thinking; but a very good night for talking to an old friend. I set to cleaning the back room, and while I dusted the bottles, wiped off the shelves, and discarded empty packing cases, I talked to Banana, the cat.

When I finished, I sat down on the high stool in front of the prescription counter and began checking my narcotics file, preparatory to taking an inventory. This file, as I call it, is really only an outsize scrapbook in which I paste all the prescriptions that call for narcotics.

About nine o'clock the store door opened and The Weasel came in. I nodded to him, noted that he seemed in a contemplative mood (his dirty gray cap was pulled forward over his eyes), but I did not get up to see what he wanted. If he comes into the store when I am sitting down in the back room, I remain seated for five, ten, or fifteen minutes after he has stated his wants. This reluctance to moving once I am comfortably settled in a chair is, I suppose, one of the more obvious signs of old age. I contemplate the act of rising before I set the process in motion.

But that is not my reason for keeping The Weasel waiting. Many of the townspeople have told me the exact words in which he couched his unflattering comment on my slowness of movement. His phraseology is not easy to forget. So I, too, can repeat what he said about me, word for word:

"Doc looks just like a woodchuck when he gets his big can parked on that chair in the back room. And he sure hates to move off it. Acts like it hurts him. Sits there holding a book, looking out over the top of his glasses, hoping to hell the customer who just came in the front door has made a mistake and will hightail it out again so he won't have to get up. I go in the store right often during the day so his fat ass won't get completely stuck to that chair."

So—when I saw him come into the store for the third time that day I looked at him, but I didn't move.

"How's tricks, Doc?" he said.

"Fine. How's tricks with you?" I said, and continued jotting down the quantities of the narcotics I had dispensed.

He braced himself against the edge of the candy counter, peering into the back room to see what I was doing. Finally he came inside and looked over my shoulder, to get a better view. There wasn't anything for him to see except prescriptions pasted flat in the scrapbook. I knew he couldn't read them, so I kept right on working, but I drew away from him. He had got soaking wet, just in the short time it took him to get from his car to the store. He gave off the smell of wet wool and an unwashed body—a peculiarly disagreeable combination of odors.

"What do them signs mean, Doc?" he asked.

"Different things."

"This one, for instance," he said, and he pointed at the letters *aa* written on one of the prescriptions.

"Different things," I said, and kept turning the pages of the book. His hands are so small the sight of them never fails to annoy me. Each time I notice them I think the same thing: a little man with a little mind and little hands.

"Aw, come on, Doc, what's it mean?"

"You go to the pharmacy college and stay four years and they'll tell you."

He didn't say anything else for a while. I went on slowly turning the pages, jotting figures down on a scratch pad.

"Say," he said suddenly, "who's P. Mearns Gramby?" His finger stabbed at a prescription.

Mearns Gramby brought that prescription in last winter when he had a slight cough. It was for a cough medicine and called for a small quantity of codeine; that's why it was in the narcotics file. Looking at the prescription I thought, He's been a walking medicine cabinet ever since he was born—eye drops for his eyes; cough drops for his throat, those expensive ones from the Liverpool Throat Hospital; and a gargle and a mouthwash, specially made up for him. He takes vitamin pills and sedatives, even a mild laxative. If he had ever asked me for advice about his health, and he never has, I could have suggested an easy, simple way by which he could have rid himself of his fussy, old-maid concern about the state of his internal organs. All he had to do was walk home from the railroad station every night when he came in from New Haven.

"Doc," The Weasel said impatiently, "who's P. Mearns Gramby?"

"Mearns Gramby. Who else in town would have that name? You do remember him, of course, the gentleman you drive up to the railroad station every morning and drive home again every night, with such loving care."

"What's the 'P.' stand for?"

"Peter. Peter Mearns Gramby. The oldest son was always named Peter Mearns Gramby. And then one of them was hanged for murder about a hundred years ago, so they stopped using Peter. The oldest sons were called Mearns, though they were all christened Peter Mearns Gramby."

Thinking about all the medicine Mearns takes, and not liking him much, anyway, made me go on talking. I was talking as much to myself as to The Weasel.

"Mearns probably coughed while he was sitting in that law office of his over in New Haven, so he went to one of those fancy eye, ear, nose, and throat doctors. And the doctor asked for his middle initial in the interests of greater accuracy and in order to give his files a touch of uniformity and also to give the office girl a little more work to do when she typed up Mearns' card. So I judge Mearns told the doctor his name was 'P. Mearns Gramby,' and cleared his throat when he said it and readjusted his pince-nez on the bridge of his nose."

"Peter Gramby," The Weasel said.

"You can't make anything out of it. That hanging for murder was more than a hundred years ago. And there's nothing staler than a murder that took place back in the eighteen-hundreds."

The Weasel started to laugh and he laughed so hard he had to hold on to the corner of the prescription counter to keep from falling down. He nearly choked and tears came in his eyes. His shoulders were hunched up so high that it seemed to me he looked more deformed than ever as he stood there shaking and shivering with laughter.

"What's the matter with you?" I said. I kept looking at the prescription, the doctor's name, and Mearns' name. The Weasel had got hold of something, but what it was I couldn't figure out.

"I knew I'd smell it out," he said finally, choking over the words. He took a filthy handkerchief out of his pocket and wiped his eyes with it. Then he patted me on the back.

"Smell what out?" I asked, shifting my back away from his hand.

And he started laughing again. I closed the narcotics book and got up off the stool, glared at him. "You listen to me. I don't know what you found out in this book, but whatever it was it's none of your business. And if I hear anything, mind you, anything, one little word of scandal that you somehow figured out from what you saw in my prescription file, I'll have you run out of town."

"What s'matter, Doc?" he said. He stopped laughing and he looked at me out of the corner of his eyes. "I thought I was one of your best friends. What would you be running me out of town for? And come to think of it, just how would you go about getting me run out?"

"You heard what I said. Now get out of here and go do your laughing somewhere else."

He waited a moment to see if I was going to add anything to what I'd said, then he left. Usually he says, "So long, Doc. Don't take no wooden nickels." But this time he headed for the door without saying a word.

Banana, the cat, came out from behind the candy counter and hissed at him and he tried to kick her in the face. And missed. He went out of the store before I could protest. I guess he would have slammed the door behind him if he'd been able to, but it has one of those automatic quiet closers on it, so the door shut behind him, making a soft sound like a sigh as it usually does.

I opened the prescription book and stared at the order for Mearns' cough medicine. There was nothing unusual about it; there are many similar prescriptions in the file. The only way in which this one differed from the others was that it now bore the imprint of The Weasel's dirty fingernail—a mark so sharp and so deep that the paper looked as though it had been cut by the pressure of his nail.

It was an ordinary, everyday cough syrup, I knew that; but I had to keep looking at it in the hope that I would see in it what The Weasel had seen. I knew, too, that The Weasel had choked with laughter because he had found out that Mearns' first name was Peter. I had no great fondness for Mearns, but I was devoted to his mother. If he were touched by scandal, it would come as a very great shock to her.

I hoped I had frightened The Weasel so badly he would not dare carry out whatever scheme had popped into his mind. But I could only sit and wait and listen; for I am too old now to turn informer—which means the threat I held over The Weasel's head was an empty one. I could not run him out of town, for I would never tell what I knew about him. He gave me certain information about himself, in confidence, and I have never yet been able to bring myself to violate that confidence, though, in a sense, my knowledge makes me an accessory after the fact. So I shall be uneasy about this matter for the rest of my life.

It is a very short story and also a very old story. I set it down here partly as a means of relieving my conscience, and partly because it lends a further insight into The Weasel.

Lennox is filled with summer hotels. Most of them face the open sea, but that is the only way in which they resemble each other. They range from flimsy, two-story buildings to sprawling, castle-like structures. The big expensive hotels are surrounded by formal gardens and staffed by tuxedoed waiters and French chefs. They have their own tennis courts and golf courses and swimming pools—though the necessity for a swimming pool at a hotel which faces the sea is something I have never been able to understand.

The Seaside Inn is a good example of the humble, two-story type summer hotel. It, too, faces the sea; but it is surrounded by small ugly houses placed so close together one cannot walk between them. It is more cheap boarding house than hotel. Flimsy wooden partitions divide its interior off into countless bedrooms. The sharp tangy smell of the sea gets lost inside the building, for it mixes and blends with the smell of the abominable food, the smell of sleep, and of too many people.

The girls who worked at the Seaside Inn came from the State Farm. They were fifteen, sixteen, seventeen years old. They were wards of the State because they had been in difficulty with the law, or because they had no families, or because they were mentally retarded—or all three. But they could wax floors, make beds, wash dishes, clean windows, do routine laundry jobs.

Supervisors from the farm paid regular visits to the inn, making certain that the girls and their employer were satisfied. It was an arrangement that profited everyone concerned: the State had fewer mouths to feed; the girls were earning money and were pleased to be spending a summer in Lennox—a welcome change after the routine of the institution where they spent most of the year; and the Seaside Inn got its drudgery done for little or nothing.

For reasons best known to himself, The Weasel struck up an acquaintance with one of these girls. Perhaps he had the normal male sexual urge caged inside his abnormal, wizened body. Or perhaps he set about the conquest of a large female as a kind of perverted compensation for his own smallness.

In any event, he made it a habit to take the girl for rides, picking her up somewhere in the center of town or just out of sight of the Seaside Inn; and when he left her, it would be at a discreet distance away from the inn.

The girl, Rose Marie, was a huge stupid-looking creature.

She had dull blue eyes, the roundest eyes I think I have ever seen. Her face was bovine in its placidity. She was at least a foot and a half taller than The Weasel.

He was always bringing her into the drugstore for ice-cream sodas; his eyes darting all over her, his small hands patting her hand as she held a straw up to her mouth. She made a loud sucking noise as she pulled the soda up through the straw. The sound seemed to delight him.

"Ah, Rosie," he would say. "Dear little Rosie. Have another."

He started buying ice-cream sodas for her shortly after the Seaside Inn opened for the season in the early part of May. And then, one hot stifling night toward the last of July (oh, yes, it can get hot in Lennox, too, and can stay hot until a thunderstorm roars down the river and cools things off), The Weasel came into the store so upset he could hardly talk.

"I got to see you private, Doc," he said. And started walking toward the back room.

I have never encouraged customers barging into my back room like that, but it was a hot night and I was too tired to object. So I followed him back there. He collapsed in the chair by the window and said, "I'm in trouble."

The instant he said it I had to stifle an impulse to laugh because he was using the same phrase women have used since the beginning of time itself whenever they discovered they were pregnant. Issuing from The Weasel's lopsided mouth this phrase was ridiculous.

"Yes? What's the trouble?"

"Rosie's going to have a baby. I knocked her up, Doc."

For days after he told me that, I couldn't laugh at anything. I kept seeing Rosie, as The Weasel called her, fifteen, a moron, a ward of the State; kept seeing her as she made beds, scrubbed floors, washed clothes and ironed them. And after the dreary drudgery of the day, The Weasel took her for rides, bought her ice-cream sodas, and sat close by watching her like a hawk as she noisily sucked chocolate sodas up through straws.

I couldn't say anything.

"What'll I do, Doc?" he said. "Give me something to give her. You gotta give me something for her to take, something to bring her around." He babbled like an idiot.

"There isn't anything to give her."

"There's gotta be, Doc. You know about drugs. You can give me something if you want to. Please, Doc. I'll pay you any price you say. Anything at all. I'll sign a note. I'll—"

"There isn't any such drug. There never was. There never will be. You'll just have to marry her."

"Me?" he said angrily. "She's a half-wit. I won't marry no damn half-wit."

"If she was good enough for you to get her in this kind of trouble," I said slowly, "then she's good enough for you to marry."

He went out of the store muttering angrily to himself. Then he turned around and came back and his eyes were darting about in his head. He stood as close to me as he could get and he kept looking behind him as though he expected someone to come up in back of him. He said, "You won't tell nobody, will you, Doc?"

I didn't say anything for a moment and he said, "That was a confidential talk just between us. Promise you won't say nothing, Doc."

"No, I won't say anything. It won't be necessary. Rosie'll tell it—sooner or later."

Then he left. He almost stripped the gears of the taxi when he pulled away from in front of the store.

I was wrong, of course. Rosie didn't tell. She came into the store about once a week with another girl. But The Weasel never came in with her again.

As the weeks slipped by, Rosie got a little larger, her belly swelling, slowly enlarging. I thought she would appear frightened, but she didn't. She had a smug, self-satisfied air and her face lost none of its placidity. She used to stand and gaze at the fountain so wistfully that one of the last times she came in I made her a chocolate ice-cream soda and gave it to her. But I walked as far away from her as I could get because that sucking noise she made with the straws was unbearable.

About the first of September I kept seeing those beach wagons that come from the State Farm. They tore down the street, almost every day, heading for the Seaside Inn. Soon afterward the news was all over town: Rosie, fifteen-year-old Rosie, was going to have a baby; and neither threats nor promises had any effect on her; she simply did not respond with anything that remotely suggested the name of the man who was the father of the child.

There was only one topic of conversation in the drugstore: Rosie.

"If they catch that feller they'll send him up for life."

"They ought to shoot him."

"Who could it be?"

Every time two females got together and started talking in low voices, I knew what they were discussing. They could start with the weather, the apple crop, or last Sunday's sermon, but they ended up talking about Rosie. "Have you heard anything more?" "No. Have you?" "No. Isn't it awful?" "I hope they catch him and horsewhip him."

I think it's an interesting commentary on the difference between the sexes; for the men always suggested shooting, whereas the females were all in favor of horsewhipping, and, I am certain, hoped it would be a public ceremony.

"They" never found out who the man was. The Weasel's passion for comic magazines served him well. He worked on Rosie's poor simple mind until he finally convinced her he was Superman and that she was pregnant because of all the ice-cream sodas she had eaten.

When pressed for information about a man, about the father of the child, she said, "Superman."

If questioned further, she babbled endlessly about chocolate ice-cream sodas. The people at the Seaside Inn had never seen her in the company of The Weasel. Neither had the townspeople. For if a customer came into the store when he was in there with her, he moved away from her. They usually arrived about suppertime when there were few people about. So there was no way of connecting The Weasel with Rosie.

For months afterward his eyes darted about in his head, faster than ever. Slowly the gossip died down. One of the local girls got in the family way; an airplane had to make a forced landing in Perkins' hay lot; and the high-school principal suddenly eloped with one of the students. Rosie was forgotten.

The Weasel and I are the only ones who remember Rosie. He has never mentioned her since that hot night in July, two years ago. I have no way of knowing whether his conscience ever bothers him. But offhand I would say he was born without that necessary appendage we call a conscience.

That night I found myself hoping he would develop a conscience and that its twinges, combined with my empty threat, would prevent him from the malicious act he had in mind when he was seized by that fit of laughter.

13

IT RAINED ALL THAT NIGHT. The next day, wind, coming straight from the northeast, pushed rain across the town in long, slanting sheets. Now and then the wind blew hard enough to lift the rain as though it were a flat layer of water to be elevated whenever the mood of the wind turned capricious; and because of this eternal shift and change in direction, the rain had a nervous, unstable quality.

Leaves were blown down from the big elm trees. They covered the streets, forming masses behind the privet hedges and the picket fences; packing in wet thick layers in the corners of the church steps. The leaves came off the trees first. They were followed by twigs and small branches. Very few cars appeared on the main street and those that did appear nosed their way along, cautiously. For the wet leaves and the branches of the trees and the slick wet surface of the macadam road made driving hazardous.

But the town taxi, driven by The Weasel, took the wet road in its stride. There was an extra flourish about the way he parked the taxi in front of the drugstore. He took his time getting out of it, too, despite the driving rain. He looked relaxed, at ease with himself and the world. He had his cap far back on his head, and as he entered the store, he pushed it even farther back.

"Hope there's no hard feelin's about last night," he said.

"Well, no. I suppose there isn't," I said, but I couldn't resist adding, "Don't you ever kick at my cat again."

"You made me mad, Doc. A man ain't responsible for what he does when he's mad. And I don't like that cat and she don't like me. So you might write it off as an accident, because I ain't ever bothered her before."

When he went out to get into the taxi, he was still ignor ing the rain, walking slowly. He had the easy manner of a man who has, at long last, accomplished some cherished and difficult project.

I stayed at the front window long after he left the store. Just before the town clock struck nine, I saw children hurrying up the street, hastening toward school. They wore raincoats and rubbers. And as usual the rubbers didn't fit, so the children ran in an awkward, duck-footed fashion, bent over, holding their feet close to the ground so the rubbers wouldn't slip off.

Comment on the nature of this storm varied. At the postoffice an argument ebbed and flowed all during the morning. One group insisted that a "line" storm caused the rain, the persistent, steadily increasing wind. Another smaller group rejected this theory, saying it was too early in the season for the line storm, and identified the storm as a northeaster, the kind that tore in from the North Atlantic and stayed until it wore itself out after a two-or-three-day blow.

In the drugstore, I pointed to the barometer Mrs. Gramby gave me last Christmas and said: "It keeps falling. Been going down all morning. According to the papers that came with the barometer this isn't any northeaster. It isn't any line storm, either."

The early morning newspaper customers laughed at me. Because I stubbornly persisted in predicting more rain, an increasingly violent wind.

"Take her back, Pop," they advised, pointing to the barometer. "Somep'ns broke down inside her."

I was right about the wind. As the day wore along, it increased in velocity. Shutters banged; and once having opened a door that faced toward the north, it became increasingly difficult to close it. Roofs developed leaks, water crept in under window sills, beneath door jambs. The trunks of the big elms were motionless, but the wind tossed the high top branches until they were doing an insane dancing—moving faster and faster.

The coves and inlets along the edges of the town crept over a wider area, slowly, inevitably; covering roads, submerging fields and meadows. Fishermen, who stopped in the store, told me Long Island Sound was a strange dark gray, almost black, in contrast to the restless, foaming edge of whitecaps that chewed at the sand, moving ever farther and farther inshore. The river was swollen to a raging torrent, for the wind whipped its surface and the steady rain kept increasing its breadth.

In the early afternoon, a gnarled and twisted apple tree that had stood behind the drugstore for thirty years lost one of its largest branches. It came away from the trunk with a tearing sound, loud enough to be heard inside the store—a sound so sharp that it was like a cry from the heart of the tree.

A young peach tree—slender, graceful, ready to bear the following year—came up by the roots and fell quietly to the ground.

Women sat near the windows of their houses, pretending to knit or crochet or catch up on the mending. Actually they were watching the storm, watching the wind ruin the privet hedges; watching it take down whole sections of picket fence; watching it destroy rose trellises and grape arbors and gates.

I could feel a waiting quality, a tenseness running through the town. It seemed to me that the beat of the rain against the windows, the ever-increasing force of the wind, had set all of us to a reluctant examination of our lives; set us to thinking about the things we had wanted and never got; set us to weighing and balancing our desires against our achievements.

There were very few customers about; for in the late afternoon the storm began to take on a quality of violence that made it easy for us to believe that this might be the last storm we would ever witness.

Mrs. Gramby's gardener, The Portegee, was one of the few people who braved the storm that afternoon. He arrived on his bicycle. I saw him pedaling down Whippoorwill Lane and wondered what could have brought him out on an afternoon like that one.

He wanted to buy a box of candy. I showed him several boxes. He rejected all of them. Finally he said, "For Neola." And then I knew that he wanted an elaborate box complete with ribbon and fancy cover.

I found the type box he wanted—a three-pound affair. After I wrapped it up, he tucked it inside his raincoat, near his chest. Then he went out and got on his bicycle and pedaled toward the Gramby House.

Storms somehow give a push to romance, and other things as well, I thought.

Shortly afterward the Congregational minister came in. He was the last customer I had that day. I saw him coming across the street, his coat-tails blowing in the wind. He bought the *Atlantic* and just before he went out the door he turned to me and said, "It's a high wind. I don't think it can do much damage. It's going to stay high up over the town."

I watched his progress as he went toward the parsonage. I couldn't help thinking that perhaps it was a high wind, but in that case how come it was reaching near enough the earth to send his coat-tails up over his head; and to make that big elm in front of his door sway back and forth down near the roots as though it were a sapling? Had he grown so absent-minded he didn't realize he'd come out of the house without his raincoat?

He went inside, closed the door, and the big elm crashed down right across the doorstep of the parsonage. Something that shocks you profoundly seems to arouse disbelief; you feel the desire to convince yourself that what you have just seen didn't happen.

I took off my glasses, ran my hand back and forth across my forehead, across my eyes, closed my eyes, opened them again; then I looked toward the parsonage.

The slanting rain, the wind, obscured the street, and for a moment I had the illusion that this wind was something I could see as it twisted, cone-shaped, right through the middle of the main street. Only of course it wasn't. It was the way trees, leaves, shrubs bent before it that made me believe I could actually see the wind.

But the big elm was, I saw finally, wedged firmly across the front of the parsonage—its massive trunk effectively blocking the door.

There have been few occasions in my life when I talked to myself. This was one of them. I kept saying: "Wind going to stay high up, is it, Rev.? Why he beat that tree by seconds. That's all. Just by seconds. By the bottom thread in his coat-tail. It was that close."

I tried to turn on the lights in the store, for it was getting dark, though it was only four o'clock in the afternoon. The power had gone off. Before I went to get my kerosene lamps, I took a last look at the street. And again it seemed to me that I could actually see the wind, funnel-shaped, tearing through the center of the town. I wondered if this storm that had come smashing, raging, thundering up out of the sea to blow itself out against the town of Lennox had not brought with it some ancient spirit of evil, long suppressed, but now free of whatever bonds had held it, free to stalk through the town—restless, mocking, powerful, creeping inside the houses to whisper in our ears.

While I fumbled with the kerosene jug in the back room, I felt this building, which houses the drugstore, move from the force of the wind. Its swaying unnerved me. For this building was built to last, to withstand the ravages of time itself. It was erected around a great central chimney; its foundation stone was quarried from local granite.

When this sturdy old building swayed on its foundation, I knew we were in for a wild and awful night. I looked out of the back window, seeking reassurance, and in the rapidly failing light I saw that the rose trellis had disappeared, the big stone bird bath was down on its side. And it was obvious that the maple tree was doomed. It was a young, strong tree, but it could not withstand the pressure of the wind. It was weaving back and forth and I watched it, waiting for the trunk to snap, thinking, Will it give in the middle, at the top, near the root?

It did none of these things. It came up all at once, root and all, in a convulsive, twisting movement dreadful to watch.

I lit the kerosene lamps and then sat down in the prescription room and started reading the Twenty-Third Psalm. I'm not exactly what you would call a religious man, but the Bible seemed to me the best book to have in one's hands on a night like that.

14

MRS. GRAMBY HAD SPENT MOST of the afternoon in her living room, sitting in her favorite chair near one of the front windows. At her orders dinner had been served much earlier than usual, for she had hoped that Lillian would decide to eat at a later hour. It hadn't worked. Lillian had come downstairs, expressing surprise at the early dinner hour, and they had gone into the dining room together. By a tremendous effort of will Mrs. Gramby had managed to carry on a polite conversation with her.

Now, at five o'clock, she was back in the chair by the window. It was quite dark.

Neola came into the room. She lit the candelabra on the mantel, placed lighted kerosene lamps on the table at the far end of the room, and then brought in another lamp and put it on the inlaid table near Mrs. Gramby's chair.

"Can I get anything for you?" Neola asked.

"No," Mrs. Gramby answered. "No, thank you." I would like peace of mind and a quiet heart, she thought, but even Neola could not get those for me, though if asked she would certainly try. And aloud she said, "Bless you."

Neola smiled at her and went out of the room.

This room is empty without her, Mrs. Gramby thought. The prisms on the candelabra swayed back and forth, emitting a faint tinkling sound. Wind crept in under the closed windows, lifted the dark red draperies. Yes, it is an empty room, uninhabited—save by defeat and loneliness.

She looked out of the window, watching the wind assault the picket fence, bend it, push it out of line, and then flatten one whole section near the gate. Her mind was on the letter. She could see it as plainly as though she were holding it in her hand: the grimy envelope, the finger marks. She could smell the faint odor of gasoline and motor oil that had assailed her nostrils the instant Mearns handed her the envelope.

She had been sitting in the dining room, sipping her morning coffee, thinking what a gray, sullen morning it was. Rain beat against the windows, dripped down the panes. It was accompanied by wind so violent that it had loosened a shutter somewhere upstairs; and the banging of the shutter was like the sound of doom—muted, portentous. Mearns had kissed her good-bye and hurried out of the house to get into the taxi.

And then, suddenly, he was back, standing beside her; his raincoat was wet, his hatbrim dripping water.

He never wore his hat in the house. She opened her mouth to protest, intending to speak sharply, partly because of her surprise at seeing him back in the room, partly because of her distaste for the gray dreariness of the morning. But his face under the hat was twisted with pain, crumpled, grown smaller and older. And she cried out, "Mearns! What is it?"

He thrust the envelope at her. Even as she drew the letter out, she kept searching his face for a clue to its contents. Then she looked down and saw that the paper was soiled, worn, and creased, suggesting it had been carried in someone's pocket, fingered again and again, read and re-read.

It would, she was almost certain, be disgusting. She read it quickly: "Darling Ed: I think I can meet you at the usual place on Saturday. Petey is going away for the weekend. Your own Kittikins."

It had nothing to do with Mearns or with her. She read it again, trying to find out what possible meaning it held for him, why it should make his face quiver, his hands shake. No. Nothing. But his eyes would tell her. She looked up at him. He had taken his glasses off, was holding them in his hand, holding them delicately by the nosepiece; and, stripped of the protective glitter of the lens, his eyes were piteous.

She looked away from him, stared at the letter. Then she knew. Because she recognized the handwriting. It was Lillian's. She had seen it on innumerable Christmas cards, on bills for dressmaking: one afternoon dress, three nightgowns, and the price, written out in this same immature hand. Lillian's hawk's face, predatory, hungry, the lines about the mouth made deep by a gnawing discontent, had bent over this piece of paper; her thin, nervous fingers had written this, had folded the letter up, had put it in an envelope.

"Oh, no!" she said.

Mearns nodded his head, and then leaned over and touched her arm as though he were seeking comfort.

"Where did you get it?" she asked.

"From the taxi-driver. Just now. He said"—Mearns paused and cleared his throat—"He said he found it and he thought I ought to have it."

"Who is Ed?"

"Ed Barrell. He runs a gasoline station on the edge of town, not too far away from the railroad station."

Ed Barrell, she thought, the man who had been on Obit's Heights, making love to young Johnnie Roane's wife, a man who didn't even bother to take his hat off when he kissed a woman.

His shoulders had been thrust forward as though the one thing in life he wanted and needed was to get back inside the young woman he held in his arms. The young woman was Gloria. Why, that meant he had had the mother and then the daughter. Horrible! No human dignity about it, like rabbits or pigeons or chickens.

I could forgive her not having children for Mearns. She is too old to have them. But this—he stands there like a man bemused, outraged, scorned, hurt beyond healing, and all I ever wanted was to see him happy.

She had folded the letter up and replaced it in its grimy envelope. When she put it in her pocket, she thought, There must be some way of comforting him. But the words eluded her.

She said, "You'll miss your train."

"I'm going now"—he cleared his throat again. "I think I'll spend the next few days in New Haven. That's what I came back for, to tell you I'd be away."

"I understand."

He started out of the room and at the door he groped for the knob, stretching out his hands in front of him, feeling for it as though he were blind. Though she knew he fumbled because he had forgotten to put on his glasses, the gesture suggested old age, uncertainty. His movements were usually quick, precise. The sight of this fumbling sickened her.

"Put on your glasses," she had said sharply. And then added, "*Will* you stop clearing your throat!" It had been due to the pain and the shock, she knew, but there, at the door, he had cleared his throat, twice in succession. And she had found herself doing the same thing. For listening to that repeated, rasping sound he made was like watching someone who had a tic. Your own muscles started to twitch.

What is he doing now? she wondered. Is he trying to rebuild the broken house of his pride by staring at his great carved desk, by dictating long involved letters to his secretary, by mentally itemizing the things he owns, by dwelling on the achievements of his ancestors?

Or is he doing this that I am doing, sitting in a chair by a window, holding himself more than usually erect? I would like to turn her out of the house now, this moment, send her forth in the storm. And just as she stumbles down the steps, about to be whipped by the wind, beaten by the rain, I would like to tell her what I think of her.

I am too old to withstand a shock like this. The veins and the arteries cannot hold this rush of blood which my heart keeps pumping through them, faster and faster; the walls of the vessels have grown too rigid.

She clenched her hand on the cane, tightening her grip until the veins stood out—thick, swollen. I will not think about Lillian. I refuse to.

There was still enough daylight left so that she could catch glimpses of the box hedge with its covering of boards. The wind had blown down the front gate, destroyed the picket fence; but it had not been able to budge the boards that protected the hedge.

How had Portulacca known this storm was brewing? Perhaps he covered the hedge because it was time to cover it for the winter. No. The boards were put in place much earlier than usual. He must have sensed the approach of the storm, known beforehand that this high wind, this cold, brutal rain, was on its way.

It was a good night to be inside, to be protected by a tight roof, warmed by a fire on the hearth. Neola had lighted the fire in the fireplace and the room was pleasantly warm. She turned her head, studied the room. A beautiful room. The light from the candles, soft; the kerosene lamps shedding a mellow glow over the old mahogany, the oil paintings, the silver.

She had loved this room, loved the house. Whenever she had awakened, early in the morning, she had listened for sounds. And faint, far-off, in the kitchen, pans would be rattling because Cook was creating some delicious breakfast dish; the cats thumped going down the stairs; and a fresh, cool breeze rustled the draperies at her windows. Those early-morning sounds were the very heartbeat of the house.

If she woke up at night, she was instantly aware of the house—beautiful in the darkness. Sometimes she got up and walked through the house at night, even going up to the attic, just to look at the rooms, cool, high-ceilinged, subtly changed because they were faintly lit by the moon or the street lamps. When the house slept, she got the feeling that Mr. Gramby was close by. He, too, had loved to roam through the house at night, to walk in the attic; for he said all men need regular doses of solitude, though few of them have the good fortune to discover its value.

Sometimes she woke up just before daybreak. She would hear the roosters crowing, perhaps the sound of a footstep on the flagstone walk beneath her window, or a bird would chirp. And she would think, The house is waking up. When the sun came out, she would lie in bed, picturing the sun shining on the brick of the house, turning it pink; and in her mind's eye she could see the tall chimneys, pink, too, as they went up and up toward the early-morning sky; and the dark glistening of the box-wood hedge close to the ground.

Yes, she had thought of this house with joy. It was now the home of a man whose wife had wantonly taken a lover. It had become a house of betrayal.

She had to look at the letter again. She knew it by heart: the smudges on the paper, the shape of the envelope, as well as the words. She reached for her cane, got up, and walking slowly, leaning heavily on the cane for support, she walked the length of the room.

Opening a small wall safe, she took the letter out and held it in her hands. Then she put it back quickly, without reading it, thinking that it was as grimy, as dirty, as the story Lillian had revealed in the few words she had written on the paper.

I must touch something else, look at something else, she thought. To sit on a night like this, a dark night full of wind, and think of ugliness, of faithlessness, of the mean in spirit—I cannot do it.

She took a string of pearls from a worn velvet case, put them around her neck. When she finally succeeded in fastening the clasp, her arms were tired. Her fingers had grown stiffer, clumsier, during the course of the day. There was something else she wanted. She reached inside the safe again, took out a diamond ring which she forced over the swollen knuckles of her little finger. Mr. Gramby had given her the diamond when Mearns was born.

Before she closed the safe, she examined the stone, turning her hand this way and that. One could easily believe that it was not a jewel at all; that it was, instead, a blazing fire which had been so cleverly encased in glass that the fire still burned—the flame flickering, giving off heat. She had told Mr. Gramby that when he gave her the ring. He had thrown his head back and laughed, saying, "I suppose it is warm to the touch." And when she said, "No. But it should be from the way it flames and flares," he had laughed harder than before and leaned over and kissed the top of her forehead and said, "Well, you wear it whenever you feel cold."

I feel cold, tonight, she thought. Then she crossed the room and sat down by the window. Why did I put on these pearls, this ring? she asked herself. Am I afraid of Lillian?

The storm beat at the windows like an evil spirit, bent on entering the house, bent on violence; and the letter lay there in the safe, the knowledge of its presence weighed against her. I *am* afraid of Lillian. This necklace about my neck—the neck shriveled but not bent, thank God, though it is old, thickened with age, slightly stiff—this ring on my hand, indicate my fear.

Women have always decked themselves out in whatever finery came within reach of their hands whenever they have known fear. The slim young girls here in Lennox carmined their lips and painted their fingernails when their husbands went off to war. They worked in factories and they fastened scarves the color of hope around their heads before they went to work in the morning—scarlet and gold and emerald and azure. It was a gesture of defiance, a refusal to reveal their fear by any outward sign—no black, no gray, no muted colors in their headgear.

She had not worn the ring since the night two years ago when they went to a concert in New Haven. Mearns had been married just about two weeks. The concert was his idea. Inside the concert hall she had drawn off her gloves. Lillian's eyes had licked over the great diamond, kept returning to it, finally stuck there, and the lines about her mouth deepened, and almost as though she could not help it, her fingers encircled her ring finger, caressing it, as though she were saying, Wait, wait, wait, you'll have one, too; you'll have this one if you wait long enough, some day it will be yours.

A sudden gust of wind made the windows rattle and rain struck the glass, making a sound like pebbles thrown against it. Then the rain died away, the wind lessened, and there was a stillness as though the storm had paused for a moment to catch its breath before continuing.

In the silence she heard Lillian coming down the stairs. Her footsteps were light and quick. They were coming nearer and nearer. There was something inexorable about her approach, nothing to stop her, nothing ever would stop her. Mrs. Gramby covered her face with her hands.

When Lillian entered the room, Mrs. Gramby's hands were

folded in her lap. She was watching the cats as they walked up and down, their tails switching back and forth, their eyes glowing in the candlelight.

"The storm seems so much worse upstairs. I thought I'd stay down here while it lasted," Lillian said. It sounded like a question, an asking for permission.

"I suppose it does," Mrs. Gramby said politely. "One is more aware of wind when one is on the second floor." She gripped her cane firmly and stood up. "I'll ask Neola to bring us some tea. And some little cakes."

She turned her thoughts away from the letter, away from Lillian. The fall rains always depress me, she thought. I have never liked the fall after the opulence of summer. It is a sad season, sad and lonely. That is why I feel so useless, so defeated. It is that, and that only.

When Neola brought the tea, Mrs. Gramby poured a cup for Lillian, and one for herself. She sipped the tea, thinking, This is proof of the great advance of our civilization, this pouring tea for a woman I despise, a woman I hate, when what I want to do is turn her out of the house. That is the point of view of a pessimist and yet, looked at in that fashion, man had come a long and futile way. He had crawled up out of the ooze and the muck only to fall back, to get up and try again, and finally he had walked, stood erect and walked, built cities, left them, gone into a wilderness, founded churches, hunted witches. Was it for this? And then there were the wars, for he fought Indians, the French, the Dutch, the English; and then later fought a Civil War, the Spanish, fought in Europe, once, and then later fought again in Europe and in Asia—yes, a long and futile way. All those layers of living between me and the day when man first walked erect keep me pouring tea for this woman instead of driving her out into the storm.

Why is she looking at me? Her eyes keep following the motion of my hand as I lift the teapot, the cup. The ring, of course. She looks as though it had mesmerized her; and as she sits there holding that cup and staring at this ring, she is like a vulture—the head thrust forward, the nose like a beak, the eyes focused on this stone in my ring with such concentration that they are slightly crossed.

"The wind is blowing harder," Lillian said and sighed.

"It probably won't stop until well after midnight. Storms like this last a long time." Mrs. Gramby reached for another cake. They were delicious. Cook had made them with butter and they were light, feathery; dissolving in one's mouth almost without chewing; the flavor lingered on the tongue; the palate cried out for more.

15

THE CAKES ARE DELICIOUS, LILLIAN. Try one," Mrs. Gramby said politely.

"I never eat sweets," Lil said. She meant to enlarge on this remark, pointing up her words with meaning glances at Mrs. Gramby's feather-pillow waistline. But a tree crashed to the ground somewhere near the front of the house, making a splintering, explosive sound, loud above the roaring of the wind and the beat of the rain. The house shuddered from the impact, the candles flickered, and the prisms quivered, sending forth streaks of rainbow-colored light.

Lil jerked herself up from the chair she was sitting in, the teacup slipped out of her hand, and hot tea splashed on her thighs. "Good God!" she said. "What was that?"

Mrs. Gramby sat still, apparently unmoved. And Lil said violently, "How can you sit there like that with the place falling down about your ears?"

"I doubt whether the house will fall down," Mrs. Gramby said quietly. "It has stood a good many years and it will probably continue to stand long after you and I are gone. That was one of the big elms in front of the house. It was a very old tree and it could not withstand the pressure of so young and vigorous a wind. When a century-old tree falls, it is only fitting that it should go down with a note of protest. The top branches undoubtedly struck the roof."

Lil gave Mrs. Gramby a long, searching look. She seems to be talking to herself, she thought. Certainly she isn't looking at me as she talks. Her manner is polite, slightly detached. She acts as though she welcomed this storm. If she's upset at the thought that the house may be destroyed, she doesn't show it. Perhaps she'd rather it be blown down than to have me stay here and live in it.

In the candlelight Mrs. Gramby's face was serene, young; the wrinkled skin looked smooth. She might go on living another five years, another ten years. And I—can I face this existence I lead for that many more years? Go on, day after day, watching Mearns take his vitamin pills, listening to him gargle his throat, and then sit silent while they talk endlessly about what happens in Europe, what happens in Asia, what happens in Africa, sit silent and ignored and left out while they talk to each other?

Can I go on year after year, listening to her slow, faltering progress through the house, the sound of the cane, the shuffling of her feet; hear that perpetual nervous clearing of the throat she has been doing tonight and which Mearns does all the time?

Sounds like that could drive you mad. They could become an obsession, growing in importance, increasing in magnitude, until finally you heard nothing else; you waited for one of those sounds, listening at the head of the stairs, at the door of the bedroom you share with Mearns. You heard her footsteps on the stairs, the awful slow progress, the sound muted by the thick carpeting but unmistakable, the cane digging into the rug and the dragging sound of her feet. You heard it outside on the flagstone walk, clear, sharp, when she approached the front door; and then you waited for that other sound, the clearing of her throat; all of you waited and you frowned, you wanted to cover your ears with your hands, but you couldn't because you might miss it, and then you would start waiting all over again until you heard it repeated.

Once, late at night, she had awakened and heard the footsteps in the attic, going up and down, up and down, the tap of the cane and the slow, dragging footsteps. She woke Mearns up. "Your mother's in the attic," she'd said. "What's she doing up there this time of night?"

"I don't hear anything," he said, and went back to sleep. But first he cleared his throat.

She lay there beside him thinking, You have destroyed me, you and that old devil dragging her feet across the attic floor. You managed, between you, to cheat me of all those things I thought I had within my grasp. But you snatched them away.

What was the old woman planning as she limped back and forth overhead? Some new way of humiliating me, of letting me know I don't belong, of showing me again that I may have a paper saying I'm legally married to Mearns, but that is all I have—just a paper?

She is the boss here, she is the one Mearns turns to for advice, she is the one that Mearns gives his money to—not me. If she could she'd sleep in the same bed with him and put me in the servants' quarters. No privacy anywhere in the house, for even in this room I share with Mearns—she manages to enter it, to crush me under her feet. What is she planning now as she walks back and forth in the attic? She may think she can drive me away, but I will not go. This is my house as much as it is hers; and I'll have it yet. I'll outlast her.

Shortly after that night when she had lain awake listening to Mrs. Gramby's shuffling footsteps in the attic, she had begun that unsatisfactory affair with Ed Barrell, meeting him once a week at his cabin in the woods. After two months they ended the relationship—without regret on either side. It had meant nothing to him or to her.

If Ed had been content to look at her, to whisper extravagant flattering words in her ear, she might have kept on seeing him. For she needed the undivided attention of a lover; needed and wanted that attention to use as a bulwark against the indifference and the hostility she had found in this house. But instead of telling her that she was important to him, that she was beautiful and witty and desirable, Ed set to work to get her undressed and in bed with him in the shortest possible time. It happened like that each time she visited the cabin.

She had hungered for the sound of pet names and endearments, and had lavished them on him, hoping he would reciprocate. But he had brushed them aside, never remembering them from one week to the next. She had asked him to call her "Kittikins." And whenever she reminded him of this special name he was to call her, he shrugged and started unfastening her dress.

That last time, the time that ended her visits to the cabin, he had stared at her saying, "'Kittikins'! Oh—damn!" There was contempt in his voice. She had never gone back after that.

She had not thought about him in months; had, in fact, dismissed him from her mind. He had left her with the feeling that she had been cheated by him, too; for he had given her nothing in return for what she had given him. But tonight she savored the thought of him.

I would like to tell Mrs. Gramby that I used to sleep with Ed, and thus she would know how much I despise her, and despise her son, Mearns. The thought startled her. Why am I thinking that? I wish I had stayed upstairs. For being in the same room with her, in this damn candlelight, with the trees crashing down and the wind howling at the windows, is doing something terrible to me.

Mrs. Gramby put the cup and saucer down on the tea tray.

Then she pulled herself up, out of the chair, paused, reached for her cane. Is she going back to sit by the window—or is she—Ah, no, Lil thought, I can't stay in here if she's going to begin that awful walking up and down.

Why doesn't she sit down? They haven't put the winter rugs in place yet and if I hear the sound of her feet and the tap of the cane on this bare floor I will start screaming and never be able to stop.

"You oughtn't to walk like that," she said irritably. "I don't think it's good for you."

"It's the best possible thing for me," Mrs. Gramby said. "Doctor Williams insists that I take some exercise every day even if it's only walking the length of the room."

If she should put her fingers in her ears, Mrs. Gramby would attribute the gesture to a childish fear of the storm. But I can't help it. I am afraid to stay upstairs by myself. And down here with her—

She covered her ears with her hands and leaned back in the chair, crouching down in it. She could no longer hear the shuffling feet, but there was a thick dull roaring in her ears; and she thought it was like going far down in the earth, going into a deep underground tunnel, and that her eardrums were rebelling against the pressure exerted on them. Then she sat up straight, for under the roaring she heard a new and different sound—not the wind, not the rain—but a wild clanging, metallic, far-off. Her hands came away from her ears. She got up from the chair, listened.

"What's that?" she said.

Mrs. Gramby stopped walking, stood leaning on her cane, frowning as she tried to identify the sound. "The church bells," she said finally. "The Congregational bells and the Episcopal bells."

"What are they ringing them for this time of night? What does it mean?" It was a wild, eerie sound, completely frightening.

"They're always rung in times of great stress," Mrs. Gramby said. She smiled faintly and said: "'It is said that the evil spirytes that been in the regyon, doubte mouche when they here the bells rongen: And this is the cause why the Bells been rongen, when grete tempeste and outrage of wether happen, to the end that the fiends and wyced spirytes should be abashed and flee—'"

She turned away from the sight of Lillian's white ghost-ridden face, and limped back and forth the length of the living room thinking. Two hundred years ago I would have said you were a witch and that you had bewitched my son. Why else would he have married you? And she continued to walk heavily, slowly, leaning on her cane.

Lil watched her slow, persistent progress, back and forth the length of the long room. How is it she always finds the most horrible quotations with which to frighten me? "The evil spirits that been in the region—" She looked around the room. It was filled with a draft so strong that the draperies moved at the windows, billowing in toward the room; and the cats kept emerging from the brooding darkness of the corners.

The house is full of evil spirits tonight and that horrible old woman in that loose black dress might well be one of them, she thought.

As Mrs. Gramby turned around, came near her, she looked at the old woman sharply. Why, she's wearing the pearls, too—the pearl necklace. The three-strand choker was tight under the wattles of her throat, half-concealed by her fleshy neck. What does she need with pearls at eighty-two, and a great diamond blazing on her finger? It was a sacrilege to place such jewels against that mountain of diabetic flesh, let them touch those misshapen joints which were swollen by arthritis.

There was another let-up in the storm, a pause. The rain fell away to a mere whisper of sound, the wind died down, leaving such a stillness in the house that she became aware of the beating of her heart. After the continual roaring of the storm, the quiet was frightening. She found she was holding her breath, waiting for something to happen.

She got up and looked out of a front window. Nothing but blackness outside—total, complete; it was like trying to look into the bottom of a well.

As she stood at the window, the storm returned taking on a quality of violence that made its previous attack seem mild. The house can't stand this, she thought, for she felt it shudder on its foundation. I'll probably die here in this room tonight with this fat old woman. I will be entombed here with her.

She moved away from the window, sat down again, huddling in a chair by the fireplace. And what did you accomplish? she thought. All those nights when you called up and told Mrs. Gramby the sewing would be late—couldn't Mearns stop for it; the pert talk, the eternal dieting, the curling of the hair, the subtle insinuating housecoats which slipped open to show a glimpse of thigh; the tea in winter and the iced drinks in summer served so graciously in the cozy living room in the little house in Westville—what did it add up to? Less than nothing; no, worse than nothing if this was the last night she'd live.

Some nights you kept Mearns way past midnight, sitting close to him on the sofa while he told you about one of his important cases, leaning just a little closer to him, acting young and silly when what you wanted was to get into bed and go to sleep. And you needed sleep so badly you could cry because you had been sewing all day long and your back ached from bending over the machine; your eyes hurt from putting some special piece of handwork, a flower or an initial on a blouse or a dress for some rich bitch who wouldn't want to pay but a fraction of what it was worth.

And you turned down customers so you could make clothes for yourself—clothes in soft colors with swift, sharp lines that showed off how slender your hips were, how small your waist, because you knew he would keep comparing your lean body with that feather-pillow figure of his mother's. You swallowed the sharp things that rose to the tip of your tongue when at Christmas he came up to the door carrying—Good God!—a book, of all things, when you had counted on a diamond bracelet, a circle of running fire to wear around your wrist; or a ring with a stone so big and so perfect it would be like looking at a hot coal.

Ah, yes, she in a black velvet housecoat—only it was velveteen—but at night under that dim light in her living room it took on the depth and richness of velvet—with a scarlet ribbon at her throat and her hair up in curls, red gold curls—she could see herself now, standing there looking at him and holding that goddamn book in her hands. The instant he handed her the package, she had known it was too big to hold a bracelet, too big to hold a ring or a necklace.

When you smiled at him, because you made yourself smile at him, you knew how the lips of a panther feel when it draws them back away from its teeth. You wanted to curse him, and instead you whispered, Mearns, you thought of me, today, at Christmas, this special day of the year. You winked back tears that were real enough because you wanted to cry at the wasted effort, at the lost time, at the aching back, the tired eyes, the wanting and never getting, the hunger for clothes, for money, for fat jewels that caught other women's eyes and held them. All of it gone, lost, and you smiled at him and patted your eyes with your handkerchief and whispered thank you, and hated him; hated the smooth polished surface of his glasses, hated the black overcoat with the velvet collar, hated the derby hat and the suede gloves he held in his hand, and the white scarf at his throat and the highly polished shoes on his feet.

You went on smiling at him, saying, Sit down, let me get you a glass of sherry, it's Christmas, it's a special day, and we will toast the snow and the Christmas carols and your gift. You poured the wine and he lifted the glass and said, Dear me, I suppose that nowhere in the world is there a wine the color of your hair, your beautiful hair. You had to sit down quickly because you had stood up to drink the toast with him and you knew the instant he said that, that he was hooked, he was yours, it would all come true, he would propose, he would marry you, and you let the words trickle through your mind, mouthing them over and over: no wine the color of your beautiful hair. As you said those words, you knew that you were holding in your hand the fat bank accounts, the great house, the servants, the jewels. They would be yours because you would become Mrs. Mearns Gramby—the very name itself, fat, rich-sounding.

What did it get her? Well, she married him if that meant anything. The other things? None of them. A mink coat, yes. But what did a mink coat mean if you had no place to wear it?

Her life had been geared to Mrs. Gramby's. "Mother doesn't go out in the evening any more. We must stay home with her."

So she wore the mink coat to church on Sundays and the women in Lennox neither knew what it was nor cared—it could have been cat or rabbit fur. No eye ate up the fur with envy, no eye hungered to own one like it. Then on Thursdays she went to Miss Susie Brandford's to play cards with Miss Susie's boarders.

From the day she married him she had lived in this house like an unwanted roomer who was so far back in her rent the landlady ignored her. She'd had three meals a day—no, two, because she never ate breakfast with them; two meals a day and a room given begrudgingly because even Mearns objected if she moved a picture in the room. Mrs. Gramby's hostile servants—her insolent cook, her silent gardener, her indifferent maid—had all helped seal her inside that one room.

If this is—and it well might be from the fury of the storm—the last night of my life, I might just as well never have been born for all I got of what I wanted.

"The wind seems to be increasing," Mrs. Gramby said.

"Yes," Lil said absently. Mrs. Gramby was the stumbling-block. Mrs. Gramby made her life unbearable. Mrs. Gramby dominated the house, dominated Mearns. "It may be the end of the town," she said.

"The end of the town?"

"The storm is uprooting trees, knocking down houses—it could destroy the whole town."

"I doubt it," Mrs. Gramby said firmly. "It is not that easy to destroy a town. Even if all the trees and houses came down, even if all of us died tonight, this place would still be called Lennox. And when it is rebuilt, and it would be, it will still be Lennox. Trees will grow, people will live here. Thus there will always be a town which is called Lennox."

But we wouldn't be here, Lil thought. Not you and me. There wouldn't be any Grambys. All your money, in banks, in safe-deposit vaults, in real estate, in stocks and bonds, would simply rot because there wouldn't be any Grambys to inherit it.

Ah, she thought, why doesn't she die? She has now reached the stage where she is completely sexless—that heavy gray mustache over her mouth, that mountain of flesh inside that loose black gown, could belong to a man just as well as to a woman.

Mrs. Gramby picked up a small cake from the tea tray, a cake coated with pale pink icing. She can't resist them—a cake, candy, pie, ice cream—anything that's sweet. But as long as she keeps on using insulin, it doesn't seem to matter much what she eats.

Suppose, though, that for some reason the insulin wasn't

ready to her hand and there was a box of chocolates right by her chair, and suppose it was Neola's day off when this happened and Cook's day off, too?

It could happen like that. Mrs. Gramby could no more resist a box of candy than she could deny Mearns something he really wanted. One of those boxes of assorted chocolates would do, the cover tilted so that she could catch a glimpse of the different coatings, creamy milk chocolate, dark brown bitter-sweet chocolate, and they would suggest the variety of centers—hard and soft, nut-filled—

And the insulin, just this one time, would not be in the table drawer, not in the dining room, not upstairs anywhere.

The idea frightened her. She tried to stop thinking about it. But each time Mrs. Gramby paused in her walking to reach for another cupcake, the thought returned. She could see the old lady's hand reaching for the chocolates just as it now reached for a cupcake—the knuckles swollen, the skin on the hand drawn tight and the brown moth patches standing out, the great diamond blazing. The hand dipped into the box of chocolates again and again, finally reached, faltering, a little shaky for the insulin, for the needle. The hand fumbled inside the table drawer, grew frantic in its reaching. The mouth full of the rich taste of the chocolate called out for Neola—silence in the house—no answer—

Mrs. Gramby turned and looked her full in the face. "Are you worried about something?" she asked.

"Of course not," Lil said. "But this storm—it's so horrible—I was thinking about Mearns over there in New Haven—"

"By this time he's probably sound asleep in the best bed in the Taft Hotel. Don't ever worry about him." Mrs. Gramby's hand hovered over the tea tray, undecided, picked up a cake coated with chocolate.

Lil saw that there were crumbs around her mouth, on the bosom of the shapeless black dress. When she chewed there was a clicking sound, as her false teeth hit against each other, making a sound like tombstones rubbing against each other, she thought and shuddered.

No, it couldn't go on like this. If she'd needed any proof, this evil, stormy night had more than shown her that she'd had her nose rubbed in it long enough. To be in the same room with the old woman and the cats was more than anyone could stand. The storm had made the cats restless. Their eyes were a hot yellow as they jumped on the chairs, the sofa, clawed at the upholstery and then jumped down again, tails switching, pointed ears battened close to their round, brutal heads.

She'd get rid of the cats first, then Cook, Neola, and The Portegee because if she was alive tomorrow morning, she was going to make the pattern for a brand-new life.

The church bells were still ringing—ominous, slow; as though they were tolling the death of the town. The sound lingered in the living room.

"Why do they keep ringing those bells?" Lil asked irritably.

"'When the bells been rongen—'" Mrs. Gramby began.

For the first time since she had come to live under the same roof with Mrs. Gramby, Lil interrupted her—rudely, impatiently, cutting off the rest of the quotation.

"That's a lot of rubbish," she said. "Someone must have died in the storm. That's a tolling for a death."

Mrs. Gramby stared at her so long that Lil turned her head away, thinking, I've shown her that for some reason, because of some decision I've reached, I no longer think it's necessary to be polite to her. She knows that I've decided that she's as good as dead.

"Perhaps you're right," Mrs. Gramby said finally. "Perhaps it is a tolling for a death." She walked the length of the room and back before she spoke again. "Death has a way of following in the wake of storms."

A sudden gust of wind hit the house with such force that it moved on its great stone foundation; the prisms jangled and the room was filled with a rush of cold air. "Perhaps you're right," Mrs. Gramby repeated. Then she said softly, "'While the earth remaineth, seedtime and harvest, and cold and heat, and night and day shall not cease.'"

Lil shivered and put her hands over her ears.

16

NEOLA AND PORTULACCA WERE ALONE in the kitchen of the Gramby house. Cook had made tea, had spiked it heavily with rum as the best means of building up an attitude of complete indifference toward the storm, and, after drinking four cups of the brew, had gone upstairs to bed.

The Portegee was sitting in the Boston rocker close to the stove; and as he rocked back and forth he stole an occasional glance at Neola. She had been sitting in a chair near the window ever since Cook had left the kitchen.

Surely there ought to be something they could talk about, he thought uneasily. This silence is unnatural. Here is a kitchen with a coal fire burning in a mountain of a stove, the coals showing red here and there through the lids, sending out waves of warmth; and candles on the kitchen table with the copper of the candlesticks glowing. Two people in the kitchen—a man and a woman and yet there is nothing but silence. A storm is raging outside, roaring and raging as it destroys trees and plants. A time like this called for talk, the talk of friends, the revelation of the deep places in the secret recesses of the heart.

He pulled on his pipe and said: "I'd better go upstairs and look for leaks. There's only one bad place so far. In the back bathroom, around the window. I got that plugged, but others may have started."

Neola nodded her head, said nothing.

As he went out of the kitchen and up the stairs, he decided that that was a pointless remark he had made. It didn't lead anywhere. He made the rounds of the windows, calking an old sheet more firmly into the bathroom window. If he could just think of the right words he could ask Neola to marry him. Other times when he'd got the proper words together, his courage had failed him. Tonight would be a good night for a proposal, but one couldn't propose to a silent woman. Silence destroyed a man.

Why was she silent tonight, anyway? Usually they talked freely. She was one of the few persons to whom he *could* talk freely, without effort, the words coming out as smoothly as when he talked to Mrs. Gramby. When he tried to talk to other people, he was gripped by an awful shyness that held him speechless.

When he entered the kitchen he said, "The windows are okay." Neola nodded again and gave him the ghost of a smile.

He sat down in the rocker, lit his pipe. Then, under the fury of the wind, under the crashing, splintering destruction that was the wind, he heard a new sound. It was the ringing of the church bells and the sound brought Neola to her feet.

"It's the church bells," she said. "Why are they ringing them?"

"I don't know—perhaps for a fire."

"Fire?"

"Bells are rung for fires and floods and storms—and for death, too."

"But who would be out in a storm like this, ringing the bells?"

He shrugged, "Storms do strange things to people. There's no telling who's ringing the bells."

A conversation like this doesn't lead anywhere either, he

thought, eyeing Neola with a certain wistfulness. She had sat down again in the chair by the window and the soft candlelight made her very desirable. Perhaps the candlelight that made her beautiful made him ridiculous, perhaps his mustachios were casting long shadows over his mouth, darkening his skin, making the color of the turquoise in his ear all wrong—the pale blue stone incongruous against his swarthy face.

He covered the turquoise with his hand, so that if she looked toward him she wouldn't see it. He had never proposed to a woman. What words did one use? Time and again he'd had the right words ready, but they had been selected for a special season of the year; spring with faint young sunlight on the crocuses or summer with the hot sun on the tall foxgloves; even for the rain, soft drops falling on the honeysuckle, intensifying the sweet smell of it. Besides, he had never been able to say those carefully selected words to Neola, despite all the thought he had put on them.

He didn't have the words for a kitchen, snugly warm, copper glowing, fire sending out heat, storm screaming at the windows and doors.

So he watched her and said nothing. She didn't seem to be nervous about the storm; her hands, brown and strong-fingered, stayed quiet in her lap. Now if she were only upset, fearful, crying, he knew the words; for once he put his arm around her, talked gently to her, comforting her, dispelling her fear of the storm, the words would form themselves. He would whisper them in her ear: I will keep you from the storm and the wind; I will build a fire that will warm you on cold and windy nights, for I love you.

But this way, with her sitting over by the window, serene and composed, this way it was impossible to find the right words.

"I'm going to look in the living room and see if Mrs. Gramby is all right," Neola said.

After she left the room, he tried to plan how it would be. Now if she would sit by the table, not by the window, sit right across from him at the table with her head erect, her hands so quietly folded in her lap, and he could see that blue uniform she wore, blue the color of the delphiniums, with the white apron so white, like a white peony—if she would sit there he would be able to dwell on the uniform. If he could keep his mind on the uniform, nothing else, just the delphinium blue and the peony white of it, why, when she came back into the room he would propose to the uniform. That way he wouldn't get confused, he would be able to say the words easily: protect and cherish and worship and water well and feed with the rich, life-giving—Godalmighty! no, he had plants and Neola completely mixed up.

Forget the uniform and the color of it which would only lead him straight to disaster. Just the woman, think about the woman, about Neola whom he loved. She was getting a divorce from Chowder Head, that no-good husband of hers, who had deserted her five years ago, gone within two months after the marriage ceremony. The divorce papers would be in her hands this week.

He knew the kind of house he would buy for her—small, with a garden for flowers and fruits and vegetables. They would have a dozen chickens, just enough to provide fresh eggs for breakfast in the morning. She could stay home instead of working. And they would manage very well. The house would have a small, blossoming kind of kitchen—not a vast room like this with countless mysterious cupboards and back entries and side doors and dutch ovens and a thousand and one windows.

The door that led to the butler's pantry opened and Neola came into the room. He watched her as she walked toward him. She's like a young tree, he thought, strong, erect, growing, the leaves perfect and free from blight.

"Why don't you sit here at the table?" he said.

"The chair by the window is more comfortable."

"Oh," he said hastily; "then, of course, sit by the window. I didn't realize. I just thought it would be friendlier—" He sighed and tapped his pipe against the coal hod. When he spoke again he changed the subject. "Was Mrs. Gramby all right?"

"She's fine. She's walking up and down in the living room, getting her exercise. She said you must spend the night. I told her I would fix up a bed for you in the back wing."

"And the other one? The hungry one? Was she all right, too?"

"Of course. What would ever happen to her so that she wouldn't be? I think she's afraid of the storm. She's sitting in front of the fireplace. With her hands over her ears. And her face"—she hunted for a suitable word—"Her face looks like sin itself."

"She's an evil woman. On a night like this she probably aches with the evil that pushes against her heart. In the old country she'd 'a' been hanged for a witch."

On a night like this it was easy to believe all manner of things, he thought. The noise itself was such that it upset one completely. What with the trees crashing to the ground, crying out as they went down, and if the trees were dying and moaning as they died, what of the shrubs he had cherished—the flowering cherry and the dogwood and the quince? He was certain that under the howl of the wind he could hear the shrubs and the small plants protesting as they died. Godalmighty, no! There were no words known to man suitable to be used for a proposal on a night like this.

Under the shrieking of the wind, the monotonous beating of the rain, he heard a new sound—the sharp splintering of glass. He jumped up, horrified. It was the roof of the greenhouse. He headed for the door that led to the back entry.

"Portulacca," Neola said, "you're not going out in the storm!" She got up and followed close behind him.

"My plants," he said. "I've got to see to my plants. The roof has gone on the greenhouse."

"You'll be killed out there. With this wind and the trees coming down, you won't ever reach the greenhouse."

He ignored her and opened the door leading to the back entry. The wind was blowing at such a rate of speed and with such violence that it seemed to be knocking against the outer storm door. Cook's raincoat hung on a hook near the door and he put it on; pulled a cap down snugly over his head; then he opened the outside door.

The wind snatched the door from his hand and then slammed it back against him, knocking him off his feet. He gripped the door with both hands, thinking Neola was right, he couldn't possibly make it to the greenhouse. He tried to pull himself erect and couldn't. By clinging to the knob and to the door, he managed to get outside on the steps and still in a half-squatting position he forced the door shut. If he crawled on his hands and knees he would be able to get down the path, for it was impossible to stand erect against the fury of the wind.

He got down the steps, reached the flagstone path. Instantly he was lost in total darkness. No matter which way he looked there was nothing but blackness in front of him. Wind tore at the raincoat, rain beat against him, yet he kept moving down the path.

The flagstones were covered with leaves, with twigs. Once he ran head-on into the branch of a tree. After that he moved more slowly, inching along, groping, lifting his hands in front of his face to be sure the way was clear. He came to the branches of another tree, thick, full of leaves. His hand reached toward it, his body moving closer to it. The path was hopelessly blocked. This wasn't a branch, this was a tree—its trunk stretched endlessly in front of him.

He turned and looked toward the house. Just this short distance he had come and he couldn't make out its outline, couldn't see even the faintest flicker of light.

What had made him come out in this storm? Even if he could reach the greenhouse, what did he propose to do there? He had no flashlight, so it would be impossible to determine the extent of the damage. If, as he suspected, one of the great oaks had smashed through the roof, there wasn't anything he could do to save his plants. He shook his head; for in his mind's eye he could see the broken pots, the crushed plants, the ruined flowers. Nothing at all that he could do about it.

It's the storm, he thought. I did what men always do in the midst of violence, I went straight toward my heart's love. But Neola—what of Neola? Did this mean then that he was far more concerned about his plants than about her?

He smiled. And he felt the sodden wetness of his mustachios lift themselves about his mouth. No, it hadn't been the plants that sent him forth into this black and evil night. He had hoped that his battle with the wind and the rain would crack Neola's calm, that her concern for his welfare would be the little bridge across which he would walk straight into her heart.

He crawled back up the path. His hands sought and found the steps. He lifted himself to his knees, grasped the doorknob. The door was locked. He banged on it. Why had she locked it? Why had she locked it? Was this an affront, deliberate, calculated? Had she locked it in order to let him know that she was not concerned about him, that he could eternally crawl about in the wind and the rain while she sat inside warm and dry? Could it be that she had locked the door to keep his unpleasant person out in the wet?

Neola unlocked the door and the wind took it away, brought it back, slammed it against him. But how stupid he was! She had locked it in order to keep it closed. He struggled to shut it and the door seemed to come alive in his hands, stubbornly resisting him, pulling him down.

Neola's arms went around his waist. They pulled together and the door came in. He hooked it securely and then turned toward her.

He had never known such a glow of warmth as he knew now at the thought of her helping him, her arms around his waist. After the black violence of the night, the surge and beat of the wind and the rain, the back entry was as calm and peaceful as a garden in sunlight. Neola helped him off with the dripping raincoat, took the sodden cap from his head. The quick deft touch of her hands was all about him, and he thought, Yes, a garden in sunlight.

"I'll go ask Cook for some dry clothes," she said and turned toward the kitchen.

"Wait," he said.

She looked at him warily and he decided that the tone of his voice had disturbed her.

If he could remember the storm, hold tight to the storm, the black night outside and the warmth and light inside the entry, the words would come. They must come quickly, too, for from the look of things outside there might be no morning for him and Neola. He had to ask her now.

She was staring at him and he almost didn't speak the words; because he knew he must look like something washed up by the storm—his mustachios hanging limp, water squishing inside his shoes, dripping from his trouser legs.

"Neola," he said quickly, "will you marry me? I love you very much, Neola."

She made a nervous gesture with her hand, as though she were pushing something away from her, and turned and almost ran across the kitchen. He could hear her swift footsteps going up the back stairs. And as he listened, he frowned and fingered the blue stone in his ear. She thinks I've gone crazy, he thought. She never even answered me.

The words had been all wrong. They were hurried, frantic words. He should have embroidered them, enlarged on them, and while he waited for her to return with Cook's dry clothes, he tried to think of new and better words.

17

IN THE ROANES' HOUSE, JOHNNIE walked the length of the kitchen, lit a cigarette, snuffed it out, peered out of a window.

"Listen to that wind," he said. "I think I ought to drive up to the store and get Glory."

"I suppose you should," his mother said doubtfully. "But the store doesn't close until six."

"I know. But from the way things look, I might not be able to make it later on."

He took another turn around the room, hesitated in front of the telephone. "I guess I'll call her and tell her I'm on my way—" He held the receiver to his ear, jiggled the hook. "The line's gone dead," he said. "I'd better get going."

The memory of last night, of the warm feel of Glory lying close beside him, had been with him all day. On a wild night such as this night was going to be, it would be fun to be under a roof of their own. Just the two of them under the one roof, lying snug and relaxed after the lovemaking, listening to the beat of the storm outside. But where? Cabins, a string of them on the

Post Road, near the overhead bridge—they'd spend the night in one of those tourist cabins.

"Don't worry if we're not back tonight," he said. "We may spend the night in a cabin, a tourist cabin." The surprised look on his mother's face made him add, awkwardly, "Sort of second honeymoon." Then embarrassment flooded through him, making him want to leave the house quickly. Hastily grabbing his raincoat and the sou'easter that hung near the door, he left the kitchen, hurried toward the garage.

The wind was stronger than he had realized. The car lurched and swayed as he drove along the River Road, the wheel twisting under his hands. He drove cautiously, afraid of skidding on the wet leaves which were packed on the road's macadam surface. He had to steer out of the way of large branches and yet keep close to the center of the road because of the water which flooded the shoulders.

When he parked the car in front of Perkins' store, he saw that the green shades were drawn at the windows, the big padlock on the front door fastened. But he got out of the car anyway, and rattled the door, looked through the windows, bending down in order to get a glimpse of the interior under the half-drawn shades. The vegetable stand was covered with netting, the drawer of the cash register was open. The store was obviously closed for the night.

Had he passed Glory on his way to the store? But he couldn't have. Her yellow raincoat was a flash of color, easy to spot on the darkest, grayest day.

He gave the doorknob a vicious tug, banged on the door. There might be someone in the back of the building; Perkins himself might have stayed late to check accounts. He knew, even while he raised his fist to pound on the door again, that the building was empty; no one would be working in the store without a light.

Where did Perkins live? He could picture the place—cows, red barn, chickens pecking in the dooryard, lilacs near the kitchen door, sheep grazing near the front of the house; disgruntled customers used to say, "Perkins keeps them sheep so he won't have to spend no money getting his lawn mowed." He could see Perkins going into the house after he finished at the store: his fat stomach hanging over the top of his belt, his hair long over his red wrinkled neck. He could picture him in the store, too; a pencil behind his ear, shapeless felt hat on his head, long butcher's coat with raffia sleeve protectors and the coat covered with interesting stains. When he was a kid he used to speculate on those stains, picking out bloodstains from beef and chicken, grass stains, grease marks from butter and lard. Perkins always smelt of barnyards and horses; and he had asthma, so he wheezed—

What the hell! this wasn't getting him any closer to the location of Perkins' house; and he was getting soaking wet, standing in the rain. He got back into the car, tried to remember where Perkins lived. He was always going there to get eggs when he was a kid. There was a small stream near the house. He had it now—it was on the road to Westville, near Oyster River.

Before he turned the car around, he put the headlights on. It was quite dark. He glanced at the clock on the dashboard—four-thirty in the afternoon and already dark—and thought there was something ominous about day being turned into night.

The car lights showed the slant of the rain, revealed the young rivers that ran along the side of the road. Water was sluicing down the windshield at such a rate that the wiper could not take care of it. He was forced to drive slowly and it irked him. He could have walked at a faster pace than the car was moving.

When he parked the car in Perkins' driveway, he noted that the drive had become a small lake. Fences were down, the lilacs had been uprooted and were blowing along the side of the house. Water from Oyster River was seeping up to the barn, surrounding it.

He got out of the car, and ran, bent over, toward the house. He banged on the front door, shouted. The wind carried the sound away. He walked around the house, found a side door, banged on it with both fists.

Perkins opened the door. "Come in," he said.

"I can't. I just want to know—

"Come inside," Perkins roared. "Can't hold the door. The wind'll take it."

Between them they got the door closed. "Let me stand on some newspapers," Johnnie said. Water was dripping from his raincoat, forming a pool where he stood.

"A little more water won't hurt. The whole damn house is leaking like a sieve. Water's coming in everywhere." Perkins looked at him with a curiosity he made no effort to conceal. "What you doing out in this storm?"

"I'm looking for Glory. I went to get her at the store and it's closed—"

"Sure. We closed up at two o'clock. There wasn't any point in staying open. Not a car moving on the street and the storm getting worse all the time. So I sent 'em all home."

"But she isn't home—"

"You sure? Ed stopped by to pick up his groceries just about the time we were closing. He offered her a lift. She must be home by now."

"Oh—well, thanks a lot," he said, starting for the door.

"Why'nt you call and see if she's got there yet? You can use my phone."

"The line's gone dead," he said. Not a single car had passed him on the way to the store. She wasn't home. She was somewhere with Ed Barrell.

"It has? Tree must have come down on the line, or a pole's

been blown over. Wait a minute, I'll try mine, see if it's working. Sometimes they get 'em fixed up right away—" Perkins picked up the receiver, listened, shook his head. "Nope. It's gone, too."

When Johnnie got back into the car, his only thought was that Glory was with Ed; somewhere in this storm, somewhere in this day that had become night, Glory and Ed were together. He steered cautiously through the lake of water covering Perkins' driveway. Last night she had been in his arms. Last night hadn't meant anything. Last night was a bone you throw a dog to keep him quiet.

Romeo Lothario Barrell, Ed Romeo Lothario Barrell, the bowlegged bastard, the bull-chested bastard, the bastard of the leaky heart, of the cigar in the corner of the mouth, of the chewed cigar and the felt hat placed at a rakish angle, would give you the shirt off his back, would share his last crust of bread with you, share his last cigarette. He would also share your wife with you. He was the Lennox Lothario, the Romeo of the filling station. He and Glory of the bright hair, of the hair like a golden net, were now Romeo and Juliet, were playing at Tristan and Isolde. If I find them I will kill them, he thought. Kill both of them? Kill Glory? No. Kill Ed? Of course, and without even thinking about it.

Somewhere in the woods, Ed had a cabin. There was a side road, a narrow dirt road, which led to it. The side road turns off from a black macadam road and the black macadam road is reached by turning left at the Post Road; and at that corner there is an overhead stop light, which swings back and forth in the wind.

He headed the car up the street, drove through the town and then on toward the bridge which led to Lyme. He knew that eventually he would reach that other narrower road, that country road; and up that country road he would find the Place, the

Place of Seduction, the Palace of Delight, which was owned by Ed Barrell.

He became aware of the rattling of the car. The wind must have blown loose every bolt, every nut; the sound suggested that even the tires and the chassis were being wrenched apart. Going across the bridge, he thought the car would turn over from the force of the wind screaming down the Connecticut River. He told himself he must remember his last thought, cherish it; because last thoughts just before going down to a deep and watery grave, sealed inside a six-year-old car, ought to be worth remembering.

Once across the bridge he found he was enjoying the storm. I hope to Christ it wipes out the town of Lennox, leaving not a single building standing on its foundation, no blade of grass, no tree or shrub to mark the spot. I hope it destroys every home down to the last shingle, every chimney, every plant; so that no one will ever know that people lived there. I want everyone to lose tonight. I want them to watch the death of the things they loved; I want them to stand at windows and huddle in doorways and peer from the shelter of barns and corncribs and see what they love blown down, violated. I want all of them to be in at the death of their dreams; held there, immovable and defenseless, as they witness the last gasp.

His hands on the wheel were violent. He slewed the car back into the middle of the road, fighting against the wind that pushed it to one side or the other. His hands, his arms, his shoulders, ached for a fight. I want to feel his thick throat between my hands, he thought. He is not fit to live. His hands with the smell of gasoline and tobacco, with the stains of the thick black grease from cars, have caressed her, fondled her breasts, encircled her waist, traced the line of her thighs.

The overhead light on the other side of the bridge was out

and he went past the spot where the road turned off. He turned the car around and went back, driving slowly, trying to see into the darkness, for the car lights penetrated the blackness only a few feet ahead.

When he found the turn in the road, he increased the speed of the car; for the trees on each side offered shelter from the force of the wind. He had driven a quarter of a mile when he suddenly slammed on the brakes. The car lights revealed the branches of a tree, a thick trunk. He took a flashlight from the car pocket, got out of the car, and examined the tree. It lay lengthwise across the road. There was no way to get the car around it.

He set out on foot. As he climbed awkwardly over the tree trunk, he thought, I'm a veteran of the rain. Been out in it for days now, tramping around. And, then, What are you going to do when you get there? Suppose she isn't there, has never been there? But where would she go? Suppose he isn't there, either; that there's no trace of either of them? They might have gone miles away, taken a train for New York or Boston.

He thought the wind was blowing inside his head, scattering his thoughts, so that his memory of this walk in the storm was of a confusion that whirled inside his skull. For there was rain in his eyes, his mouth, trickling inside his ears; the raincoat hung heavy on his shoulders and his body was hot and clumsy under it.

He tried to keep Glory and Ed Barrell out of his thoughts by concentrating on his physical discomfort, only he always came back to them. Dry clothes and a roof over one's head were essentials. Out of a tub, dry yourself off; wash your hands, dry them off; wash your head, dry it off. Dryness an essential—to be warm and dry was a kind of paradise. Last night he had lain with Glory in his arms, smug, falsely secure, grinning at the world and hoping it got soaked. Tonight he was out in the wild dark, in the wind and the rain, because she had gone from him. Man always hunts a roof, a woman and a room—one and the same thing.

He braced his body against the wind, stooping a little. There were twigs not leaves underfoot, sometimes the branch of a tree. The flashlight revealed the slant of the rain, perpetual, never ceasing. No painting ever achieved that quality of wetness. Could it? Perhaps. But no black like this, a black without shadow, even the light from the flashlight was swallowed by it. The evil black world that was the night, eating up the candlelight.

Somewhere, at one side of this road, was that other dirt road; that road which led to Ed's Place, the Palace of Delight. Get lost easily in this blackness. Road should be on the right. Kill him. How? Why always the thought of choking him? End the corrupt and evil flesh—was that the idea? Hands destroying it? Should wear gloves. Would it be warm to the touch? Would the big blood vessel in the throat beat against his hand, revealing the very life's blood of him, the dirty corrupt blood?

How did one find a road in the dark, a country road, a narrow dirt-brown road? I wouldn't go on living with the knowledge that he was alive somewhere, anywhere in the same world with me. Step on a snake, don't you? If a snake has two legs and wears a felt hat and smokes cigars tilted at an angle in his mouth, you step on that snake, too, don't you?

And Glory—what afterward? Nothing. Kill him. Nothing else matters. Why kill him? Why not turn back? There is a point where man's instinct for survival stops him—but there is, too, a point beyond that. What about it? Nothing beyond it.

Glory was a name, a body—bright hair under a lamp, bright hair in the sun, in the light of the moon; bright hair that you wanted to hold to your heart. So you lost her. You—

Christ, where was the road? He stopped, turned back, climbed over the trunk of a tree and stopped again. He couldn't remember whether the tree in front of him had been there when he traversed this section of road before. Had it just come down? Did I crawl over this tree once before and not remember doing it? Am I so eaten up with rage and despair that I pulled myself over this tree trunk without being aware of it?

He waited a moment, trying to decide and couldn't. He started walking again, muttering to himself: a fire and a roof and a woman; food—well, yes, taken for granted, always food. Yes, learn to turn your head in a crib, focus your eyes, move your fingers; learn to grasp with your fingers, to pick up, to hold; learn to creep, to crawl, to walk, to climb, to run; learn to talk—so that you can propose to Glory.

He found the narrow dirt road only because he hugged the edge of the macadam road, leaning over, examining it, holding his flashlight low to the ground, as he searched for an opening that would lead off between the trees.

There were more branches, more leaves on this road. Small shrubs lay across his path. Occasionally he left the road, and went through the underbrush to avoid an uprooted tree. It was the slow, clumsy progress of a nightmare, for the road slanted upward.

His legs began to ache from the effort of the slow uphill climb against the pressure of the wind. His raincoat got caught on shrubs and trees; thorny branches slapped against his face; and wind tore at the snagged places in his raincoat. He could hear trees crashing to the ground deep inside the woods; and once somewhere not too far behind him.

When he reached a clearing, he paused, tried to look around him. The road ended where he stood. There were fewer trees here, the undergrowth had been cleared away. Ed's cabin must be somewhere in this open space, but its outline was not visible in the darkness.

He walked forward, quickly, then slowed down, for he had tripped over a root, almost fallen. Where was the damn place? No light revealed it. He walked back and forth, covering an ever-narrowing circle. Then the blackness ahead of him took on a deeper quality, seemed to bulk more solidly.

It was the cabin. He could touch it with his hands. He walked around one side of it, hoping to see a light; turned the corner of the building.

And as he turned he saw a faint, yellowish light, coming from a window. He looked into the room and nearly dropped the flashlight. Ed was sitting at a table, feet thrust out in front of him. He was alone. But the table was set for a meal, two places, one in front of Ed, the other place was unoccupied. Who was it for? The plate in front of Ed was empty; someone had eaten half the food on the other plate—remains of spaghetti, a slice of bread—

Was it Glory? Ed turned his head toward some other part of the room. And then Glory came into view, carrying two thick white cups, steaming cups, probably coffee. She put them down on the table.

Ed put his arm around Glory's waist. She bent over him, kissed him. Then she was sitting on his lap. She was wearing a man's wool shirt and nothing else—legs bare, thighs bare, the shirt open. Ed's hands went under the shirt, caressing her breasts, and she laughed and turned toward him; pressing her body close to his.

Johnnie's first impulse was to jump into the room; the force of his leap would smash the window. Then he decided, no; he would find a door, he would walk through it and confront them. They thought they were safely hidden away here in this cabin on this stormy night.

He ran away from the window, seeking a door; thinking it must be on the other side of the building. In his haste he stumbled, fell flat; and lay on the ground trying to get his breath back. What was he doing here, blundering about in the rain?

Why didn't he get up and go home? The thought of leaving Ed and Glory unmolested filled him with rage. He felt as though he were a part of the storm itself—a wild thing, let loose to destroy; so filled with the desire for destruction that it was choking him. Hate was swelling and pushing inside him, goading him on until he had become what he was at this moment—an animal on all fours.

The thought brought him to his feet. He started around the building, continuing his search for a door. He had taken only a few steps when he realized that the flashlight was not in his hand. He had lost it when he stumbled over the root. He turned back, feeling along the ground, seeking for it. When he didn't find it, he lowered himself to his hands and knees, searching every inch of ground.

His hands found leaves, twigs, the sodden earth. Wind plucked against his hands as though trying to remove them from the ground. He wondered if the center of the earth was warm and started digging, and then drew his hand back when he became aware of what he was doing, and said aloud, "Are you trying to crawl back into the place from which you came, the very earth itself?"

He pulled himself erect. He didn't need the flashlight. If he followed the building, feeling his way around it, staying close to it, he would find a door.

The shingles were rough under his hands, splintery. He turned a corner, thinking that the workman who laid these shingles had held the nails in his mouth, had let go with regular strokes of his hammer as he pounded them in place. While he worked in the hot sunlight in this little clearing, he had paused to look at the sumac, the bayberries or the wild cherry; and whistled as he worked because the air was clear and the sun was warm on his shoulders. He probably conjectured about what would take place under this roof some night—the girl, young and wanting and waiting, and the man, eager and hungry—

An unknown workman had hammered these shingles in place in order to keep rain and wind away from Ed and Glory. He had cut the openings for door and windows so that soft yellow light would shine through to the outside; so that the animal who was outside, snuffing about the building, moving slowly on all fours, would see the yellow light and would be doubly conscious of the outer darkness into which he had been cast.

His hands found only the shingles, they came across no opening for a door. He turned another corner and went away from the building when he made the turn. He came back to the building, feeling for it, hands outstretched.

He found the door, the smooth panel, the knob. The doorknob was cold to the touch. He paused there with his hand on the door, listening.

18

JOHNNIE ROANE PUSHED THE DOOR of the cabin open, stepped inside. The room was warm. He identified the smell of bacon, of kerosene, of tobacco. Homey, he thought, tight and snug like two bugs in a rug—man, woman smell mixed up with the other smells.

Glory was sitting at the table facing the door. The sudden rush of air through the opened door made her say, "The wind—" and then she looked up and saw him. She didn't finish whatever she was going to say, her mouth stayed open, the lips moving, but no words came out. She shoved her chair back from the table. The chair scraped on the floor.

"Don't get up," Johnnie said.

Ed turned around in his chair with an awkward movement. If he was frightened, Johnnie could not see any sign of it in his face. He didn't say anything. He got on his feet, quickly, and the chair that he had been sitting in fell over on the floor.

Glory said, "The storm—I couldn't get home—Johnnie—don't—"

He heard what she was saying and ignored her, walking toward Ed, seeing him magnified; the cigar, in his mouth, black, enormous, symbol of lechery. Even before he reached Ed, he knew that he would hit him in the mouth first.

He clipped the cigar out of Ed's mouth and then hit him hard on the chin.

Ed's hands, quick, violent, came at him, seeming to materialize out of thin air. And he thought to himself, I'm a goddam fool, what made me believe he wouldn't hit back? Ed hit him squarely in the stomach, then in the chest, so that he grunted, backed away, hunting for an opening and found it.

He hit Ed on the jaw, the nose, ducked away again. He watched Ed sidestep, thinking, Where'd he learn to fight, he's a professional, goddam him. This time Ed came in slowly, and he waited for him, exulting in the thought that he had hurt him; the bastard's hurt. He threw caution out of his mind; intent on reaching Ed's jaw again, he walked straight into a blow, saw it coming too late to dodge it, felt his chin give under the impact, and went down on the floor.

He took his time getting up, planned his next move. He'd back away and pretend he was hurt, he'd fight slowly, cautiously. Because he knew he could beat Ed. Ed was years older and those added years would kill him, here, tonight, in this cabin. I can take my time and kill him, he thought, beat him up for an hour; using slow, cautious, hammer blows to beat him to death.

Glory had moved to another part of the room. She was sitting on a bunk in the corner. The expression on her face held him motionless. Her lips were parted, she was bending forward, her eyes fixed on him. He had seen that same expression on her face when they used to go to the movies. She would sit on the edge of the seat, not moving, lapping up the gaudiest kind of melodrama; so entranced that you knew that as she watched the picture she had transformed herself into the glossy heroine on the screen. He knew a moment of such revulsion that he felt physically sick.

The wave of nausea was followed by a burning anger that brought him to his feet. The instant he stood up, Ed lifted his fists, ready to fight again. The sight made him forget about the cautious plan he had worked out. He waded into Ed with quick, fast blows; hitting him on the mouth, the chest, in the stomach, the mouth again; not dodging but slugging it out.

He sent a right to Ed's chin, expecting that Ed would dodge it, but he didn't. There was a faint astonishment on Ed's face as the blow landed; and then he fell, sideways, clutching at his chest as though he were trying to tear it open to admit the passage of air.

Johnnie stared at him. The bastard had passed out. He lifted his foot intending to smash in his face, his ribs, his belly as he lay there on the floor. He would grind his carrion flesh into nothingness.

There was a stillness in the cabin, a hush. He heard the wind faintly, now; and the branches of a tree, scraping against the roof. He knew suddenly that he couldn't do it. He tried to force his foot toward Ed's face. Impossible. Out of the question. Why was it out of the question? He had intended to kill Ed. Yes, but not this way, not by kicking him to death when he was down. Much as he hated him, hated the sight of him, he couldn't bring himself to finish Ed off. You're a fool, he thought. The color is coming back in his face, in his lips. He will be on his feet in a few more minutes. He will continue to live under the same sky with you, will go on smoking his obscene cigars while he fondles your wife. But even if he were on his feet, I couldn't kill him. I am not an executioner.

He turned away from Ed. He felt as light-headed and dizzy as if he had been standing on the edge of a precipice, ready to plunge over, when he was suddenly pulled back. He could still see the long, sheer drop down which he had very nearly fallen.

Then he remembered that Glory was in the room. She must have realized what he meant to do when he had stood over Ed, foot drawn back. She hadn't moved. She was sitting on the bunk, in the same position, bent forward. As he looked at her the expression on her face changed. She's coming out of that trance, he thought. The movie is over and the house lights have been turned on. In another minute she's going to scream because there's a speck of blood on Ed's chin and it's real and not make-believe.

Her breath came out in a long sigh, but she didn't scream. She got up from the bunk to kneel beside Ed, loosening his collar, unbuttoning his vest. She reached in his pocket for a small bottle. He stirred, sat up; and she handed him the bottle, watched him closely as he opened the bottle, shook out a small dark pill and then swallowed it.

Then Ed waved her away and got on his feet. He sat down in the chair by the table; his hands were shaking, but he managed to light a cigar.

Johnnie turned his back. I don't have to look at him, he thought; and I don't have to leave my wife here with him.

"Put your clothes on," he said to Glory.

"Johnnie, you don't understand," she said softly. "You see I got caught in the storm and my clothes were soaking wet so I—"

"Go put your clothes on."

"They're not dry," she said. "I can't put on—"

He came close to her, gave her a little push. "Go put 'em on."

She went into another room, closing the door behind her.

We've both seen her without her clothes on, Johnnie thought. Why the sudden modesty about getting dressed in front of us? Perhaps she thinks there would be something wrong about both of us seeing her naked at the same time; one, alone, is okay; many of us in succession, alone, would also be okay.

He followed Glory into the bedroom. It was furnished simply but efficiently, he thought. Just enough equipment for seduction: a brass bed, a chest of drawers and a chair near the bed. Glory's skirt and sweater, a pink slip and stockings, were draped across the back of the chair. They were unwrinkled, obviously had never been wet.

He closed the door, leaned against it.

Glory said: "I don't see what you got so upset about. You come in here and start fighting with Ed and—"

"I saw you through the window," he said, and his voice broke. "He was dandling you on his lap—you naked—you loving it—"

She looked frightened. "I told you I got caught in the storm," she said quickly. "And he brought me here to dry out—"

"You must think I'm a damn fool," he said, and slapped her across the face.

He lifted his hand to strike her again and she put her arms around his neck. The soft hair brushed against his face, faintly sweet. He closed his eyes, thinking, You could ride straight into heaven on a smell like that, just drifting, floating up.

Then he pushed her away from him. "Don't do that," he said.

"What's the matter?"

Her eyes were full of tears, her face innocent, lovely; somehow beseeching. And for a moment he wavered; he could take her back, they could start all over again, they could be happy together. She loved him, she was clinging to him, wanted him.

Wouldn't he ever learn? This was Ol' Lightnin's daughter, Young Lightnin'. A half-hour ago she was Ed Barrell's and now she was willing to be his, but only because she was afraid of him. He didn't want her on those terms; or any other terms. Tell her. Get it over with.

"I'm through," he said. "We're through. You and me."

"But, Johnnie—" She came close to him, tried to put her arms around his neck again.

"Get the hell out of here," he said, pushing her away. Because if she came near him again, just a little closer, with her hair brushing against his face, he would forget that she was a liar and a cheat; a dissembler and a wearer of the false face of love. He would forget and he would take her in his arms again and hold her tight, loving her.

"Go on! Get out!" he shouted. He saw the fear in her eyes. He thought she was going to run out of the room; and he urged her on in his mind: yes, run, coward that you are, shadow of a woman, worthless cheat.

She paused with her hand on the doorknob and shouted back, "Yes, I slept with Ed. And I'll do it again." Her face at that moment was like her mother's face the day she found them on the porch, sitting in the glider, their arms wrapped tightly about each other. The voice was the same, too, ugly, emerging from lips that curled back in a snarl.

"He's a man," she said. "And you're not. I wouldn't go on living with you if I was to be paid for it."

The final insult, the crowning touch, he thought. Why should it hurt? But it did. He pushed her away from the door, opened it and went quickly through the room where Ed was sitting.

The instant he stepped outside the cabin, wind and rain assailed him. He groped his way along, seeking the road. He felt as though some part of him, some vital part, had died there in the cabin. Well, Ed and Glory could hold a wake over whatever it was; they could sit up with the body, Gloria in her nakedness, and Ed puffing smoke from his obscene cigar.

It seemed to him that he was hours trying to find the road. He had no flashlight, so he had to feel his way, stumbling over tree trunks, picking himself up and going on, fighting every step of the way to get back to the place where he had parked the car.

We die a little every day, with the ticking of a clock, he thought, but tonight I did enough dying to last straight through to eternity.

He came on the car suddenly; he had climbed over what seemed to be the millionth tree trunk to find the car on the other side of it. When he got inside he turned on the headlights. Then he blinked, for he had grown so accustomed to darkness that the light hurt his eyes. He stared at the branches of the tree. They showed yellow-green, almost translucent in the flood of light.

This is where you came in, he thought. You're right back where you started. He couldn't decide what his feelings were—hate for Ed Barrell? No, not wholly. Hate for Glory? More ache than anything else; a pain that would stay with him for a long time—not sharp, but dull, uncomfortable; and whenever it rained like it was doing now he would become aware of a throbbing inside him—unbearable, persistent, like the throbbing of an old wound.

Tomorrow, he would go to New York, taking the first train out. New York was what he wanted. Part of what he wanted. That you get, the other part, the part called Glory you lost. Die a little? Live a little? Yes, but it never quite balanced. The ache of the dying lingers over and beyond the living.

He stepped on the starter. There was no response from the engine. Too much water, drowned in water. He curled up on the front seat, put his head on his arms. This was as good a place as any to spend the night; he had a roof over his head and he had once at some earlier moment in the evening waxed philosophical on the subject of roofs—and women. Forget it, relax, go to sleep. After all, he was still whole and all in one piece. Not quite in one piece. Only on the surface. We will not go into the detail of what the wreckage inside is like.

You are now, he told himself, a veteran in every respect; a veteran of that other war, the one between the civilians and the soldiers; a veteran of the never-ending battle between the ones who stayed at home and the ones who went away.

Rain drummed on the roof of the car, beat against the windows. And then faintly, far off in the distance, he heard the sound of the church bells. They toll for a death, he thought. But whose?

As he listened to the sound, he got the feeling that the storm had sent waves of disillusion through the town, starting with the trees; revealing the rotten heart in the seemingly sturdy maples; the soft weak places in the elms.

The storm had sent Glory, slender, bright-haired, smiling, running straight in the direction of her heart's desire. And he had come stumbling after; he, too, heading straight for the thing he wanted most.

There's but to do and die, he thought; there's not to reason why. I only know I lost her; lost the illusion, the soapbubble dream of her.

He turned off the car lights, sat in the dark, listening to the bells; thinking, yes, Jack and Jill, pail of water, up the hill, Jill fell down, and yes, yes, you came tumbling after.

Shortly after Johnnie had left the cabin, Glory came out of the bedroom, looked around cautiously. "Has he gone?" she asked.

Ed Barrell nodded his head, staring at her. He'd had the mother, cold like ice; and now he'd had the daughter, a born tramp if there ever was one. He had waited a long time, longer than usual, before he made the first tentative move toward lovemaking. He had had the feeling Glory might be as frigid as her mother. Yet something kept telling him she would be okay. And she was. Too bad that boy had come blundering in here tonight.

"He'll probably talk, you know," Ed said.

"No, he won't. And if he does it won't matter. People will say he's gone queer in the head like a lot of other soldiers."

"How will you straighten it out with his folks?"

She shrugged her shoulders. "There isn't anything to straighten out. I'll just stop living there and move into my own house. I'm through with him after tonight."

He put his arm around her waist, caressed her cheek. "Are you sure?"

"What do you think?" she said, and bent over and kissed him, confident that she could straighten it all out, very easily, very simply.

19

ABOUT MIDNIGHT THE STORM BEGAN to blow itself out to sea. It left the town with reluctance. A drizzling rain hung behind long after the gale had disappeared.

I went to bed at a little after midnight, and lay awake for a long time, listening to the patter of the rain on the tin roof of the back room.

When I woke up the sun was out, filling the room with strong, brilliant light. I know that I am not giving you any idea of the kind of morning it was—crystal clear, shining. It might have been the morning of the first day—the day of the Creation—a morning designed for a world that had not yet known pain and sorrow.

I got up and, opening one of the front windows, leaned far out to look at the street. The elms were down everywhere; their enormous roots now reached toward the sky. The picket fences were down, shutters were gone from the houses, and windows had been blown in. Sections of roofing, railings from piazzas were strewn over the lawns. There was a rowboat on the town green and the urn that had held the geraniums lay on its side near the boat.

And overhead—well, the sky was like the inside of a Chinese bowl, pale blue with delicate drifts of white cloud across it. The air was so sweet and so clear it suggested one of those spring mornings when you wake up early and you can tell by the smell of the air, the feel of it against your face, that spring has come back again; you hear a bird singing softly, somewhere in the distance, and you think that the time of the singing of birds has come; you say a small prayer of thanks, under your breath, that you should be alive and awaken to find such a morning.

But the bright morning, the arching, tranquil sky, the soft air, could not wipe out the nightmare memory of the storm. As I looked at the sun shining on the church across the way, I remembered the awful tolling of the bells; remembered, too, the hideous howling of the wind—a wind so strong it had moved those massive bells back and forth as though they were made of straw. Thus the bells had tolled the death of the trees.

The leaves of the huge old elms were still green. They fluttered in the breeze. For there was a breeze, a quiet, small breeze. It was all that was left of the evil wind that had beaten against the town, hour after hour, during the night.

As I stood there at the window, Johnnie Roane came down the street. He climbed over tree trunks, crossed the street, crossed back again to the other side, picking his way through the litter and the débris. His shoulders were bent. He was walking slowly, his pace that of a very old man.

Just as he passed beneath my bedroom window, he looked up. Perhaps some unconscious movement I made attracted his attention; or perhaps he felt that someone was looking at him. He had a bad bruise over one eye and another on his chin. His face bore that quiet, waiting expression one associates with old age.

He made no gesture, called out no greeting, but kept doggedly on his way; climbing over trees, pausing now and then to push branches aside. His raincoat was torn, his trouser legs were a mass of wrinkles.

I watched him go down the street and I couldn't help thinking that it was ironical that they had to call that girl "Glory." I could have given her a more appropriate name, a one-syllable name that summed her up and would have left no doubt in anyone's mind as to what she was. So he, too, had been uprooted by this demon-begotten storm, pushed faster in whatever direction he had been traveling. Whatever he had sought in the storm, he had not found. I could tell by that slow, old man's walk he had acquired. The bells had tolled the death knell for the trees and for Johnnie Roane's lost youth. As long as he lived, he would never again have that young, eager look on his face.

Shortly after that, the sound of saws could be heard throughout the town. The sound continued all of that day—a rough, grating sound as steel went through the live green wood of the big trees. Highway trucks carted the trunks and the branches away; and by late afternoon a car could navigate the main street.

The customers who came into the store talked about the storm and nothing else. Most of them bought candles and flashlight batteries and wicks for kerosene lamps because it was obvious it would be a week or two before the electric light people got their wires and poles put back and in working order.

About five o'clock I saw Lil Gramby picking her way along Whipporwill Lane, lifting her feet high like a cat walking through water. She came into the store and stood by the candy case, eyeing the few boxes of chocolates on display.

"How do you do," she said.

"How are you?" I said. I was reading *Progress and Poverty* at the time and I laid the book down with some reluctance, waiting to hear what she wanted. I didn't get up, on the off chance that what she wanted would be right there in the back room where I was sitting.

"I want to get a box of candy," she said.

I showed her the few I had on hand, pointed at one of them, saying, "Here's a nice assortment."

She took the box over to the front window and held it out, at arm's length, in order to read the list of contents on the back. In the strong sunlight her hair was a brassy color.

"This won't do," she said finally. "It's got too many hard pieces in it."

"Here's one that's all soft centers. Won't stick to your plate." I don't know why I said that except that she obviously needed glasses and wouldn't get them for fear they would make her look old; and I had a sudden desire to let her know that I was well aware she had reached the age when most people have false teeth. "I didn't know you ate candy."

She frowned. "Sometimes," she said, and then added hastily, "This box will be all right."

As I wrapped the candy, I inquired about Mrs. Gramby.

"She's fine now. The storm last night seemed to upset her, but she's calmer today."

"That's funny. I've never known her to be upset by storms. She's seen a good many of them."

She didn't answer, and I said, "Storm hurt the place much?"

"Some of the trees came down and most of the shrubs were uprooted. Nothing very serious."

"Trees are rather important," I said mildly.

"They are to some people," she said.

When she left, I stood in the door watching her teeter down the front steps. She wears shoes with extremely high heels and her skirts are very short and also very narrow. From the back she looked like a young woman, twenty-five or so.

Once on the sidewalk, she turned around and looked at me. The sight of that pinched, avid face of hers, and those long, deep hunger lines around her mouth, made me shiver. At that moment she might have been a hundred years old instead of forty-five or forty-six.

20

IT WAS QUITE LATE THAT afternoon when Glory finally reached Perkins' store. She found Mr. Perkins near the back of the store, standing on a stepladder, hunting for kerosene lamps.

She loosened the scarf from around her throat as she approached him. "Mr. Perkins," she said, "I thought I ought to tell you about this, frankly and right away. Just in case you heard a different story." She waited a moment to see what he was going to say; he was staring at her as though he were puzzled. Good, she thought, he hasn't heard anything. "Johnnie and I are through—" she said it dramatically.

"Through?" he said, startled. He came down the ladder. "Through?" he repeated. "Why, he just got home from the army. He was looking for you out at my place yesterday afternoon. How—"

"Looking for me?" she said quickly. "Why—why—he must be crazy. He knew where I was. He was supposed to meet me up at Ed Barrell's place. Ed offered it to us—a sort of second honeymoon—" Her voice broke. "He knew where I was—" she repeated.

"Don't talk about it if you don't want to, honey," he said, patting her hand.

"He—" She didn't go on talking; instead she unwound the scarf, watched Perkins' eyes dilate as they fell on the dark bruises on her throat, wondering if he could detect that they were not real. She had carefully painted them on early that morning, in Ed's bedroom. He had helped her. They were compounded of iodine and a bit of cold cream.

"Did Johnnie do that?"

She nodded, watching him. "I'm just covered with bruises—" Her voice dropped so low Perkins had to bend over the counter to hear what she was saying. She turned a little away from him. "Everywhere—bruises—just everywhere—"

"He oughtta be run out of town! I'd like to get him in my barn with a horsewhip. He—"

"No," she said. "He's just home from the army." Then she added gently, "He's—he's not really responsible."

"I guess you're right," Perkins said. "Another one of those veterans who's gone queer in the head. But I'd still like to get my hands on him."

"And I loved him so—" Glory said. She leaned against the counter as though she lacked the strength to stand erect. "His folks won't believe anything against him. It makes it awfully hard."

"Why'nt you come stay at our house? We got an extra room. You ain't got to stay with his people."

She smiled at Perkins—a small smile, piteous, helpless. She could tell from the expression in his eyes exactly how right the smile was; and also from the way he blinked and swallowed. He would tell his wife that Glory was a brave little girl and that

that skunk Johnnie Roane had tried to kill her in a fit of rage; given to them like so many of these veterans who think they're still driving B-29's over Tokyo or something. The story would cling to Johnnie; it would crop up wherever he went; queer, not safe, not all there, Glory left him, tried to kill her, dirty skunk.

"That's so nice of you, Mr. Perkins. And if it won't be too much trouble, I'd love to stay with you and Mrs. Perkins."

"It won't be no trouble at all," Perkins said, swallowing hard.

"I'll put my smock on now and go to work."

"You sure you feel like it?"

"Yes," she said. "It's better to work when you're unhappy. It helps you forget your troubles."

She moved briskly behind the counters, checking stock. It was hard to keep on looking lost and sad, she thought. Because she didn't feel that way. She felt triumphant. She had more than paid Johnnie back for choking her, for slapping her in the face, for pushing her away from him as though she were dirt. When Momma heard anything about all this, she would be living at Perkins'. Then, as soon as the people got out of the house she and Johnnie had lived in, she'd go live there. It had been very easy. She was rid of Johnnie, she had Ed, and she could keep the job at the store.

Her satisfaction lasted until The Weasel came in. He walked over to her counter and said, "How's tricks, Glory?"

"Okay." If I act as though I'm awfully busy, she thought, and don't talk to him, he'll go away. I don't want him staring at these bruises I painted on my neck. He's the kind would reach over and rub them to see if they would come off.

"How's Ed this afternoon?" he asked.

"How should I know?"

"Ha, ha!" he said, and laughed so loud that Perkins looked up, surprised, and nearly fell from the ladder.

"Ain't you the one for a joke, though?" The Weasel said. "I seen you this afternoon, climbing over that tree that blocks Ed's road. You didn't know that was me in that car, did you?"

He crossed the store, heading for the counter where Perkins was. He looked back at Glory over his shoulder; his glance, sly, knowing. Then he winked.

21

MRS. GRAMBY PAUSED IN THE doorway of her living room. She had the uncomfortable feeling of having lost track of time, just since yesterday. Sometimes it telescoped, shortening so that she could not place an event in time. Sometimes it lengthened out, stretching ahead of her, frightening her. She now thought of time only in terms of Lillian.

It had been a beautiful morning, so beautiful that one doubted one's memory of the violence of last night's storm. Ordinarily she would have relished the serenity of the morning, for a gentle breeze was sweeping through the house. Sunlight, coming through the small-paned windows, had made a wavy pattern on her bedroom floor, enlivening the muted colors of the Chinese rug. But she had thought this was the day after Mearns had brought Lillian home—a bride; and she had stiffened with a fury that remained in her for the balance of the day.

Now she was thinking that time stretched ahead of her; that for a thousand years she would have to go on living under the same roof with Lillian; go on building up the smooth surface of politeness between them.

The thought made her infinitely weary. She could see Lillian at the dining table, Lillian in the halls, sitting in the living room. Lillian was a dead weight that would hang across her shoulders for limitless stretches of time; and her shoulders were too old, too tired, to carry even so much as the weight of her clothing.

Nonsense, she thought. It's the stuffy air in the living room. I am not carrying the burden of Lillian's weight. This bad air is making me breathe deeply and quickly. The Bates girl had lighted the lamps, one on the inlaid table near the front window, another at the far end of the room; and the candelabras, too. Candles and kerosene lamps exhausted the oxygen in the air so one had to breathe more deeply in order to fill one's lungs. The quickened breathing was making her heart beat faster.

The girl had been wise not to light the fire in the fireplace; for the room would have been unbearably warm. The Bates girl was wise and willing; but she couldn't help missing Cook and Neola and Portulacca on Thursdays when they were out of the house most of the day. Cook, of course, came back late at night. But Neola wouldn't be back until tomorrow morning. On their day off she always felt as though a loyal army had moved away, leaving her to face the enemy, alone.

That was probably what was wrong with her now. She had been alone in the house with Lillian most of the afternoon. And she had got the feeling that Lillian had been listening to her every movement, waiting to hear her steps on the stairs, the closing of a bathroom door, a sigh. It was a ridiculous idea, for Lillian had stayed upstairs in her room, with the door closed, until dinnertime.

After dinner Mrs. Gramby had gone upstairs to take a nap. But she had not slept. She had heard the Bates girl leave by the side door; and then later she had heard Lillian moving quietly about in the living room. Then Lillian, too, had gone out, banging the front door shut. If I had been asleep the sound of that heavy door being closed with such force would have awakened me.

Tonight, for a few hours, I will be free of her haggard face. By the time she returns from the whist game at Miss Susie's, I shall have gone to bed, thank God. Tired as I am, I could not spend another evening looking at her, being crushed by the burden of her guilt. She has disillusioned Mearns, completely and with finality; for she cut away his pride and his self-esteem and his belief in himself, cut them away from him with a sharp-edged knife. She has destroyed him—for men are destroyed by the knowledge that their wives have been intimate with other men.

Could this have been my fault, she wondered. I carried on an open battle against her, pushing her back and back, pushing her out of his life, day after day, week after week. I did it deliberately because I could never forgive her for marrying him. It was not difficult to do. I think faster than she does; and so I found a thousand ways in which to punish her for having had the temerity to marry him.

She sat down in the wing chair by the window; her mouth was trembling; and the hand which rested on the cane was shaking, uncontrollably. She gripped it with her other hand, forcing it to remain quiet; and she felt a tremor sweep through her body.

This sorrow of Mearns' has made me older, she thought. I have taken to standing, staring into space, while I think. And I do it though standing is painful, making my knees, my thighs ache unbearably. Yet I stood there bemused, aware of the painful tingling in the soles of my feet, but making no effort to sit down.

At this moment time bears bat wings; it is swooping about

me, shortening and shortening. She could see Mearns and Lillian being married in the church. She had turned her head away, staring out of the long windows at the leaves of the trees. I tried to make the best of it, she thought; to pretend a cordiality I did not feel, but Lillian sensed my hostility.

Yes, it may all have been my fault. After the ceremony Lillian and Mearns had gone to New York for a two weeks' honeymoon. Then they came back here to live. When I saw Lillian, leaning on his arm as they walked up the path to the front door; saw her brushing against him, kissing him, patting his cheek while she talked baby talk to him, I could not bear it. The sight of those cold eyes under that beflowered hat, the sound of her shrew's voice carefully pitched to tenderness, nauseated me.

Lillian had been living in the house just two days when she said, "Mother Gramby, I think I'll order new draperies for the living room the next time I go to New Haven. These are much too dark."

What else could I have done? If let alone she would have relegated me to a chimney corner in my own house. And I said sharply, "You'll do nothing of the kind. You will not change one thing in this house. If you cannot live in it as it is, then you and Mearns had better go elsewhere."

She had known that Mearns would not go anywhere else to live. It was not wholly devotion that held him in this house; it was also a lack of expense—no rent, no maids to pay, nothing. So Lillian had lived in another woman's house; and the other woman had told the help that not a chair was to be moved, not a bedspread changed or a picture put in place, unless she, Mrs. Gramby, ordered it done. Thus she had pushed Lillian into a corner and kept her there.

It was at that moment that she noticed there was a box of candy on the inlaid table beside her chair. She stared at it in surprise. It had been there on the table when she sat down, but she had been too engrossed in her thoughts to notice it. She lifted the lid, drew the box closer to the chair. Selecting a chocolate, she ate it quickly; then another, and another, without pausing to wonder who had put the box on the table.

What had Mearns been seeking when he married Lillian? Excitement? Passion? She made a wry face. Perhaps. But what he got was a small-town dressmaker, a cold, calculating woman. He must have been disappointed, for he had never given her an allowance. Every penny Lillian had got from him had been humbly requested and he had seen to it that she received it with a proper show of gratitude. His making her beg for money may have been the means he used to revenge himself for her coldness.

If she were someone else's daughter-in-law, I would say that I could almost see how she came to intimacy with that bowlegged man. For she must have been desperately disillusioned, too, what with the bedroom door kept open at night, the cats stalking in and out, the cats sleeping on her bed; no money of her own, no place of her own in another woman's house. When did she see that man; where did they meet? It wouldn't have been difficult for Lillian to meet him, anywhere, any time. I never cared where she went or what she did; how she spent her days; so long as she understood her place in my house.

But did I have the right to put her in some special "place"? I disliked her from the moment Mearns married her, and showed it. I won and I lost—at the same time. No, I lost a little more than I won. If revenge was what she wanted, she has it now. Mearns will never get over this.

She could see his face so plainly—crumpled, bewildered, frightened as he went out of the house to get into the taxi. She was tired, too tired, to think about Lillian any more. Her thoughts had become a confusion of images, of remembered sounds, of faces—last night's storm with the trees crashing down, rain beating against the windows, wind howling down the chimney, mixed with the phrases in Lillian's letter and with the vision of Mearns getting back into the taxi, his back bent, his shoulders slumped.

She picked up a book, tried to read. Mearns' face kept coming between her and the pages. She put the book down, nibbled another chocolate, eating it slowly. They hadn't really discussed the letter. He had gone out and got into the taxi and his face and hands had been quivering like those of a very old man. She wished he would come home soon. But there were no trains or buses running since the storm; and he had said he would be gone a few days. What was he doing now? Was he thinking of Lillian, despising her?

Lillian would live in this house. She would, eventually, live here and order Neola and Cook and Portulacca to do her bidding. No, she would probably get rid of them, insulting them when she gave them notice. The thought made her pull herself up from the chair. She got the letter from the safe and re-read it.

The slightest effort left her feeling exhausted, indescribably old. She leaned heavily on the cane as she stared at the letter. She put it back in the safe, closed the door, locked it. There was nothing she could do about it.

She resumed her seat by the window, reached for another chocolate, closed her eyes as she ate it. I could go to sleep sitting here, she thought. I suppose I feel like this because I know there is nothing I can do about these things that are wrong; these things that will take place after my death. But there was. She could make out a will. She thrust another chocolate into her mouth, thinking, I must stop eating these; but they are so delicious, the rich chocolate taste is on my tongue, far back in my throat, lingering there, somehow comforting, soothing.

Yes, I can make out a will. And the will could cause certain changes in the town. But her *reason* for the thing she would do would be vengeful. Could good come out of evil? People were a mixture of both. The town was like that—neither all good nor all evil. Lillian? Could one say the same thing about her?

Lillian had brought Glory, her daughter, up; seen her safely married. But that was because she knew the only way to free herself of the responsibility for Glory was to marry her off to some respectable young man.

It doesn't matter, anyway. We're all mixtures of good and evil. Who am I, Bertha Gramby, to be sitting in judgment on another woman? I am an old, old woman, with not too much longer left for living. Don't you see that I'm busy, don't bother me; can't you see I'm busy dying? Who said it? Don't interrupt me, can't you see I'm busy dying. Someone, recently—no matter.

What had made her think of dying? I suppose it is only natural to think of death at my age. Your bones tell you that you don't have too much longer left. What would it be like? Would it come swiftly and with violence; or would it be like drifting off to sleep—a slow delicious relaxing?

Mearns would be sorrowful, of course. They had been devoted to each other—but he would be all right; he would be financially secure. It was the one thing a parent liked to be sure of before death. The knowledge that one's children would be safe, that one's flesh would not go cold or hungry, was reassuring.

She reached for another chocolate; her hand hovered over the box, moving slowly toward one that was wrapped in gold tinfoil. When she touched it, conjecturing on what taste sensations were concealed by the shiny wrapper, she began to wonder where the box had come from. There was never any candy in the house these days; not since Doctor Williams had raised a fuss about her eating it. Mearns would not buy it, even if he were here and had known she wanted candy. If Neola knew there was a box of chocolates in the house, she would not place it on the living-room table.

As she unwrapped the gold foil from the chocolate, Neola's disapproving, slightly sorrowful face seemed to take shape before her eyes, to come between her and the candy. She popped the chocolate into her mouth, quickly.

Had Lillian placed this box here on the table? Tonight at dinner, the lines about her mouth had been deeper, the eyes were harder, more watchful. Her manner had changed, too. She was no longer obsequious. She had issued imperious orders to the Bates girl. The girl had resented the sound of Lillian's nagging voice and had stared at her with a sullen expression.

Mrs. Gramby pushed the box away with an irritated gesture. Of course Lillian had put the box there, knowing that she couldn't resist its contents. But for what purpose?

It was an effort to lean forward and open the table drawer. She felt as though the flesh had grown so heavy on her bones that it would be impossible for her to move. She couldn't help thinking that she was caged inside a mountain of flesh; and she was aware of a drifting, languorous feeling that urged her back toward the chair when she would move forward.

She felt inside the table drawer for the bakelite case that contained the insulin and the hypodermic needle; and not finding it, she bent farther forward, thinking, I must have pushed it far back in the drawer. I will have to get up and pull the drawer all the way out.

The thought of moving was unpleasant. If she sat still, leaned back in the chair, she would go to sleep. The thought of sleep tugged at her. It was like a hand beckoning to her to walk around a corner; a hand that promised sunlight and grass rippling in a gentle breeze, and the subdued sound of birds far off in the trees that surrounded a meadow.

Why, I must have been asleep, she thought. She gripped the cane firmly and pulled herself up out of the chair. The nearness of the table surprised her. From the amount of energy she had used in order to reach it, she had thought she would have to walk the length of the room and actually it was only a step. There must be something wrong, she thought; distances blur and lengthen out. Even this room that I know so well seems all wrong.

She studied the room; her glance wandering from the fireplace to the prisms on the candelabras, to the cats who blinked at her—their eyes yellow, wide open—on to the long windows at the other end of the room. The trouble was that they had moved Mr. Gramby's casket. Why had they done it?

Then she shivered because she knew that time had telescoped again, shortening, shortening, until it seemed only an hour ago that Mr. Gramby had lain in his casket at the end of the room. His flesh had changed. The only familiar thing about him was the long sweep of the nose—its arrogance accentuated by death. The room had been filled with the odor of lilacs. He had loved them; so she had had great masses of them brought in from the garden. "Lilac blooming perennial—"

Why am I standing here? she thought. I am so tired and yet I stand here. Then she remembered that she was going to reach far back in the drawer for the bakelite case. She pulled the drawer out full length, then took it out of the table; and holding it in her hand, she stared at it. It was empty.

The surprise of finding the drawer empty kept her standing, staring down at it, not believing in its emptiness; expecting that some trick of sight, some momentary failure of vision, would pass and she would see the case, would open it and find the needle, the insulin, the little bottle of alcohol, the cotton—

"I am Bertha Gramby," she said, aloud. "I am old Mrs.

Gramby as they call me here in the town. I am standing in my living room, holding a table drawer in my hand. I am looking for a case containing insulin—"

It was not there. She looked again and it was not there. She felt a little foolish at having spoken aloud, but the sound of her voice had reassured her. The bakelite case was gone.

And as she realized what it meant, the muscles of her hand and arm relaxed. The drawer went out of her hand, landing on the floor. She sat down in the chair, glad to sit, for she could feel all of her muscles relaxing. In another moment she felt as though she would have gone to sleep standing up.

She closed her eyes, leaned far back in the chair. Her heart was beating heavily, slowly. As she listened to the sound of it, she became aware of the silence in the house; the house stretched around and above her—vast reaches of empty space undisturbed by voices or by a football.

Her mind returned to the insulin. But I need it now, she thought. I have to have it. I've eaten all that candy. I must telephone to Mr. Fraser and he will send insulin and a hypodermic needle and send it quickly. She leaned forward, ready to get up, and then settled back in the chair, for she remembered that the telephone was not working.

There wasn't anyone in the house. This was Neola's day off. She would get a flashlight and walk down to the drugstore. Most of the tree trunks had been pulled aside so there was a clear path. She wouldn't have any difficulty. It wasn't a long walk.

In another minute I'll get up, she thought. I'll sit here and rest and then I'll go to the drugstore. Her head nodded, she dozed. Then she jerked her head erect, fighting the feeling of weariness, the desire for sleep.

She was aware that she was breathing as though she were asleep—long, slow, deep inhalations of air. Her heart seemed to have slowed, too. Its beat was strangely soothing, not at all painful. It was like a hammer being swung in slow motion against her chest—but the hammer was cushioned so that the blows were like something nudging her—slow, so slow, so forceful, growing slower, harder, hitting harder.

She knew a moment of panic. This is what death is like, she thought—a great weariness, an inertia that creeps over one almost unaware, paralyzing the impulse to motion. She acknowledged the fact that she could not get up out of the chair, would never be able to. She would die in this chair by the window. It was nothing to fear, for death was just a slowing-down of heart and breath—perceptible, recognizable. No nightmare terror bringing with it a convulsive tremor of muscles and nerves, but just this quiet, slow, rather pleasant slipping away.

She thought of Mearns and regretted that she had left so many things undone. Lillian would have the house. She told herself, even dying you think of this house as though it were a world which Lillian would inherit.

I have done what I ought not to have done, and for those things which I have not done which I ought to have done, please God—it went something like that; but she could never remember it correctly; not that it mattered now. "Ought not to have done," it was like the ticking of a clock, slow, regular, rhythmic.

I didn't make out the will. I have never made a will. Perhaps Mearns, perhaps—she moved her hands—too difficult. Any kind of movement was out of the question.

Then she thought, "Who shall have mind on thee after death, and who shall pray for thee?" It seemed to her that the words had been said aloud in the room, gravely, slowly. Would Lillian pray for her, Portulacca, Mearns, the town—would any of them pray for her? Neola would. She was sure of that.

But the town would forget her—the privet hedges around the

houses, the apple trees and the pear trees in the back yards, the uncut hay fields, the corn with the tassels turning brown, the mock orange and the syringa, the long gentle curve of the river, the lanes and the narrow country roads—all of them would forget her. Why not? What had she ever done for the town, the trees, the curve in the river? The people in the houses, the houses with the clapboards painted white and the blinds painted green, they would forget, too—easy to forget an old woman—

A selfish old woman. Ah, no, not that. But had she ever done anything save for herself and for Mearns? She had given freely of quotations and that was all. Many times in her life she had paused to censure someone by saying, "'Time shall come when thou shalt desire one day or one hour for thine amendment and thou wottest not whether thou shalt get it.'"

Now the words were being said to her and she could not bear them. If only she had one more day, just one more day. She turned her head toward the window, nothing but blackness outside—no lights, no movement, no voices. She was cut off.

If she got out of the chair, got the flashlight—but she couldn't. The drowsiness was like a wave, soothing her, lapping around her, saying that she only needed to sit quietly and she would find herself in a peaceful place. "Sooner or later delicate death—" Time seemed to be stopping, the telescoping, the lengthening-out had ceased.

"Thou shalt desire one day or one hour—" She did not know whether she had spoken the words aloud or whether she had thought them inside her mind. She made a tremendous effort and forced her hand inside the pocket of her dress and slowly pulled out a handkerchief. For a long moment she sat staring at it, and then, with an effort that left her panting, exhausted, she looped one end of the handkerchief through the crocheted pull on the window shade.

Someone might see it and wonder at it, and come in and find her before it was too late. Though the chances were that they would not. She leaned back in the chair, closing her eyes. Her head fell forward on her chest. The only sound in the room was the curiously deep, regular sound of her breathing.

22

I REMEMBER WHEN ELECTRIC LIGHTS WERE first installed in the town of Lennox. My father, whose reaction was fairly typical of the period, objected to them as being a wicked invention of the devil, expressly designed to ruin man's eyesight—the light being too harsh; and to soften his moral fiber. He predicted a general lessening in self-reliance because the use of electricity would eliminate a whole series of character-building tasks.

When I lit the lamps in the store that night, four of them—one at the cigar counter, one at the candy counter, one at the fountain, one in the back room—I could not help thinking that I much preferred having my moral fiber softened and my eyesight ruined by using electricity. I had spent an hour washing lamp chimneys, trimming wicks, and filling lamps. In spite of this, I could not read because their soft yellow light was hopelessly inadequate—most of the store was in darkness. There was, too, a smell of kerosene in the air, a smoky odor that stayed in my throat and nose, making me cough.

Because of this dim light, I did not recognize Neola when she came in later in the evening. The doorway was so shadowed that I could not tell whether it was a man or a woman who had opened the door. There was such haste about her entrance that I received the impression that whoever it was had not walked in, but had been thrust in by some enormous pressure which fairly blew them through the door.

Neola's skin is dark brown, and she had on a dark coat. Even after she was inside and moving toward me, I could not identify who or what she was. I saw a hurrying figure coming at me so fast that I instinctively moved back, away from the counter, close to the shelves behind me.

"Mr. Fraser," she said. She was panting and her voice, normally low in pitch, was high, excited.

"Yes?" I peered at her, frowning; recognizing her, but puzzled by the haste of her movements and by the excitement in her voice.

"It's me. Neola. Mrs. Gramby's sick. Doctor Williams wants you to come right away and bring these things with you."

She stuck one of Doc's prescriptions practically into my eyes. I held it near the lamp, reading it.

"And please hurry."

"I am hurrying. But I've got to know what I'm hurrying *with*, haven't I?" I spoke sharply because illness in one as old and stout as Mrs. Gramby is likely to be fatal. Doc's list puzzled me. He wanted physiologic salt solution, five per cent solution of sodium bicarb, and plain insulin—Mrs. Gramby uses protamine zinc insulin, I thought, wondering why he had changed it—a very strange list indeed.

Neola was walking up and down, up and down. That kind of nervous movement bothers me. It distracts my attention. Part of my mind was listening to the sound of her light, quick step and the other part of it was rechecking Doc's list.

I started asking her questions in the hope that once she began to talk, she would talk freely, and thus relieve the tension that was making her pace the floor.

"What's the matter with Mrs. Gramby?" I said, walking toward the back room.

She followed me as far as the edge of the candy counter and stood still, watching me as I made up the solution of sodium bicarb.

"I don't know," she said. "She was sitting in that chair by the window. I thought she was asleep when I first went in. But I couldn't rouse her. So I went and got Doctor Williams."

"I thought this was your day off. What were you doing there tonight?"

"It is my day off. I went out for a walk and I saw a handkerchief in the window. We always pull the window shades to a certain point all over the house. When I walked by, it seemed to me there was something wrong about the living-room windows. So I went back again, and walked up close and then I saw that someone had tied one of Mr. Gramby's best linen handkerchiefs to the curtain pull. I went inside to find out what it was doing there."

"Mmmm," I said. She made a nervous movement that suggested she was going to start that hurried pacing of the floor again. So I said, quickly, "How is it you were out walking with all the trees down? Seems like a queer night for a walk."

She frowned, hesitated, and then said, "I was trying to make up my mind about something."

"Walking helps sometimes." I took a package of insulin from a shelf near the door, and then checked each item on the list. As I wrapped them up, it occurred to me that if Neola had something on her mind, and if this was her day off and The Portegee's day off, then she had gone walking in order to decide whether she would marry him. It has to be a weighty matter to send one out walking through unlit streets, stumbling over the trunks of uprooted trees.

I reached this conclusion because I remembered the whopping big box of candy The Portegee had purchased, recently. Recently? It was yesterday, the morning of the storm. But it seemed as if a year or more had passed since then. Lil had bought a box of candy, too. When was that? Just this afternoon. The Gramby House must have an unusually large supply of candy in it—especially so since no one there ate the stuff.

"You think it's Mrs. Gramby's heart?" I said.

She shrugged her shoulders. "I don't know," she said, frowning.

"You didn't have to wait for me," I said. "You could have gone back and I'd have been right over."

"Doctor Williams told me to take his car because I could come and go much faster. He wanted me to bring you back to help him get her up the stairs."

When I told her I was ready to go, she went out of the door, ahead of me, running. I locked the door and hung my emergency sign on it, the one that reads, "Have patience. Back as quick as possible."

I hadn't got the car door closed before Neola started the engine. She evidently didn't let the clutch take hold because I've never heard such an outrageous sound of gears being stripped as we pulled off. The car gave a jerk that nearly snapped my neck in two.

The Gramby house is almost at the corner of the Post Road and Whippoorwill Lane. It is within spitting distance of the store because Whippoorwill Lane is a short side street, straight as an arrow. It begins at the Post Road and ends in front of my door. But that ride with Neola was undoubtedly the longest and roughest ride I'll ever have and live to tell the story. She drove Doc's car as though it were an unbroken, wild horse. We went forward in sudden darts and dashes, swooping suddenly from right to left.

Tree trunks that had been pulled to one side of the road suddenly loomed up right in front of the headlights. Neola would yank the wheel in the opposite direction and the next instant we would be heading straight for disaster on the other side of the road. I was too startled to protest.

We took a breath-takingly sharp turn into the Post Road. This brought us out on the left-hand side of the road. Neola pulled the car to the right and then abruptly back to the left and slammed on the emergency brake. Thus we suddenly arrived at a dead standstill in Mrs. Gramby's driveway.

Neola was half out of the car before I could speak. And though I was desperately worried about Mrs. Gramby, I stopped Neola long enough to say, "Neola, did you ever drive a car before?"

"No, I didn't. This is the first time," she said quietly and hurried off toward the house.

At sixty-five a man is too old to start riding around in a car that is being steered by a female who's never had her hands on a wheel before. My knees had gone so soft and rubbery that when I tried to get out of the car I just sat right back down on the seat. I was mad enough to kill Doc Williams. Finally I hauled myself off the seat and started toward the house, thinking that Doc was getting old and foolish and that this was one time I was going to tell him exactly what I thought of him.

Doc was standing in front of the fireplace in the living room with his hands folded behind his back and his mouth pursed up, as he looked in the direction of Mrs. Gramby's chair. She was slumped over in it and at first glance appeared to be asleep. Doc looked so worried that I decided I would postpone telling him what I thought of him for sending Neola to get me.

"Got everything?" he said.

"Yes."

"Let's see if we can get her up the stairs."

"I'll fix the bed—" Neola said.

"It's all fixed. I fixed it, and filled the hot-water bottles while you were gone," Doc said.

It was then that I noticed the strange sound of Mrs. Gramby's breathing. I thought she was asleep and breathing deeply and regularly. But her cheeks were flushed, her head fallen forward, and she was so relaxed that she looked completely lifeless.

Between us we got her up the stairs and on the bed in her room. It was not an easy job, for she was a large woman.

"What is it?" I asked just before I went out of the room.

"It could be diabetic coma. But it isn't, really. It's her heart. She's been badly frightened some time during the last couple of days," Doc said.

There was no further reason for me to stay there. I should have gone back to the store, but I wanted to know that Mrs. Gramby was going to pull through before I left. So I went downstairs and waited in the living room.

I had been sitting in a chair by the fireplace about twenty minutes when Neola came in the room.

"Has she come around yet?" I asked.

She shook her head. "He said it might be quite a while."

"Funny she should go into a coma. Doc always said she had a mild form of diabetes."

She didn't answer. She pulled a small table around in front of the chair where I was sitting. I noticed that she kept glancing at the table by the window. After she left the room, I walked over and looked at the table, too. The box of candy Lil had bought was lying there—the whole top layer was gone.

Mrs. Gramby was very fond of chocolates and Lil knew it; but there must be something more than that involved.

Neola came in with an armful of wood, started a fire in the

fireplace. Once she had it blazing, she stood there poking at the logs.

"You'll put it out that way," I said and walked over and took the poker away from her.

"The insulin was always there in the table drawer—a black bakelite case that contained alcohol and needles and a syringe and cotton—everything she needed for an injection. And it's gone," she said.

"Gone?" I looked at the table drawer lying on the floor. I had noticed it, but I thought that somehow in the confusion of finding Mrs. Gramby it had fallen on the floor—don't ask me how.

"Yes. Doctor Williams says that's what frightened her so. She couldn't find it and she was here alone and her heart isn't too strong anyway."

"Where's Lil?"

"She plays whist at Miss Susie Brandford's on Thursday nights," Neola said and left the room.

I knew Lil to be a hard woman, not overscrupulous, but I must confess I had never thought her capable of murder. I suppose one would call it murder—at least the intention was there.

Neola re-entered the room carrying a round silver tray which she placed on a small table near the fireplace. "I thought you'd like a cup of tea," she said.

After I finished drinking the tea, I very nearly went to sleep. It was warm in front of the fire, the tea had soothed me. My eyes were half-closed and I saw the room as a long space filled with a soft flickering light that was reflected in the burnished surface of the mahogany sofa, in the crystal prisms of the candelabras, in the long lustrous draperies at the windows. The light from the lamps and the candles and the fireplace was not strong enough to illuminate all of the room. There were deep shadows in the corners.

As I sat there nodding, I kept thinking that it was out of such shadowed corners that murder crept. This was a friendly gracious room, but a box of candy had been left on a table to tempt a diabetic old woman who loved candy and who would become panic-stricken if the insulin she thought she needed was not ready to her hand.

It was quiet in the room, save for the crackling of the logs and overhead an occasional footstep muffled by the thick carpet on the floor of Mrs. Gramby's bedroom. The cats made no sound. They were sitting hunched over, feet tucked under them—two on the sofa opposite me and one in Mrs. Gramby's chair by the window.

The silence induced a reflective mood in me. My thoughts slipped along easily; now here on the firelight, now there on the cats. Finally they settled on Mrs. Gramby.

I have often expressed a dislike for females. But Mrs. Gramby was as fine a specimen of humanity as I have ever known. Had she been younger I would have married her. But she was almost twenty years older than I; and it would have been a most unsuitable match.

With each passing year she grew a little stouter; until finally her excessive weight slowed her movements to the point where she was more and more dependent on her cane. She was one of my best magazine customers. For years my day was made brighter because she came limping into the store, shortly before noon, saying, "Good morning, Mr. Fraser. And what have you for me to read today?"

After much discussion she would select a copy of *The Atlantic* or *Harper's* or some other good magazine.

There is something very flattering about being called "Mr. Fraser" in a town in which one is known as "Pop." I accept the latter title with what grace I can muster, for I recognize it as a palpable indication of my approaching old age. It suggests a portly figure, bifocal glasses, and an upper plate; and to my intense dismay I have acquired all three.

But to return to Mrs. Gramby—her taste in books and magazines changed after Mearns and Lil were married. She took to reading the most arrant trash—love stories, detective stories. She borrowed them from my circulating library at the rate of two or three a week.

When she returned these implausible novels, her only comment was, "Please give me two more." Yet she had a fine mind for a female (or a man either, for that matter)—inquisitive, retentive, logical.

I read one of those books after she returned a package of them. The kindest statement I can make about it is to say that it offered a momentary escape to a person who desperately needed to escape from some unbearable here-and-now. I decided that Mrs. Gramby was using those novels of romantic love, of impossible feats of detection, in order to escape from the fact of Mearns' marriage, to escape from the reality of Lil's presence in her house. If she could have viewed Mearns from my front window, of a Sunday morning, she would not have been surprised and shocked by his marriage.

On Sundays Mearns always walked down to the drugstore to buy a number of newspapers. Whenever he picked up a copy of *The Tattler* he would say, "I'll take this along for the servants."

The Tattler is a weekly newspaper which specializes in unpleasant stories of sexual perversion and promiscuity. It is the only paper I have ever seen that prints the detailed verbatim testimony in divorce cases.

Mearns read *The Tattler* with avidity. I could look out of the front bay window of the store and see him reading it; holding the theater section of *The New York Times* in front of it, his glasses sparkling in the sun, his head thrust forward almost inside the paper. To this day I do not think he knows that my store window is so located that I could look right over his shoulder.

Thus I was not taken unaware by his marriage. I am certain that he expected Lil's lean shanks would offer him the same hot excitement he had found recorded in *The Tattler's* shabby pages. He should have known better. Females who have the kind of cold and calculating look that Lil had never whole-heartedly respond to love-making. They always have their minds focused on what they can get out of it.

Mrs. Gramby grew older and slower after Mearns married Lil. I tried to imagine what it would be like to live with Lil. It is one thing to have a grasping female as your dressmaker; it is quite another and more serious matter to suddenly acquire her as your daughter-in-law.

If Mrs. Gramby died, it would mean that Lil's presence in this house had finally led to murder.

I knew I ought to go back to the store, that Doc Williams and Neola would take care of Mrs. Gramby. But I did not move. I was waiting for Lil to come back from Miss Susie's. I wanted to see the expression on her face.

23

THERE WERE TWO CARD TABLES set up in Miss Susie Brandford's living room. Lil, who made the fourth and necessary person on Thursday nights, sat at one of the tables with two old ladies and a Mr. Wormsley. Her fingers had developed an annoying clumsiness. Each time it was her turn to shuffle, the deck of cards slipped between her fingers. Twice she had clutched at them, quickly, awkwardly, and the entire deck had fanned out on the floor.

The second time it happened, Miss Susie's roomers helped pick up the scattered cards, sighing and groaning as they bent over. The sight of their hands, reaching for the cards, set up a nervous quivering in Lil's stomach.

They were such hideously old hands, she thought, the joints swollen, the nails thick and ridged, the skin at the wrists loose over the bone. They might have been Mrs. Gramby's hands, reaching toward life, clutching at life, eluding and denying death as they reached out.

When she extended her hand to receive the cards, her mouth was dry; her body was wet with perspiration. She fanned her face with the cards, trying to dispel the sudden flashing wave of heat that had enveloped her.

Miss Susie looked up from her crocheting. "You must be having a hot flash, Lillian. You're just about the right age for 'em," she observed maliciously. And then with more kindness in her voice she said, "Want me to open a window?"

Lil shook her head, too distracted to resent Miss Susie. If she only knew what was going on inside the Gramby house at this moment, she could rid herself of the nervousness that was plucking at her hands, pinching her stomach. She hadn't done anything so awful. She had simply helped Nature take its course. Mrs. Gramby was a greedy old woman. She wasn't responsible if Mrs. Gramby lacked self-control. All she, Lillian, had done was try to make certain that she wouldn't go on being cheated out of the things that were rightfully hers. She had always been cheated. But not any more.

As the game progressed, Mr. Wormsley went through the cards at the end of each hand and shrilly asserted that one of these nights he'd find somebody had cheated, and glared at Lil. Each time he said it the old ladies tittered; and Miss Susie smiled as she jerked the crochet hook back and forth through the twine.

Lil began to feel as if she had been sitting in Miss Susie's living room for the last century; listening to the tremulous voices of the old ladies; trying to pay attention to the whist game, while her thoughts were concentrated on Mrs. Gramby. Cook might have returned right after she left the house; or the old woman might have stared at the box of candy in cold surprise and never touched it; might at this moment be sitting in the big chair by the window, calmly reading.

She wished she had stayed at home. The old ladies were looking at her, noting her shaking hands, her nervousness. But she had to come here. It was the perfect alibi. And so tonight, for the first time, she had come to Miss Susie's without resentment.

When Mearns had first insisted that she take the place left vacant by his mother, who no longer went out at night, she had been furious. She had been afraid to defy him openly, so she had meekly acquiesced. For a year and a half she had played whist here. Once a week.

To be shut up in the house with his mother was bad enough. This was worse. Miss Susie's ancient roomers always gave her the feeling that she had been entombed while still alive. That feeling was heightened tonight; for as she looked at them she kept seeing Mrs. Gramby. All of them resembled the old woman, in one way or another. No, they didn't resemble her; they merely suggested her presence because they were so old. Even Miss Susie, who was so thin her bones threatened to come through her wrinkled skin, suggested Mrs. Gramby; for when she talked Lil could hear the faint click of her false teeth.

At nine o'clock, Miss Susie said complacently, "I hear Glory and Johnnie have separated."

"You heard what?" Lil said angrily.

There was a little murmur from the tables. Mr. Wormsley bent forward, the old ladies laid down their cards.

"Yes," Miss Susie said. "I was up in Perkins' store, late this afternoon, and Mr. Perkins told me Glory's going to live at his house. It seems that Johnnie beat her something terrible; tried to choke her to death. So she's left him." Miss Susie looked down at her crocheting, ripped out a few stitches. She was aware that the roomers knew she had not yet reached the climax of the story and she took a perverse pleasure in keeping them waiting. Finally she said: "The Weasel says she was up at that Mr. Ed Barrell's place during the storm. I believe he saw Glory coming out of there. Didn't you know anything about it, Lillian?"

"No," Lil said shortly. "And I don't believe it." She hadn't paid much attention to what Glory had been babbling about day before yesterday. Was that what she had tried to tell her? What had

Glory said, anyway? Something about Johnnie wanting to go to New York. That was all.

Glory needn't think she was going to come and live with her. There wasn't any room. And even after the Gramby House belonged to her, Glory was going to have to shift for herself. She had made her bed, now let her lie in it. Ed Barrell. What did he have to do with it? Did Glory know that she and Ed had once been—well, friends? Men have a loose way of talking when they're in bed with a woman. Ed probably told Glory. Glory might be planning blackmail. She wished she would start something. She just wished she'd try it.

"Let's get on with the game," Lil said abruptly. "It's your play, Mr. Wormsley."

It was ten-thirty before Miss Susie folded up the dishcloth she was crocheting and stuck the crochet hook in the ball of twine. Watching her, Lil thought, Thank God the night is nearly over. In another minute I would have flung the cards in their faces and run out of here.

"It's bedtime," Miss Susie said.

Lil pushed her chair away from the card table. The old ladies tried to hold her a few minutes longer, in order to put off the moment when they would have to go to bed. But she ignored them, saying, "Good night. It's been a pleasant evening."

In the hall outside, she put her coat on, picked up the flashlight she had brought with her. She felt in the pocket of her coat, making certain that the bakelite case was still there. It couldn't be anywhere else, yet she was so nervous she knew she would continue feeling for it. Her fingers found it. She kept her hand on it so that if Miss Susie's inquisitive eyes should note the way her pocket bulged, Miss Susie would think it was bulging because she had her hand there.

Miss Susie opened the street door for her. "You're in an awful hurry tonight, Lillian. Is Mrs. Gramby feeling all right?"

"She's fine. You asked me about her when I first came in. Remember?"

Then she left, walking so swiftly that she stumbled over the branch of a tree and muttered, "Damn it." Miss Susie's second inquiry about Mrs. Gramby had sent a prickling fear through her. Long before she reached the Gramby House, she was looking for lights in the windows. She thought she saw a faint yellow light at an upstairs window but she was not certain.

When she reached the driveway, she stood motionless, suddenly aware of two things: there were lights in Mrs. Gramby's bedroom; and there was a car parked in the driveway. She directed the beam of the flashlight on it and saw that Doctor Williams' roadster was crossways in the drive; the front wheels were at a crazy angle, suggesting that he had arrived in such a tearing hurry he wouldn't even take time to park it properly.

She looked up at the light in Mrs. Gramby's room, thinking, I don't know whether she's alive or dead. I don't know who found her. I have to go into the house and I am afraid. I must have been crazy to do a thing like that. What made me do it?

She walked slowly up the flagstone walk, paused with her hand on the door, closed her eyes. She had to get her face straightened out. Should she be surprised or not show anything or what?

Footsteps were coming up the walk behind her. She wanted to turn around and see who it was, and couldn't. She stood still, one hand on the doorknob, waiting, expecting that a hand would fall on her shoulder, a heavy hand; and that she would hear a man's voice say, "You're caught. You didn't get away with it. Come along."

Instead, Cook's high-pitched, sibilant voice said, "Is there something wrong?"

He was standing so close to her that his voice was a hissing that sounded directly in her ear. She could smell the wine he had been drinking. The need to get away from him impelled her through the door, into the hall, and then the sound of his footsteps close behind her sent her straight on into the living room.

The room seemed to be full of people. All of them were staring at her. She had the feeling that the moment before she entered, they had been talking about her, and she wanted to run up the stairs, run away from this room full of strangers. Then she saw that they were not strangers. Doctor Williams was standing in front of the fireplace; Mr. Fraser, the druggist, was sitting in the middle of the sofa, his hands folded across his stomach, and the light from the fire gleamed on the smooth surface of his bald head; Neola was standing in the center of the room and, though this was her day off, she had on a dark uniform and a white cap and apron.

They looked as though they were held in a spell of some kind, not moving, not talking; but staring at her with an open question in their eyes, an accusation. She was aware that Cook had walked past her. He, too, was now standing in the room, watching her. His eyes were small in his fat, insolent face. They were like—what—like a pig's eyes.

Though she knew she ought to keep her wits about her, ought to keep her mind on these silent, staring people, she began thinking about Mike, the white pig she'd raised. It was years ago. She had decided that a pig was an economical way of providing meat for her and Glory. So she bought a baby pig. To her dismay he consumed great quantities of food. As he grew larger, she developed a deep dislike for him. His gluttonous appetite, his impatient grunting if not fed on schedule, made her want to beat him. But she dared not club him because he represented food and was therefore too valuable to injure.

His little eyes had followed her every movement, just as Cook's eyes were doing now. When she opened the back door and walked quietly down the yard, carrying his food, he was always waiting for her, having somehow sensed her approach. He would stand close to the bars of the pen, staring at her; his little eyes, alert, greedy, his jowls quivering; and his fat pig's face was as stubborn and as arrogant as though she were a paid servant who had been a little late in serving his meal.

She jerked her eyes away from Cook. Doctor Williams seemed the least hostile of them all, so she looked at him and said, "Is—is there anything the matter?"

Doctor Williams cleared his throat twice, teetered back and forth on his heels, and said, "Well, yes, and no."

She waited for him to continue, but he didn't say anything else. Mrs. Gramby wasn't in the room. If she didn't ask about her they would think it strange and if she did—no, she had to ask. Why didn't some of the others break this awful silence? She hated them for their silence.

"Is Mrs. Gramby sick?" she said hesitantly.

"Yes, she is," Doctor Williams said. "As a matter of fact, it is a wonder she is not dead. But—she isn't. Apparently the age of miracles has not yet ended. She'll be in bed for a while, but she'll be all right."

Lil turned toward the door, thinking, I'll go upstairs and lie down. Am I sorry—regret, relief? I don't know. I don't even know what made me do it. That storm last night, and her walking up and down and the cats—it got too much—I don't know. At least none of them will ever know what happened. Should I offer—no, yes—because if I don't—

"Is there anything I can do?" she asked, pausing in the doorway.

Doctor Williams shook his head. Perhaps I ought to ask what happened, she thought. No. Because after all the old lady had a bad heart and it could have been almost anything; better not ask. But she couldn't help glancing at the table. The drawer was on the floor. Then they knew that the insulin was gone. She suddenly remembered the bakelite case in the pocket of her coat. It made a bulge there. That's why they were staring at her. They knew. She was worse off now than she was before. She had destroyed herself, but the rest of them—the tomcats, the insolent help, the old lady—they were indestructible. They would never die.

Cook sat down in the chair by the window, in the chair where Mrs. Gramby usually sat. He was staring at the box of candy on the table. There was contempt in his little eyes, on his fat, stubborn face. She thought the way his plump hands, in the yellow gloves, were resting on his cane was a further indication of his contempt for her.

"Get out of that chair!" she said. Her voice was out of control; it was high in pitch, kept going higher. "Get in the kitchen where you belong."

Cook didn't move, didn't answer. He simply shifted his stare from the box of candy to her face; his too-small eyes concentrating on her face. She shouted at him, "Get out of here! Get out of here! You damn bohunk!"

"Now, Lil," Pop Fraser said. His voice was disapproving.

Cook settled back in the chair. "You go to hell," he said softly.

She took a quick step toward him and Doctor Williams grabbed her arm. "You're upset, Lil," he said. "You'd better go upstairs and go to bed. I know there's nothing more unnerving than a murder that doesn't quite come off."

I'll pull him out of that chair myself, Lil thought. I'll kick him back to the kitchen. I'll use his own cane on his fat rump. She tried to twist out of Doctor Williams' grasp and then she stood still, forgetting Cook; because her mind had echoed Doctor Williams' words: "A murder that doesn't quite come off."

He had said "murder." That was the word they would use when they told Mearns about it. There was no question but what they would tell him.

She shook off Doctor Williams' restraining hand, aware that they were looking at her, watching her face, waiting for what she was going to say.

Turning her back on them, she went out into the hall, started up the stairs. She had to deny it, quickly. She forced herself to turn her head, look down into the room. Doctor Williams was frowning at her and she said coldly, talking to him, "I don't know what you mean."

Upstairs, the hall was dark. She had to use her flashlight. The door of Mrs. Gramby's room was ajar. There was a dim light near the bed. She paused outside the room, listening. Mrs. Gramby was breathing softly, evenly, as though she were asleep.

Walking down the hall toward the bedroom that she shared with Mearns, she kept thinking, "A murder that doesn't quite come off." Then it wasn't a murder at all. But the intention was there. The Grambys would use that against her, threatening her with it.

She lit the kerosene lamp that stood on the bureau and then closed the door. Glory would pick a time like this to leave that Roane boy. Glory probably thought she was coming here to live, had perhaps counted on it. Glory was an empty-headed fool.

She's exactly like me, she thought. They say you shouldn't ever put all your eggs in one basket and that's what I did. That's what Glory's done. But Glory had no reason for doing it. She's irresponsible. She always was. She'll just have to lie down in that bed of rocks she's made for herself; and get used to it the best way she can.

What can I do now? I don't care what they know, I'm not going to leave here. I don't care what they think or what they say, whether they tell Mearns or not. They'll have to put me out because I'll never leave of my own free will. I know the Grambys—mother and son. Don't I know them, though? Know them well enough to hate them. But they won't put me out. The Gramby pride wouldn't allow them to. They couldn't bear what people would say.

I'll go on living here as though nothing had happened. I'll sit and wait it out. One of these days she'll die, of her own accord, and then I'll be Mrs. Mearns Gramby and boss of this house, and the first person I'll kick out of it will be that fat pig of a cook.

She undressed, blew out the lamp, and got into bed. One of the cats scratched at the door, mewing gently. He'll never get in here tonight, she thought.

The cat yowled, making a sound so loud and so unpleasant that she covered her ears with her hands. He would probably howl outside the door for hours. She uncovered her ears to listen. His cry was outraged, as though he were possessed of a malicious human intelligence. Let him claw at the door and caterwaul until his throat was raw, until his claws gave out.

There was a knock at the door. "Come in," she said, startled, and sat up in bed.

The door opened. "Leon III wants to come in," Neola said. "We were afraid the sound would disturb Mrs. Gramby."

Before Lil could protest, she heard the sound of the door being shut. She could not see the cat, but she heard him mewing in an annoying, satisfied way. Then he jumped up on the foot of the bed. She pulled her feet up close to her body, buried her head in the pillow, disregarding the damage she was doing to her curls. Leon III was purring. It was a more unpleasant sound than his mewing; and she pulled the blanket over her head to shut out the persistent buzzing. She could still hear it through the covers, a sound so loud it suggested all his internal organs—his lungs, stomach, throat, heart—were vibrating in an obscene song.

The vibration seemed to pass from the cat into her, creeping up the bones of her feet, to her legs, to her thighs. She sat up and with a sudden swift gesture of her arm threw him off on the floor.

There was a thump when he hit the floor. He made an angry sound in his throat, a shrill outraged cry, and then he hissed at her. Almost immediately afterward, he jumped back on the bed. She could not see him, for the room was dark, but she was certain he was sitting up straight, near the foot of the bed, glaring at her.

Finally she located the yellow glow of his eyes and she drew the covers close about her throat. Then, appalled at the thought that he might leap at her face, clawing it while she slept, she pulled the covers over her head. And as she lay there, shuddering, she started to cry.

Cook spent all of the next morning making beef broth for Mrs. Gramby. The Portegee came into the kitchen, carrying an armload of wood, and paused to watch Cook sample the broth. Then he turned to Neola, grinning. "He's tasted it ten times so far, when I brought in coal, when I brought in wood for the downstairs fireplaces, when I brought in flowers—"

Neola interrupted him with a gesture. "Don't tease him," she said. "This is a special broth. He says it'll give her strength."

The Portegee said, "Maybe," and started up the back stairs, his back bent a little from the weight of the wood.

Neola watched him, thinking, That's the way he will look when he's an old man, not quite bent over, but a little sagged from the weight of his years. He's got such a good heart; and there is so much of hate in this house, so little love—

She sighed and, picking up a tray, placed a white cloth on it. She would use the best silver, the Meissen china, and one of the old thin goblets; and perhaps Mrs. Gramby might show some interest in food when she saw the tray. With roses in the small

Crown Derby vase, and the vase, here at the side, the tray was quite beautiful.

"I wonder where Portulacca found the roses," she said.

"Him?" Cook shrugged, tasted the broth again. "Ah!" he said, "a little bit of heaven. Him? The Portegee?"

"How did he get to be a little bit of heaven?"

"I speak of the broth," Cook said with dignity. "But that Portulacca, that man would find a rose in a mine far under the earth. Flowers call out to him. Why would you wonder about him finding them? Ask how a hunting dog finds the partridge, ask how a bee finds the nectar." He paused, stirred the broth gently, added an infinitesimal sprinkle of salt, tasted it again. "Or ask how a man finds a maid," he said slyly.

Neola ignored him. How did he know that she and Portulacca were going to be married? He couldn't know. She hadn't known it herself until this morning. She had made up her mind to refuse him the next time he asked her because she didn't believe in the possibility of a happy marriage, not after being married to Chowder Head.

But Portulacca met her in the hall. She was carrying Mrs. Gramby's breakfast tray—nothing but liquids and all of them untouched. And he took the tray out of her hands and put it down on the table under the long gilt mirror, and right there in the upstairs hall he put his arms around her and kissed her and told her that he loved her. "You looked so sad I couldn't help it," he said afterward.

She supposed it was the storm and the nearness of death and the sight of Mrs. Gramby lying there so weak and so unhappy; and Mr. Mearns coming home this morning and he and his wife sitting in the living room like frozen people, not talking, afraid of each other and afraid of their fear; and the hush in the rooms as though there had been a death in the house. Portulacca stood there in front of her, warm and alive; and his arms were protective and gentle; so that she said, yes, because she couldn't help herself. And she was glad that she had said yes.

"When is the wedding?" Cook asked. And when she looked at him in blank surprise, he said, "Your wedding. You and that Portulacca."

"How did you know?"

"I am supposed to be blind as well as deaf? And dumb along with the blindness and the deafness? I am neither the one nor the other nor the third thing. When I see him come down the stairs, his mustachios beaming, the turquoise in his ear singing a song, and I see you come down with a song leaping in your face, and he looks at you and smiles for nothing and you do the same, then I suppose I am to think that you and he have been fighting. Bah!"

"I don't know just when we'll be married. But it'll be sometime soon."

"That is good," he said and turned his attention back to the broth.

24

THREE DAYS LATER, WHEN THE trains and buses started running, these things happened in the town of Lennox:

The Weasel took Johnnie Roane up to the railroad station in time to catch the morning train for New York. They had both been silent as they passed through the town. Now The Weasel was watching Johnnie take a worn suitcase out of the back of the car. He shoved his greasy cap a little farther over his eyes and spoke for the first time. "Well, Mac," he said gruffly, "don't take no wooden nickels."

A peculiar kind of farewell, Johnnie thought. "Okay," he said. "And thanks."

He walked to the end of the platform to wait for the train, trying to make his mind a blank. But he couldn't. Images streaked across it. He saw himself itching to get off the train, going nuts with impatience as it slowed down at Lennox; and then, finally, he couldn't wait any longer but jumped off before the train came to a complete stop. Jumped off, carrying his hopes and dreams right out in plain sight, dangerously unprotected, for he was cradling them in his hands. A man is a fool to try to carry anything as ephemeral as a dream around with him. Fragile and light, yes, but excess baggage.

You're dodging as usual, he thought, ducking even the saying of her name. Glory. Say it. Repeat it. Glory. That's her name. She was the soapbubble, the dream, the illusion, the bright hope.

The train came around the curve belching smoke as it slowed down. He followed the course of the smoke, watched it disappear, floating out of sight in the sky.

As he looked up, his face lost a little of its bitterness. The sky arched high over his head, blue, serene, limitless; puffs of white cloud were drifting slowly across its surface. A sky like that reached endlessly over the world, he thought, covering a world so vast and so complex that if a man were to seek out his rôle in it he would not have time to brood over a lost illusion.

The train stopped. A conductor swung himself to the platform. "Let 'em off," he said. He helped two women passengers alight. Then, "Bo-ard," he said. "All a-board."

Johnnie Roane went swiftly up the train steps. He did not look back.

Later in the morning, the town taxi driven by The Weasel stopped in front of the Gramby House. The front door opened and Mrs. Gramby emerged. She was wearing a long black cape. She leaned heavily on her cane and she was supported on one side by Neola and on the other by Cook.

Her progress down the front steps was slow, painful to watch. When she reached the flagstone walk, she stopped and looked about, noticing with dismay how many trees and shrubs were missing.

It took The Weasel and Cook and Neola to get her inside

the taxi. Once she was seated, Neola started to get in the front of the car.

"I don't need you," Mrs. Gramby said sharply.

"But, Mrs. Gramby, someone ought to go with you—"

"I haven't yet reached the feeble-minded stage where I need a keeper following me around."

"But Doctor Williams said you weren't to get out of bed. You're sick. Your hands shake. Please—"

"Get out of the car immediately," she said.

The Weasel waited until Neola was on the sidewalk before he started the motor. "Where you want to go, Mrs. Gramby?" he asked.

"To the Town Hall. I will be in there about a half-hour. I want you to wait for me."

"Sure thing."

She had intended to keep an eye out for the damage that had been done by the storm; instead she went to sleep. When the car stopped, she thought the voice saying, "Mrs. Gramby, Mrs. Gramby," was that of Doctor Williams. But it was The Weasel and he was peering at her with an expression of great concern. He had the car door open and his head was thrust far inside, his small beady eyes were concentrated on her face.

"Oh, yes," she said. "We're here, aren't we? I must have fallen asleep."

She hitched herself forward, nearer the car door. The Town Hall steps were longer than she had remembered them. They seemed to go up and up and up.

The Weasel followed her glance. "Wait a minute," he said. "I'll go down in the basement and get one of the fellers. With me on one side and him on the other, you can make it up them stairs without no trouble."

Before she could protest, he had walked away, disappearing

around the corner of the building. If there is anything I cannot bear, it is to make a public spectacle of my infirmities, she thought. While he is gone I can get out of the car and I shall be inside the Town Hall before he returns.

Getting out of the car was more difficult than she had expected. When she finally reached the sidewalk, she was panting. I simply cannot hurry, she thought. Never again. That illness added years to my age; right now I must be all of two hundred years old. I can scarcely move, and as for the steps—

She was looking up them with a kind of despair when The Weasel returned accompanied by a broad-shouldered man who tipped his hat and said, "Good morning, ma'am."

Their progress up the steps was slow, halting. The long cape hung heavily on her shoulders. She had to lean against both men for support. They paused frequently while she caught her breath.

When they reached the top step, The Weasel said, "We'll wait out here and help you down. You won't have no trouble the rest of the way. All the offices is on this floor."

"Thank you," she said.

She glanced inside the auditorium. It was a big bare room. Chairs lined the walls. There must have been a dance here recently, she thought. The fall of the year was a good time for dances and parties. These days the girls wore long-skirted dresses on special occasions, a pretty style. The party clothes they wear are so graceful, the skirts sweeping the floor. Their other clothes are too short, showing all the ugly part of the knee, sometimes glimpses of the thigh. So few women have pretty knees, usually too fat or too thin, the bone ugly there at the joint.

Mr. Gramby said my knees were so perfect they should have been immortalized in marble. He also said that it was a pity it could not be done, but he would be forced to shoot the sculptor afterward so it was out of the question. Then she thought, This comes with age, this standing bemused, thinking of something that happened long ago, while the urgent task that had been uppermost in your mind slips away, forgotten.

Now where would his office be? Probably the least desirable one, in a corner somewhere. She walked the length of the long hall outside the auditorium, putting on her glasses to read the names on the doors—the tax collector, the public health nurse, the judge of probate, the town clerk. The sign on the door at the end of the hall said: David Rosenberg, Counselor-at-law.

A voice said, "Come in," in answer to her knock. If he was surprised to see her, he did not show it. He said, "How do you do," very politely and helped her into a chair, slipped the cape over the back of the chair.

"I've come to make my will," she said, thinking, He's much too thin, he needs to eat more.

Ed Barrell lighted a cigar, then leaned against one of the pillars in front of the Town Hall. The Weasel looked at him admiringly and said, "How's tricks, Ed?"

"All right." Ed blew out a cloud of smoke. "She going to be in there very long?" He gestured toward the door behind them.

"Nope. Just a little while. You in a hurry?"

"Got to get back to the fill."

The Weasel noticed that Ed was breathing kind of hard. The stairs must have got him. "Kind of lost your breath, ain't you?"

"The old pump isn't so good," Ed touched his chest. "Had a lot of trouble with it lately."

"That so?"

"Yeah. Doc Williams says I ought to take it easy. He's trying to get me to stop fooling around with cars. Says a man with a bad heart ought to find something easier to do."

The Weasel searched his pockets for a toothpick, found one,

and carefully inserted it in his mouth, approximating the angle of Ed's cigar. "Well," he said, twisting the toothpick from one side of his mouth to the other. "I've heard of plenty of old men who died before their time, right after they took to running with young girls. Their backs was weak to start with, and there's nothing like a young strong female to completely break down a old man's back. So if a feller had a bad heart in the beginning, I should think it was liable to bust up in pieces any time after he started playing indoor games with some young tender female flesh as partner."

Ed frowned, flicked ashes from his cigar. The Weasel looked out at the street, waiting for some response. Ed evidently wasn't going to rise to that one.

He tried another tack, speaking softly: "I hear Glory's getting ready to leave the Perkinses and move into her own house. That'll make it real nice for her friends, what with winter coming on and all. It'll be cozier than a cabin in the woods. There's nothing like a small house, with a new heating plant in it, to make for solid comfort."

Ed made a restless motion with the hand that held the cigar; still no answer. The Weasel said: "I never did understand that business about Johnnie beating the hell out of her. The way he looked when he left town this morning, it musta been the other way around."

I'll twist his tail just one more time and then I'll let him alone, he thought. If I push him too hard he'll leave.

"Funny how Glory and Lil are so much alike, even to having the same piece of—"

The Weasel stopped talking because David Rosenberg had come out of the building, was saying something to them.

"Mrs. Gramby would like you to act as a witness to a document she is about to sign," Rosenberg said, looking at Ed.

"Sure, sure," Ed said, so surprised that his cigar fell out of his mouth.

"You mean me, don't you?" The Weasel asked.

"You're the taxi-driver, aren't you?" The Weasel nodded and Rosenberg said, "Mrs. Gramby asked for the other man, not the taxi-driver."

She's making out her will, The Weasel thought, as he watched Ed and Rosenberg go through the door. He stared at the cigar. It was still burning. The ash grew longer as he looked at it. Wonder why she asked for him to witness it and not me. He stepped on the cigar, carefully flattening it out, and then kicked it off the floor of the portico.

Mrs. Gramby signed her name to the will, aware that the town nurse and the janitor and the man with the broad shoulders were standing close behind her chair, watching her.

Then the town nurse picked up the pen, wrote her name on the document in a thin spidery hand: Grace Sloane. The janitor signed next: John Roagan. The broad-shouldered man was last. He held the pen awkwardly, formed his letters by pressing it deeply into the paper: Ed Barrell.

She frowned, trying to remember why the name was familiar. He had thick shoulders, a short neck, dark hair. Her eyes traveled the length of his body—he was bow-legged. Ed Barrell. This was the man Lillian had written the letter to, the man Lillian used to stay with whenever Mearns was in New Haven overnight.

The shudder that went through her left her feeling sick and dizzy, left her heart racing. She had leaned on his arm for support; coming up that long flight of stairs her enormous weight had pulled him down toward her. He had braced his body to receive her weight, put one arm around her waist. His hand had grasped her elbow. Each time she paused to catch her breath she had relaxed against him. He had panted, too, something obviously wrong with his breathing. He had gulped in air and his sour tobacco-smelling breath had been in her nostrils.

She closed her eyes, leaning back in the chair, hating the thought that she had been helped by someone so despicable. She could see him again, making savage love to that young soldier's wife—what was her name? Gloria—up there on Obit's Heights. She remembered the forward thrust of his shoulders, the burrowing motion of his head. Dear God, the man was an animal. And she had come up the stairs, slowly, oh, so slowly, moving ponderously because she was old, senile, helpless; she had come up the stairs leaning on his shoulder—

"Are you all right, Mrs. Gramby?" David Rosenberg asked.

She nodded her head, but she did not open her eyes. "Yes, thank you. My breath—" She paused. "Sometimes I lose it."

If only I could summon the strength to tell that young lawyer to send him away, she thought, to send away that animal who calls himself a man. The young lawyer will help me down the stairs, such a long flight. His face, can tell by his face, what is it like, the eyes so gentle, the mouth so sensitive, the long sweep of the forehead, the soft hair. It is in the picture over my bed, the painting that Mr. Gramby bought me in Italy. Why do they all of them, it is very strange, they all look like the young Christ; the medieval artists must have used—or no, perhaps some expression of sorrow in the eyes makes it the same—

A hand felt for her pulse, a cool, dry hand. She opened her eyes. The town nurse was bending over her. She snatched her wrist away from the cool-feeling fingers. "Don't do that!" she said angrily. "I close my eyes whenever I am thinking. And I do not want you poking at me. One is entitled to privacy in the pursuit of one's thoughts."

Anger made her get out of the chair quickly. She jerked the

cape into position around her shoulders, glaring at the nurse, at the janitor, at Ed Barrell. Then she turned to Rosenberg and said, "You have done much good in the world."

He looked startled and murmured, "Thank you."

She left the office, walking purposefully. The Weasel stepped forward and grasped her elbow as she came out of the door. She looked at him as though she were puzzled. "I find you everywhere," she said. "Even in my thoughts. You reach them before I do."

"Yes'm," he said blankly, and the toothpick slipped out of his mouth.

Ed Barrell grasped her other arm and she turned and smiled at him, saying, "I never expected to have so distinguished a companion for a walk. It is, sir, a very great honor."

Ed tried to catch The Weasel's eye. But The Weasel stared straight ahead, refusing to look at him.

They started down the stairs, moving slowly. On the fifth step from the top Mrs. Gramby paused to rest and she became aware of Ed Barrell's body braced against her own, supporting her. Her face puckered. He smelt of gasoline, his sour tobacco breath was in her nostrils.

I am too old, she thought. I had gone so far back in the past that I thought I was talking to the Bishop. He visited us the year after we were married; and we went for a long walk, all the way to the boat dock. In place of him I find this animal who has broken my son's heart and I am leaning against him, my body, old and worn-out, is close to his.

The Weasel and Ed Barrell thought she was moving forward in order to go down to the next step. They relaxed their bodies, stepped forward, too. But instead she was jerking her arm away from Ed Barrell's hand, pushing his arm from her back.

She drew away from both of them with a violent motion that threw them off balance. Ed tried to grasp her elbow and she shoved him in the chest. Then she lost her balance, falling forward, down, down, down. Her huge body entangled in the folds of the voluminous black cape. The cane made a thin rattling sound as it went down the stairs ahead of her.

Ed Barrell had one foot extended in front of him, reaching for the next step, when Mrs. Gramby pushed him. He jerked himself backward at the edge of the steps and for a fraction of a second he balanced there, his hands and arms raised as though he were clutching at the air for support.

Then he, too, started falling down the stairs. He tried to stop himself and couldn't. He was aware that his heart was plunging madly inside his chest, striking painful blows, so that he stopped breathing, consciously stopped breathing in order to ease the pain. He began to think that this fast, whirling, downward plunging was like making love to Glory. It was like reaching and reaching for the very heart of the world, the heart he had sought inside a woman's body, a never-ending forward thrusting which could not cease until he found respite, surcease. He never had found it, but he had to keep on trying because he was certain that some day he would find what he had sought. Want and get but never enough; the urge never quite satisfied, always present. Glory had come closer to quieting the urge than any of the others.

He closed his eyes, took a deep, shuddering breath, and the pain in his chest made him gasp. Yes, it was like making love to Glory. Down and down and down like this, falling, falling, drop in space; hit and stop, roll over and go down again; and then the drop, sheer, straight down, no pause. Perhaps he was going to find it now, the thing he had sought for so long. There seemed to be a hush all around him. It was like entering a vacuum, an enclosed unoccupied space, alone there, something waiting for him there. Then his body hit the concrete sidewalk with a dull thud.

The Weasel, smaller, slighter, more agile than the others,

went down three steps, reached for his balance, found it, stood still.

It had happened too fast. He couldn't follow it with his eyes, or his mind. He stood motionless, staring down at the pavement, his mouth open. He made a small piteous sound in his throat.

"Oh, Jesus," he whispered. "Oh, Jesus!" and he covered his eyes with his small hands.

25

MRS. GRAMBY AND ED BARRELL died, there on the sidewalk, in front of the Town Hall.

These sudden deaths and the departure of Johnnie Roane were talked of in the town for weeks afterward. A conversation that took place in the drugstore the next day was fairly typical of what was being said. The speakers were men:

"What do you think she was doing at the Jew lawyer's?"

"Who knows? Maybe she was out of her mind. She'd been sick ever since the storm."

"Wonder why death always comes in three's. My father used to tell me that. "Death always comes in three's," he'd say. "You mind what I tell you." He was right, too. It's happened again right here in the town."

"But it wasn't three. Only two—Ed and old lady Gramby."

"You got to count Johnnie Roane in there. He isn't dead, but he's gone, isn't he? He's lost to the town. He'll never be back again, not after the way Glory was running with Ed Barrell. So it's a kind of death. I tell you death always comes in three's. We've lost three people."

This last statement was followed by an uneasy silence, the

speakers pausing, as if to consider the town's loss. Then they started talking again:

"Folks will miss Ed more than the other two."

"I don't see how you figure that."

"He was more human. Why, Ed would give you the shirt off his back."

"Maybe. But at the same time he'd take the shirt off your wife's back and all her other clothes, too. It don't exactly balance."

"Just the same, folks'll miss him more. The town took a kind of pride in him. Now you take that Roane boy; nobody ever got to know much about him. Even as a kid he never was much of a hand for talking, always had his nose stuck in a book. Then when he just about got grown good, he went off to the war. And Mrs. Gramby was so old and so lame you couldn't help thinking she was more like a landmarker than a human. And that big house and all that money helped set her apart from the rest of us. But everybody knew Ed. He was always up there by the Town Hall so folks could pass the time of day with him. And even the ones who didn't know him had heard about how he chased women. He was like a institution."

"Wonder what made him so hot after women?"

"Be hard to say. It was kind of like a disease with him. And nobody's ever yet figured out why one man catches a disease and another one don't. No, it'd be hard to say."

"Wonder why death always comes in three's—"

It was exactly two weeks after the storm when Mrs. Gramby's will was read, on a gray day not unlike the day that preceded the storm. Wind was blowing straight from the northeast—cold, persistent; but instead of carrying the threat of rain there was a tingle in the air that suggested snow might be in the offing.

To my great surprise I had been informed that I was named in

Mrs. Gramby's will and was therefore among those persons invited to hear the reading of the will. I was putting on my hat and coat, about to leave the store to go over to the Gramby House, when The Weasel came in.

He was wearing the same suit he had worn to Mrs. Gramby's funeral—dark blue serge, and obviously seldom worn, for the pants had a horizontal crease mark halfway down the leg where they had hung over a hanger. He had on an out-of-shape gray felt hat. He kept tugging at the hat, using the same gesture he uses when he settles his cap on his head.

The effect of the hat was curious. His beady eyes were half-concealed by the brim so that his glance seemed sharper and slyer than ever, almost as though he were peering out from under a curtain, stealing quick, darting glances at you before withdrawing out of sight.

"Hi, Doc," he said. "I'm in the Gramby will."

I am not certain whether I was more startled by his having forgotten to say, "How's tricks?" or by the sight of the hat he wore, or by the fact that he was included in Mrs. Gramby's will.

"So am I. I'm on my way there now."

"You are?" he said, surprise in his voice. Then he grinned. "Well, come on," he said quickly. "I'll drive you over. Glad of some company, too. Mebbe with you along the sight of all them stuffed shirts won't make me sick to my stomach."

We found a very uncomfortable-looking group of people in Mrs. Gramby's living room. They were not talking to each other, either. Judge Peterson, the executor of the late Mr. Gramby's estate, was sitting bolt upright in the wing chair by the window. Mrs. Roane, Johnnie's mother, was sitting directly across from him. The expression in her eyes was so sorrowful that after I shook hands with her I looked away from her, quickly.

Mearns and Lil were seated on the sofa near the fireplace. Lil glared at The Weasel when he entered the room. I think she started to raise an objection to his being there, and didn't because The Weasel said, "How are you, Lil?" and snapped the elastic of his bow tie against his throat, in a nonchalant gesture that suggested he would be only too happy to exchange insults with her.

Father McGregor, the Catholic priest, was sitting on the sofa next to Mearns. His long legs were crossed, and he had his arms folded on his chest.

The only relaxed-looking person in the room was David Rosenberg, the lawyer. He was standing in front of the fireplace, holding a sheaf of papers in his hand. By contrast the rest of them looked as though they had been frozen in the positions they had assumed when they first sat down; so that now they could not move, could not speak. Lil kept her face turned away from Rosenberg.

Mearns got up, greeted us nervously, said, "I think there are plenty of seats," and sat down again. This was done so quickly that he might have been a jack-in-the-box, moving up and down because of some mechanical control.

I sat down at the far end of the room. The Weasel drew a chair up close to me, as if for protection, and started biting his fingernails.

Once we were seated, Mearns jumped up again and rang for Neola. When she came to the door he said stiffly, "Please ask Cook and Portulacca to come in."

Meanwhile, in all that roomful of people there was not even a whisper of conversation. Judge Peterson stared out of the front window and tapped his fingers on the arm of the wing chair. Mrs. Roane kept her eyes on her lap. She was fingering a fold in the material of her dress; and I wondered if she was thinking about Johnnie and remembering that young, eager look he had on his face when he was a kid.

Lil kept her head turned away from Rosenberg, which meant

she was looking straight at Father McGregor, and the good father's face slowly reddened. I don't think she realized she was staring straight at his chin. He kept lifting his hand to his chin, under the impression that there was a speck of dirt or a smudge on it, and he tried to remove it, furtively.

Then Neola came in, with Cook and The Portegee walking single file in back of her.

"Come and sit down," Mearns said. He waited until they were seated and then sat down himself, turned to Rosenberg. "I think we're all here now, Mr. Rosenberg. You can begin."

Rosenberg started reading in a low voice, "I, Bertha Laughton Gramby—"

Lil's face was—well, anticipatory, to say the least. She frowned when she heard the list of bequests. Cook, Neola, and The Portegee were to receive one thousand dollars apiece. Five hundred dollars was to go to The Weasel. Mrs. Gramby had referred to him as "Mr. Weasel," and explained the bequest as being in appreciation of his careful driving and for the chivalrous assistance he had so cheerfully offered to an old woman. The Weasel, for the first and only time since I've known him, looked embarrassed. I thought he was going to get up and bow, but he didn't.

Lil's lips tightened to a thin straight line when she heard that Johnnie Roane was to receive six thousand dollars, payable in monthly installments which were to cover a period of four years.

Then she made a protesting sound in her throat, for Mrs. Gramby had left her pearl necklace to her "beloved friend Annie Lowther Roane"; and her diamond ring to me—identifying me as her devoted admirer, Mr. George Fraser, the druggist.

Lil jumped to her feet and said, "She—"

Mearns pulled her back on the sofa. "Let him finish," he ordered.

The tone of his voice surprised me. It was harsh, masculine.

Lil's face turned a deep red. This sudden crimsoning of her skin made the brassy curls on her head seem a horrid color. She kept quiet, but she glared at Rosenberg as though she hated him; and a muscle in her cheek started to twitch.

Rosenberg went on reading, "The land on the main street, formerly known as the Gramby Pasture, is hereby given to Saint Peter's Roman Catholic Church, to be used in any way the church desires—"

Then his voice slowed. We all leaned forward, concentrating on the words. He paused once and looked up before he went on. It took me a moment to understand the sense of it, mixed up as it was with "whereases" and "heretofores." But Mrs. Gramby had willed the Gramby House and its contents to Cook, Portulacca, and Neola, along with five hundred a year for its maintenance. There was a clause which stated Mearns was to have the cats and any other three items in the house which he especially valued. The remainder of her property, stocks, bonds, real estate, was to go to Mearns.

Lil jumped up, and, standing well out of reach of Mearns, shouted: "She was crazy. I can prove it. And he put her up to this"—she pointed at Rosenberg. "It was that dirty Jew. He ought to be arrested. He—"

Rosenberg did not even so much as turn his head. He was lighting a cigarette and he kept his eyes on the match.

There was a dreadful silence in which I became aware of the sound of The Weasel's breathing. It was quick, jerky. I looked at him and he was nibbling at his thumbnail, putting it in his mouth and taking it out. In his excitement, his jaws were moving just as if he were chewing food, and pausing in between to swallow.

Cook broke the silence. He pointed one of his fat fingers at Lil and, speaking slowly and with great dignity, he said, " 'Thou foul sinner, what hast thou to answer thy reprovers, thou that so ofttimes hast offended thy God and so ofttimes deserved hell?'"

In addition to having a marked foreign accent, Cook's voice is sibilant, so when he said this he sounded as though he were hissing at Lil.

She lost the last tattered remnant of her self-control and screamed at him, "You pig! Go wallow in your kitchen, go wallow in the dirt of your kitchen where you belong."

Cook stood up and shouted back at her, "Watch your tongue, you foul beast! My kitchen is clean. It is always clean. My food is clean—" Then his voice died away. He stopped talking to listen to Lil.

We all listened to her. Words came tumbling out of her mouth so fast that it was impossible to separate them. She might have been speaking one sentence. Her voice was hoarse with rage as she said:

"All of them are crazy—they talked about Mr. Gramby until I thought he was alive, not dead—I was always expecting to meet him on the stairs, here in this room—everywhere—because that horrible old woman thought he was still alive—I tell you she was crazy—no car—plenty of money—the cats—always eating —I won't have niggers living here—this is my house—that fat old bastard with the diamond—that slob of a woman with the pearls—that nasty cripple—pigpen Irish—everybody in the will but me—I am the one—" As she spoke her voice gained in volume, its hoarse tones echoing through the high-ceilinged room.

Since then I have often wondered why Mearns let her go on screaming her insults at us for so long. Perhaps he wanted the rest of us to know what she was really like. Or perhaps he was too appalled to protest. I really don't know. As to the others, Mrs. Roane had covered her ears with her hands, Judge Peterson and Neola were standing up, and Father McGregor was staring at

Lil as though unable to believe the evidence of his ears. Cook closed his eyes and what with the way he was scowling he looked like a frowning Buddha. The Portegee was opening and closing his hands, forming them into fists.

Lil must have shouted at us for all of five minutes before Mearns got up from the sofa. He grabbed her by the arm and shook her, "Keep quiet!" he roared. She opened her mouth and screamed and he covered her mouth with his hand, pushed her toward the sofa, forced her down on it, held her motionless there. And still she tried to scream, to talk under his hand. He took his hand away and slapped her across the face.

"Keep quiet!" he shouted again. His voice thundered in the room. The sound startled me, for it was so like his father's voice, and it was the first time I had ever heard Mearns speak in that fashion.

The Weasel ran his finger under his collar as though it were choking him. He nudged me and whispered behind his hand, "Hey, Doc! I wouldn't a missed this for a million dollars."

Lil stopped screaming. She took a deep, shuddering breath. I imagine that at that moment she saw the house and the pearls and the diamond, saw them slipping out of her grasp. And because they meant so much to her, she fought to regain control of herself. The effort made her face turn pale.

When she spoke, her voice was shaking, but she was able to pitch it to a conversational tone. "But, darling," she said. Mearns scowled when he heard the word. "You're going to contest it, aren't you?"

"No," he said coldly. "I helped Mother plan her will."

"You helped her? You mean you want these awful people in this house?"

"Yes. They loved her. They love this house. They will enjoy living here."

Lil moved closer to Mearns, put her hand on his coat-sleeve.

At that moment Cook made a derisive sound, a sound which I believe is called the raspberry. Lil glanced toward him. He was staring at her, the expression on his face was contemptuous. The vulgar sound that had issued from his lips, the insolence of his manner, destroyed the thin surface of her self-control.

"Well, I'll contest it," she said. Her voice was ugly. "I'll go to Court and I'll prove she was crazy—that she was in her second childhood—couldn't control her bladder—thought her husband was still alive—I'll break the will—" She was beginning to scream again.

Mearns interrupted her, "You'll do nothing of the kind. Don't you remember? Don't you remember about Ed? And the letter that says, 'Petey will be away'?"

It has been my experience that all females react in the same way when cornered. Lil Gramby was no exception. She was hard-boiled, healthy, known to be strong as a horse, yet she leaned her head back against Mrs. Gramby's empire sofa and quietly fainted, sliding down to the floor. It was a beautifully timed faint, but her face had too much color in it for it to be the genuine article.

Rosenberg and Mearns picked her up and laid her on the sofa. Neola ran to get aromatic spirits of ammonia.

There was so much confusion that I knew no one would miss us. So just as Lil sighed and fluttered her eyelids, The Weasel and I left.

The Weasel did not speak as he drove through Whippoorwill Lane, though his lips kept moving, as though he were talking to himself.

He followed me into the back room of the store, watched me take off my hat and coat. I was leaning over to pat Banana, the cat, when he suddenly said, "Hey, Doc, what's 'chivalrous' mean?"

"Gallant. A gentleman in the old-fashioned sense of the word.

Polite to old women and babies and children. Even generous to, and considerate of, other men." I looked at him curiously and added, "Though I must say I fail to see how Mrs. Gramby came to that conclusion about you."

I don't think he heard the last part of what I said. If he did he ignored it.

"Oh," he said. He pulled the felt hat down over his forehead, using the same gesture he uses when he tugs at his cap or settles it on his head.

There is a mirror on the cigar counter, one of those standing mirrors that men use for shaving. I placed it there in the hope that someone would buy it. It didn't sell. But I let it stay on the counter because the customers, male and female alike, enjoy admiring their faces in it.

The Weasel walked over to this mirror, bent down, and studied his face for about five minutes. Then he straightened up and said, not looking at me, "Well, I hope Banana will have a easy time when she has her next batch of kittens."

Just before he went out of the door he said, "Don't take no wooden nickels, Doc."

About the Author

ANN PETRY (1908–1997), novelist, short story writer, and writer of books for young people, was one of America's most distinguished authors. She graduated from the Connecticut College of Pharmacy and returned to her hometown, Old Saybrook, Connecticut, to work in the family pharmacy. Marrying in 1938, she moved to Harlem in New York City, where she wrote for *The Amsterdam News* and *The People's Voice*, performed with the American Negro Theatre, studied art, and began to publish short stories. Her critically acclaimed first novel, *The Street* (1946), became the first book by a Black woman to sell more than a million copies. Returning to Old Saybrook to raise her daughter, she went on to write the novels *Country Place* and *The Narrows*, and the collection *Miss Muriel and Other Stories*. Her works for young people include the historical novel *Tituba of Salem Village* and the middle-grade biography *Harriet Tubman: Conductor on the Underground Railroad*.

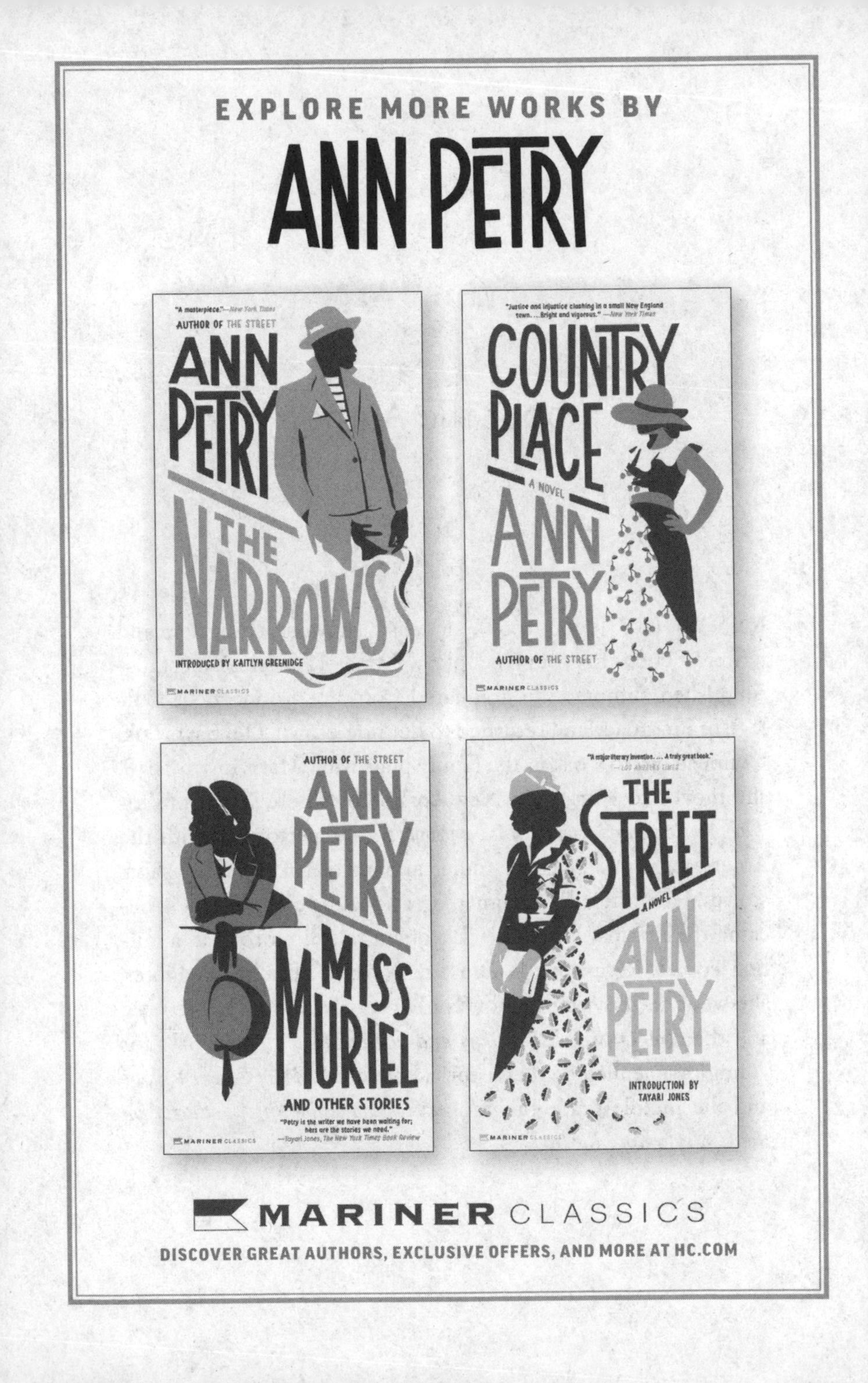
EXPLORE MORE WORKS BY
ANN PETRY
"A masterpiece."—New York Times
AUTHOR OF THE STREET
ANN PETRY
THE NARROWS
INTRODUCED BY KAITLYN GREENIDGE
MARINER CLASSICS
"Justice and injustice clashing in a small New England town. . . . Bright and vigorous." —New York Times
COUNTRY PLACE
A NOVEL
ANN PETRY
AUTHOR OF THE STREET
MARINER CLASSICS
AUTHOR OF THE STREET
ANN PETRY
MISS MURIEL
AND OTHER STORIES
"Petry is the writer we have been waiting for; hers are the stories we need."
—Tayari Jones, The New York Times Book Review
MARINER CLASSICS
"A major literary invention. . . . A truly great book."
—Los Angeles Times
THE STREET
A NOVEL
ANN PETRY
INTRODUCTION BY TAYARI JONES
MARINER CLASSICS
MARINER CLASSICS
DISCOVER GREAT AUTHORS, EXCLUSIVE OFFERS, AND MORE AT HC.COM